Signatures

AJ Humphreys

Andrew Adams

Angel Ramon

David K. Slater

Derek Thomas

Dylan Wells

Jay Bower

Joseph Murnane

Jules Terry

Lisa Breanne

Mari Pittelman

Matthew Lutton

Mel Kitching

Stephanie Huddle

Zaq Cass

Jyl Glenn

Savannah R. Fischer

PHOBOPHOBIA

FACE YOUR FEARS

CURATED BY

JYL GLENN &
SAVANNAH R. FISCHER

Paperback ISBN: 979-8-9919908-1-3

Cover Artist: Savannah R. Fischer

Editor: Jyl Glenn

Interior Formatting: Jyl Glenn

First edition 2025

Jylannah forever

CONTENTS

INTRODUCTION

Dear Reader,

Woof.

xoxo,
Betty

EISOPTROPHOBIA

BY MARI PITTELMAN

Mirrors are dangerous and tricky things. I didn't always know that in a traditional sense, but I was always uncomfortable around mirrors and avoided them as much as I could. I couldn't put my finger on why they bothered me, but they did. It was impossible to avoid them completely, but even if I could have, they'd always show up in my dreams. No matter the type of dream I was having, I always happened upon one at some point. That's usually when the dream would end, right before I could see myself clearly. I was worried there would come a day where I didn't wake up in time. That the image in the mirror would come into full focus and I didn't know why, but I desperately didn't want to see it.

For a long time, all I knew was that mirrors made me feel weird. I did, however, eventually come to understand at least some of it. It happened one morning when I was about fourteen years old, and the weird feeling I got from looking in mirrors was replaced with terror. To this day, I still don't know who she is. All I *do* know is when I looked at myself in the mirror, the person looking back at me wasn't me. Maybe, if I hadn't been so fixated that morning when I was young, I would have missed the signs. And then it might have gone on unnoticed for a long time. Hell, there's a chance I'd still be none the wiser today. Because, the thing is, she was good. She was really, really good. But her mimicry wasn't perfect. That morning, as it happened, she was just the tiniest bit slow.

The morning I saw her, I had been in the bathroom watching my Aunt Caroline get ready for the day. I loved the process she went through to put herself together. It was like magic. She looked like a completely different person, and she acted like one too. Aunt Caroline always woke up angry. I'd hear the sound of the alarm clock and then shortly thereafter, between the persistent squawks of said alarm, there'd be a loud groan and a "for fuck's sake." The blaring would suddenly cease, and she'd stomp her way to the shower, muttering and swearing about her lot in life and promising herself today was the beginning of the end of this era. I'd stay in my room, in bed, until I heard the hairdryer turn off, and then I'd sneak into the bathroom to watch all of the pieces come together. She'd talk to me while she got ready, giving me kernels of life advice on whatever topic she felt inspired by that morning. And after she'd put on her makeup (she called it her "war paint"), and her perfectly styled outfit, she'd spray herself with her perfume. While it took all of those pieces to manage the effect, the true magic was in the perfume. It was a beautiful, elegant scent that smelled of vanilla and sandalwood with a touch of citrus. As the mist of the fragrance settled over her, she'd take a deep breath, smile at me, and the transformation would be complete.

That morning, I was sitting on the edge of the bathtub, watching her through the mirror as she meticulously painted individual strands of eyebrow to fill in her sparse ones. While mirrors made me uncomfortable, I knew it was silly and was trying my best to outgrow that fear. Aunt Caroline had—on more than one occasion—berated me for my childish fears and I'd learned to keep them to myself. Watching her reflection in the mirror never seemed to bother me as much as watching my own reflection. She was explaining to me the importance of looking perfect down to the very last detail. That perfection in your appearance was difficult, but extremely important as even one wayward strand of hair could ruin the entire effect. Aunt Caroline firmly believed that aesthetic perfection was the key to success, and her tool kit to achieve that goal included makeup, hair products, and lots of designer clothing. As she finished her eyebrows, she turned and smiled at me.

"How do I look?"

"You look beautiful, Aunt Caroline," I replied with a grin

She frowned and said, "You know that's not good enough, Jackie. What's out of place? Tell me right now."

"Nothing, Aunt Caroline! I promise! You do look perfect," I tried to reassure her, worried if my incorrect choice of words was going to throw her off track. One too many times I'd said something wrong, or she'd been frustrated about something she saw in the mirror, and she'd taken off her makeup, ripped off all her clothes, and gotten back in the shower to start over again. This made her late for work, and that would make her angry. When Aunt Caroline was angry, she wouldn't let on until after work when she'd come home, silently stalk straight to her room, and not come out until the following morning. Thankfully, this morning she just smiled and asked if I was sure.

"Yes, Aunt Caroline. I promise. You do look perfect. You are perfect and so beautiful."

"Thank you, darling" she cooed and kissed me on the head.

She swept out of the room and headed to the kitchen and, feeling this was a chance to work on facing my fears, I timidly centered myself in the mirror. I grabbed my aunt's hair brush and watched my reflection smooth away the tangles. As I ran the brush through my hair, over and over, my nerves started to tingle. The usual sensation of being watched that I experienced every time I used a mirror crept up my spine. I turned to see if Aunt Caroline had come back down the hall without my noticing. But of course, she wasn't there. She could clearly be heard fixing her coffee in the kitchen at the end of the hall. Turning back to the mirror, I resumed brushing my hair and looking for imperfections. Focusing on the task at hand usually helped distract me from the fear. I frowned as I watched the tangles smooth away and concentrated on becoming more perfect and more beautiful with each stroke. Still, I couldn't shake the feeling of being watched. A sense of unease sprouted in the pit of my stomach. I glanced at the door, again, and, seeing nothing, turned to the tub behind me. I studied the walls and the ceiling, looking for anything out of the ordinary. Yet, I found myself even more uncomfortable with my back to the mirror. I turned quickly and studied the mirror again. Was there something in the background I hadn't noticed? No matter where I looked, I couldn't pinpoint the source of my growing unease. Deciding I no longer wanted to be alone in the bathroom, I looked at myself one final time from the bottom of my feet up to the top of my head. Wanting to confirm that I did, indeed, look perfect. Pleased with the results, I locked eyes with my reflection one final time and that's when I spotted it. Just the slightest hint of a delayed blink. A split second where I was looking at the closed eyes of my reflection. I shouldn't have been able to see my own eyelids shut, but I swear that's what I saw. My reflection had blinked just out of sync with me. Wide-eyed, I took a small step back. As my focus drew back and I began to take in my face as a whole, I noticed the corners of my reflection's mouth dropping down, into place. It was as if I'd caught the tail end of someone hiding their smirk. I hadn't been smirking. I knew for a fact that not even a hint of a smile had crossed my face since I'd stepped up to that mirror. I gaped at my reflection, eyes widening even further, and again noticed the mimicry was slightly delayed. The words "no way" slipped from my lips and that's when she winked at me.

With a sharp "eep!" I darted from the room and bolted down the hall, desperate for the safety and company of my aunt. But she was gone. When I reached the kitchen, expecting to find her sipping her coffee at the counter, I found the room empty. As I turned frantically around looking for her, panic fueled adrenaline began to spread throughout my body and I yelled "Aunt Caroline!" as the tears welled up in my eyes.

"What?" She snapped as she came back inside through the front door just off the kitchen.

As soon as I laid my eyes on her, and I knew I wasn't alone, the tears fell freely. Her irritation disappeared and her eyebrows came together in concern.

"What is it honey? What's wrong?" She demanded.

I didn't know what to say. She was never going to believe me, and any attempt to tell her what I'd seen would probably just annoy her more.

"I don't feel good." Was all I could muster in response.

"Oh honey, I'm sorry to hear that. You need to stop crying and pull yourself together, though. You're an ugly crier and nobody respects ugly people. How many times have I told you that?"

5

She grabbed a couple tissues and handed one to me.

"Blow your nose" she ordered as she dabbed my eyes with the other tissue. Tossing it in the trash, she pulled a hair brush out of her purse, resting on the counter, and began roughly attacking my hair, which was somehow still tangled.

"What were you even doing in that bathroom this whole time? You still look like you rolled out of bed."

"Ow!" I complained and tried to step away, though she held me fast.

"I don't even know why you bother watching me dress every morning if you aren't going to take any of my advice." She lectured.

"There!" she said. "Now you look presentable enough. Would you like to see? Go look in the mirror."

"No!" I said, a little louder than I intended to.

She stared at me for a moment before she turned around and grabbed her coat. Putting it on, and snatching up her purse, she warned me to keep track of the time and not miss the school bus when it arrived in twenty minutes. With instructions to have the kind of day I deserve, a weird expression she'd taken to using lately, she kissed my cheek and glided out the door.

As I stood in the kitchen, with the sound of the closing door fading into the silence of the house, dread and discomfort filled the pit of my stomach. It would be another twenty minutes before the bus would be there to take me to school. Normally, I'd use that time to read or watch tv, or finish getting ready if Aunt Caroline had spotted any imperfections on her way out. Normally, I loved that time to myself. That morning, though, I couldn't bear the thought of spending another minute in the house alone. I put on my jacket and my backpack, picked up my lunchbox and, out of habit, started toward the bathroom again.

Remembering what I had seen earlier, I abruptly turned back and slipped out the front door. I didn't need to worry about locking it, as it was always locked. There was a key hidden in the flowerpot by the door that I used to let myself in when I came home from school. Aunt Caroline said it was more practical to do it that way, since I'd probably just lose the key if she gave me my own. I sat down on the stoop to wait for the bus and tried to understand what had just happened. Despite the sunny day it was supposed to be, it was still early, and the shadows had me surrounded. Lost in thought, I barely heard the bus arrive and I jumped at the tap of the horn. Relieved to have the distraction of school, I hurried onto the bus.

🦷🦷🦷🦷🦷🦷

The day moved along relatively normally, and for a while, I was able to forget what happened that morning. By the early afternoon, I had all but convinced myself I had simply been tired that morning and I had let my imagination run away with me. I had a habit of doing that, much to Aunt Caroline's frustration. She said I was always living in my own head, and she wasn't wrong. It wasn't intentional. My mind has always been a busy place, and it gets very loud which can drown out the world around me. I was experiencing exactly that as I scolded myself for my wild imagination that morning. A reflection of myself in a mirror that's not really me? How silly is that? Of course that was me in the mirror. What else could it have been? What a completely absurd thought. Being tired was absolutely the explanation for my experience. What was a little harder to explain was the fact I knew I had brushed my hair, but Aunt Caroline had said I still looked a mess. Was my imagination really that powerful that I could imagine brushing my hair without actually doing it? That was, admittedly, a bit harder to believe. Was Aunt Caroline just nitpicking? Maybe, but I really felt those tangles when she brushed them out. None of it made any sense.

As I stepped through the locker room door to change for gym class, all of my confidence disappeared. I had expected the locker room to be full of girls getting ready, but I found myself alone. I glanced at the clock and noticed the time. Daydreaming had made me late again. Panic bloomed in my chest as I ran to my locker to change. I dressed quickly and headed toward the door to the gym. Halfway there, I decided I needed to use the restroom and quickly used the nearest stall. I stood at the sink, after washing my hands, and splashed some cool water on my face. I desperately needed to get myself together and get to class. I lifted my head to glance at myself in the mirror and found my reflection grinning back at me, head tilted to the side, eyes endless pits of black.

I gasped and stepped back. Her grin widened as rows of needle-sharp teeth revealed themselves. She straightened her head and slowly lifted a hand and waved at me. Just a little twitch of her fingers and then she slammed her palm against the glass. Her fingers were long and thin with massive claws that shrieked as they slid across the glass. She hit the glass over and over as her grin grew impossibly wider. She appeared to be laughing but no sound reached my ears. As the pounding continued, the glass began to crack and lines like spiderwebs crawled across the mirror. Horrified, I screamed as the mirror shattered outward and my reflection began to crawl through it towards me. I fell back into the lockers behind me unable to tear my eyes from her. And now that the mirror had shattered, I could hear her. She was screaming and laughing at the same time. I'd never heard anything like it before. It made my soul tremble. Pure

8

madness spilled from her lips as she desperately tried to claw through the small mirror. She snarled and spat and screamed and laughed while I cowered in the corner. I was hyperventilating and crying when everything went black.

🦷🦷🦷🦷🦷🦷

I woke up not long after, alone, in the nurse's office. I was laying on a cot, in a darkened room, with a cold compress on my forehead. I tried to sit up and groaned as my head throbbed. I laid back down and covered my head with the compress again. *What happened in that locker room? Had I fainted from a panic attack and hit my head on the lockers?* The door clicked as someone entered the room and softly walked to the desk in the opposite corner. I heard the chair creak as they sat down and began clicking and typing at the computer. Comforted that I was not alone, I relaxed a bit and felt myself drifting off to sleep.

"Sweet dreams, Jackie," someone whispered inches from my ear. I felt their breath tickle the tiny hairs inside my ear and I jumped, tearing the compress from my eyes. There was no one there. There was no one at the desk either. The room was empty. Deciding that I'd rather be in class than alone in this room any longer. I stood up, and my head thudded. I waited for the blood to stop pounding in my ears and made my way out into the hallway. I hadn't paid attention to the time, but there had to be just another couple of hours of school left. My head throbbed, but I could get through it.

As I stepped out, I found the hallway dark and abandoned. Not just devoid of people but legitimately abandoned. The floor was covered with dust and debris from the decaying walls and ceiling. The lockers were rusted and covered with graffiti; cobwebs decorated the doorways to decomposing classrooms. I moved down the hallway unable to rationalize what I was seeing. This was completely impossible. I had to be dreaming. I must have hit my head when I stumbled away from that horrible thing coming at me through the mirror, knocked myself out, and I was having a weird dream. I stopped in the doorway of one of the classrooms and spotted a bundle of something laying in the middle of the floor, writhing with rats. I screamed and some of them scattered. One darted straight toward me and I bolted down the hall as blood thundered in my ears.

Dream or not, I didn't want to spend another moment in there. I reached the end of the hall and turned left, toward the hallway that would take me to the exit. As I ran down the dark and abandoned corridor, I noticed the sound of another set of footsteps, rapidly moving down the hall I'd just come from. A roiling panic bubbled to the surface and the instinct to flee grew unbearable. I ran faster and the now familiar snarling and scream-laughing noise the thing in the mirror had made began to echo down the hall behind me.

I screamed again as I reached the end of the hall. Unwilling to look back and face my pursuer, I sprinted around the corner expecting to find the security desk and the doors marked *exit*. My salvation. Instead of the security desk, I found myself at a dead end with an unmarked door. I reached out and touched the handle and pulled my hand back with a hiss. The handle was so freezing cold it burned. Panic thundering in my chest, I pulled my arm into my sleeve so I could use the end to cover my hand. Without time to think any harder about it, I snatched the door handle in my now thinly protected hand and turned the knob, hoping it wasn't locked. The latch clicked and the door swung open. As the door swung outward toward me, the footsteps and the horrible noises of my pursuer stopped. I quickly glanced behind me and found myself alone.

I turned back to the yawning door and inky black darkness greeted me. So solid was the black behind the door, that the light from the hall had no effect on it whatsoever. Rather than illuminate anything, the light seemed to just bounce off. It was impossible to see what was inside, much less get a sense of the dimensions of the room. I reached around to the wall hoping to find a light switch, but instead, my hand felt nothing but air. I reached further inside and where the wall should be was empty space. I moved to the other side of the doorway and again couldn't find the wall on the other side of the door. Confused and reminded a bit of the TARDIS from Doctor Who, I touched the exterior of the walls on either side of the door. They were solid and very much existed on my side. They just didn't seem to exist on the other side of the door. I had no desire to venture into that black abyss, but feeling as if I had no other choice, I carefully set one foot past the threshold and my foot sank slightly into a sticky substance on the floor. It made a squelching noise, and I lifted my foot up and pulled it back into the light. A thick, tar-like goo covered the sole of my shoe. I put my foot back down in the darkness and moved it slightly, testing the friction to see if walking was even possible. The substance wasn't slippery, and I was pretty sure I could walk without slipping. So, with a deep breath, I ignored every instinct telling me not to, and I stepped fully into the blackness behind the doorway.

Once inside the space, the door slammed shut behind me and laughter echoed. I screamed again and tried to turn back toward the door. But it was gone and replaced with empty space. Pure adrenaline and panic exploded in my chest, and I began to sob.

"Help!" I screamed into the nothing around me. "Please, I just want to wake up."

Screaming laughter was the only reply. I cried harder and sank to the disgusting floor below me covering my ears. After what felt like an eternity of crying in the darkness to the sound of insanity, the sound abruptly ceased. I removed my hands from my ears and wiped my eyes and spotted a soft light in the distance. Taking deep, shaky breaths, I slowly stood and began making my way to the light. As I drew closer and the light became clearer, I realized the light was coming from around a corner. Though it seemed far off in the distance at first, I reached the source of the light much faster than I had anticipated. I turned the corner and found a mirror.

Though instead of my own reflection, I was staring into the bathroom at home. Aunt Caroline was standing in front of the mirror, staring down into the sink. As I watched her, the thing that had come after me in the mirror crawled into the bathroom behind her. My reflection crouched on the floor behind her, head cocked to the side, black pits where her eyes should be. Her grin stretched so wide it looked like it would split her head in half, and her razor-sharp teeth dripped with blood. I began pounding on the mirror, screaming for Aunt Caroline to turn around. To run and save herself. But she couldn't hear me. Of course she couldn't hear me. No one ever heard you in these moments in dreams. But panic had overridden my common sense, and I knew this thing was going to hurt my aunt. Aunt Caroline didn't hear my pounding. She looked directly at me but clearly couldn't see me as she continued to primp and preen in the mirror. Aunt Caroline couldn't hear or see me, but my reflection could. She turned her head and fixed her black voids for eyes directly on me.

The scream laughing echoed all around me at an ear-splitting volume, and yet, Aunt Caroline continued to admire herself in the mirror. My reflection lifted her fingers in the same little wave I'd seen earlier that morning, claws glinting in the light of the bathroom. Then she leapt, grabbing Aunt Caroline from behind and turning her around. I heard my aunt scream as she came face to face with my reflection. My reflection screamed and sunk her claws into Aunt Caroline's eyes, popping them like grapes. Blood sprayed my reflection in the face, and she cackled with glee. Snarling, she dragged her nails down my aunt's cheeks shredding the skin and muscle and exposing the bone. More blood splattered my reflection, and the black voids of her eyes began to glow red. With a new found ferocity, she grabbed Aunt Caroline by the head and ripped it from her body. With a scream she threw the head at the mirror and instead of bouncing off, it sailed straight through and hit me in the stomach.

I sank to the ground and the head plopped on the floor. Her mangled eyes, hanging from the nerves, rested on her savaged cheeks as the head lay at my side. I tried to crawl away in horror but bumped into something behind me. Turning to look up behind me, I found my reflection standing above me, face covered in my aunt's blood. She screamed and lunged for me. A pure bolt of terror wracked my mind and, again, everything went dark.

ᗯᗯᗯᗯᗯᗯ

I woke up in my bed with a pounding headache. I slowly opened my eyes and was relieved that the room was bathed in the brilliant colors of the morning sunrise. I glanced at the clock and saw it read 6:30 AM. I couldn't remember coming home after school. I couldn't remember anything about the day before except the weird hallucination I'd had

13

in the morning, and the insane nightmare. That probably wasn't a good thing, but other than the headache, nothing else appeared to be wrong with me, so telling Aunt Caroline seemed unnecessary. I had about fifteen minutes before Aunt Caroline would get up to shower, and if I wanted to tackle the headache without getting a lecture on not drinking enough water, I needed to take the medicine now. I got out of bed and tiptoed to the bathroom to sneak a pill from the cabinet. I opened the door and turned on the light. I screamed at the sight of my headless aunt, lying in a heap on the floor. Blood streaked the walls and pooled on the floor. I stared in disbelief at the carnage and then lifted my eyes to the mirror. My reflection stood there, covered in blood, holding Aunt Caroline's head by the hair. I couldn't hear the scream laughing, but I knew it was echoing in the nothingness of the space my reflection occupied. Then, she stepped away and my reflection was replaced with my real reflection. I stood there, covered in blood, with a maniacal grin spreading across my face. In my right hand, I held Aunt Caroline's head, and in my left, a butcher knife. The cackling began echoing in my ears again, and I realized it was coming from my own mouth.

ᗤᗤᗤᗤᗤᗤ

That was six years ago. And now I'm here, in this windowless room devoid of everything except a cot and a toilet. I sit here with nothing but my thoughts to entertain me for most of my day. Except for the exercise period when I go outside with the other girls. Most of them don't believe my side of the story. They don't believe me about my reflection. I don't blame them, though. It's pretty hard to believe. I guess I should consider myself lucky they just think I'm insane. Otherwise, they'd have sent me to prison and thrown away the key. And I don't think I'd do well in prison. Too many people. Too much noise. Here, in my room, it's always quiet. There are no mirrors, though. Which is inconvenient as it would give me an opportunity to prove my side of the story. Though, she probably wouldn't show up anyway. She never did when I tried to explain it to the police, the attorney, and the judge. That's how I wound up here.

There's this lady in here, named Deborah, who won't shut up about how she needs a mirror and a new hairdresser. The way she explains it, her hairdresser had gotten possessed by the devil and cut her ear (which is why she stabbed him fifty-seven times with his own scissors). She keeps insisting that it's uncivilized to live the way we do without access to mirrors. We need mirrors to be able to improve our physical flaws, and right now, we need to see that we look like hell. She drives me absolutely crazy with that bullshit. It's the exact same mentality Aunt Caroline had. I try not to socialize with any of the wackos in here.

My only friend is the guard who brings me my breakfast in the morning. We talk about a lot of things. We talk about life and love, and he keeps me up to date on the gossip around the facility. He even believes me about what really happened to Aunt Caroline. He told me he'd seen his reflection move independently of himself. And he'd even seen his own reflection murder his cousin on vacation in Hawaii. It hadn't left the body behind though, so everyone thought he just went missing. This morning, when he dropped off my breakfast, he told me that they're turning the basement into a dance studio with floor to ceiling mirrors all along one wall. I laughed and said that it was a good thing then that I wasn't allowed out of my room except for the exercise period. Then he told me that he'd messed with the paperwork, and I was now scheduled to take dance classes in lieu

15

of my normal exercise period. I'd be in a very small group. Just me and Deborah and the instructor. I looked up at him and into the black pits where his eyes should have been. I smiled, showing my needle-sharp teeth and told him I thought that was a dangerous idea. He grinned as his eyes glowed red and said we'd just have to wait and see.

2

GLOBOPHOBIA

BY MEL KITCHING

There was only one thought on Kristen's mind as she tore apart photos of the happiest day of her life. The wedding was beautiful, with no budget to hold them back because Alec's mother forked over the money to cover whatever they wanted. Now she sat at her dining room table, removing pictures of her mother-in-law and cutting up the photos she lingered in. It wasn't because Stacy ruined their wedding. She didn't wear white or try to steal the show like Kristen had heard of some mothers doing, in fact, she looked stunning in a silky navy-blue dress with gold jewelry. Her dress was very classy and appropriate for her age, as were the hair and makeup styles she had chosen. There was nothing inherently wrong with the photos themselves. It had everything to do with Kristen's mother-in-law, because she had attempted to murder her son's wife. And Kristen had plans to return the favor.

Months earlier, Kristen anxiously picked the flaky peeling skin from her chapped lips, fiddling with the tiny pieces of dead skin cells in between her thumb and index finger before flicking it onto the floor of her living room.

This was a habit she formed years prior. Her doctors called it a symptom of anxiety, a coping mechanism, or more recently, one doctor said it was a form of self-harm. She hated that term. *Self-harm.* Kristen would be on the hunt for a new therapist soon.

Alec approached the front door, returning from work right on time. Kristen heard his heavy work boots on the porch, ramping up her anxiety, until she realized she had ripped a piece of skin from her lips that wasn't quite dead yet leaving a ripe spot. The doorknob turned and Alec walked in with a smile plastered across his face and a small to-go coffee cup in hand.

"I brought you coffee," he said as he removed his boots and placed them on the shoe rack. Taking his shoes off with one hand wasn't the easiest task but he knew his wife hated it when he tracked any remnants of his workday across their cream-colored carpet, so he held onto the coffee rather than taking it to her until he was down to his off-white socks. "So, what did you want to talk about?"

Kristen looked down at the floor, finding a piece of dark lint that she focused on as she racked her brain for a way to communicate what she needed to tell her husband. She bit her lip, forgetting about the sore spot and silently cursing herself as her front tooth grazed the wound. *Just say it,* she thought to herself. *Rip the band-aid off.*

"I'm pregnant." Those two words hung in the air like humidity in the summer, unlike the coffee, which was now a dark brown stain in the shape of a cloud on the carpeted floor.

Months later, Kristen sat down on the worn leather sofa awkwardly. Her growing belly was becoming quite an interference with her comfortability, and she figured she was showing faster than other women of the same gestation. Her due date was still over four months away, but she felt that maybe since she had been pregnant once before, it caused her to grow faster this time around, making it seem as though she were a lot further along than she was.

As Kristen reminisced on her first pregnancy, a short, grey-haired woman entered the room. She wore bifocals with a beaded chain strap that connected one side of the lenses to the other. "Kristen, hi! My name is Shari. It's so good to meet you. And congratulations, by the way!" The therapist gave a warm, inviting smile and offered up her right hand. Kristen skeptically took it, matching her pace as she shook the old woman's hand.

"Thank you. I'm twenty weeks along. We are finding out the gender today!" She exclaimed, anxious to get out of this appointment and head to the next, more exciting one of the two. Alec would be joining her at the obstetrician's office after work. He usually wouldn't leave early, but this was a big appointment, not just one of the routine checkups where they measured his wife's stomach and asked if she had any questions.

"Oh, wow. Twenty weeks? You look like you're ready to pop!" Kristen flinched and started to lose her breath. Her head began to spin as she clutched at her chest and made a break for the door of the small office, stopping at the receptionist's desk on her way out to tell them *next time they should make sure to read a patient's fucking chart ahead of time*!

She cried the whole way to her doctor's office. As soon as Alec arrived, she ran straight into his arms, tears leaving watery streaks across her perfectly made-up face.

"Hey, hey! What's wrong? What is it?" Her husband asked. He took her in his arms, neither of them acknowledging the sweat and grease-stained clothing he wore, forgetting everything else in that moment. "Baby, it's supposed to be a good day! We're here! At our anatomy scan. And our baby is perfect so far."

"I know, I know. It's not that. It was the new therapist. She used *the word.*" She cried into his neck, still shaky and sweaty from her previous interaction with her new therapist. Since she had left that appointment so early, she was way ahead of schedule for the next appointment at the obstetrician's office, so she sat in her car and pulled out the memory book that she took everywhere with her while she waited for her husband. The bubblegum pink scrapbook exhibited a flashy title, the letters outlined in glitter with sparkly butterfly stickers surrounding it. On the front of the book encompassed by the butterflies was the name *Lilly Mae.*

Lilly was Kristen and Alec's firstborn. She was what you might call a 'happy accident' as the two were unmarried and Alec was still enrolled in welding classes at night, working as a line cook during the day, trying to make ends meet. But when those two pink lines popped up, nothing else mattered for the couple. They would make this work. They would be a family.

The memory book held countless photos, beginning with the earliest of ultrasounds where little Lilly looked like a jellybean in Kristen's womb, and then the next one where suddenly the baby Jelly Belly had sprouted arms and legs. The photos continued, the next one being their favorite. *It's a girl!* The words read across the glossy black picture.

More photos lined the pages along with small keepsakes, such as the hospital bracelet Kristen wore when she gave birth, the first locket of Lilly's hair that they had to cut, her footprints in dull black ink, and more. Kristen continued to sob as she made her way through the pages on the floor of Lilly's bedroom, which would now become the new nursery. She was still having a hard time accepting that she would need to replace everything in the room, erasing Lilly's existence in their home aside from the photos and the book she had made. The accident happened two years ago, the bedroom sitting untouched ever since, collecting dust specks that stuck out like a sore thumb when the sun shone into the room.

Alec brought his wife back out of her thoughts. "I'm sorry, babe. We'll find you a good therapist. A good match. There *is* one out there." He took her hand and led her into the obstetrician's office. One hour later the couple left the building, both smiling from ear to ear. Another girl. They decided they would call her Daisy.

"You know Isaiah? From work?" Alec asked as they lay in bed together at the end of the day. Kristen put down her dark romance novel, intrigued at where her husband was going with this.

"Yes, sort of. Why?"

"I think his wife is a therapist. Elise is her name. We spoke to them for a minute at the company picnic last year." He looked into his wife's eyes, studying them for a reaction, but they remained blank. "So, I was thinking maybe you could talk to her. Under the table. I think it's worth a shot."

"Oh, um, okay," Kristen replied. She didn't like the sound of this. A woman she barely knew? How was she supposed to open up to her? Sure, she'd be doing the same thing with a regular therapist at an office, but there wouldn't be that lingering awkwardness of 'my husband knows yours,' plus if they kept things off the record, did she have any rights, any protection? Or was Elise free to blab all about Kristen's fears and anxieties to whoever might listen?

Pop. Kristen jumped out of bed at the sound, screaming wildly.

"Alec! Alec, did you hear that?" She struggled to catch her breath, her chest tightening with each passing second.

"Hear what, Kris?" He asked. He knew the obvious answer, but he didn't personally hear it himself, he just knew there was only one sound that could make his otherwise sane wife have a full-blown panic attack at eleven o'clock at night. "Baby, this is getting out of control again. I really think you should consider talking to Isaiah's wife. I'll call him tomorrow."

Kristen sat across from Elise at the best coffee shop in town three days later, both her hands wrapped around her cappuccino, trying her best to focus on the conversation in front of her instead of the little boy behind her who was talking about his upcoming birthday party excitedly with his mom.

"I just want you to know it wasn't your fault. Things happen, it sounds like it was a freak accident, Kristen. I think you are a wonderful mother, and everyone knows you would never intentionally hurt a child," the woman said. Those words made Kristen tear up as she thought back to that day. She spent so much time blaming herself, it was nice to hear someone remind her that she wasn't at fault. Lilly was only three years old, attending the birthday party of a little girl that went to the same daycare. "I'm going to leave her here while I grab some groceries!" Kristen told the parents of the birthday girl. *No worries,* the mom said, *she's in good hands.*

The likelihood of a child choking on a balloon is higher than one might think. For such a small coffin, Alec and Kristen made sure little Lilly had the biggest headstone they could afford. There wasn't a day that it wasn't decorated with flowers and stuffed animals, and they visited every Sunday afternoon. They often took lunch and sat down picnic style so it would feel like they were having a meal with their late daughter.

"And mom? Can we go to the store that fills up the balloons for you with the special air that makes them fly to the ceiling?" The little boy behind the two women asked. Kristen felt her chest tightening, clutching at it with one hand and at her spinning bead with the other. Elise reached out to soothe her, but she was already flying out of her seat, figuring Elise could foot the bill for their coffee.

Things worsened over the course of the next few days. It seemed like everywhere Kristen went she saw, or heard, or even *imagined* the dreadful objects. She would wake from a deep sleep, totally convinced she had heard a *pop*. She dreamt repeatedly of her daughter, tossing and turning all night restlessly.

Avoiding balloons was a lot harder than it seemed. New shops displayed "Now Open!" signs with balloon arches, children carried balloons tied to strings on the sidewalk, helium balloons were sold with the 'get well soon' cards in the store. For years Kristen kept her fears at bay with therapy session after therapy session, techniques she learned to keep her panic attacks under control, and oftentimes just staying home. She didn't *need* to get out much other than to the grocery store and appointments, since she worked from a small corner of her home with a desk and a cheap laptop the company provided.

Alec's mother planned a baby shower for the couple. Although they already knew the sex of the baby, they hadn't told anyone else, so Stacy wanted to incorporate a gender reveal into the celebration as well. They yearned to celebrate something after all of the tragedy their lives had endured, and since Stacy offered to throw the party for them, they couldn't pass on the offer. Stacy and Kristen weren't close per se, but Kristen liked that Stacy had money and would provide them with these sorts of things, even if her intentions weren't from the heart but rather a place of wanting to flaunt her wealth. It didn't matter to Kristen because it was one less thing she had to worry about.

"I want it to be a total surprise," Stacy informed the couple as they sat over dinner and drinks, a lemon water for Kristen and wine for the others. "I'll have everything all set up and ready, you two just show up! We'll have light refreshments, games, I'll take care of it all. You just put together a list of guests and I'll send out the invites." Kristen was skeptical of this. She would like to have *some* part in the planning process, but Stacy wasn't a woman you argued with, especially if it was at the expense of her bank account.

A few weeks later, Alec and Kristen stepped into the event venue, completely in awe of the scene before them. The baby shower was perfect, themed 'a berry sweet baby' to keep things gender neutral. Kristen didn't *love* the fact that she didn't get to help plan the celebration, but she never doubted her mother-in-law's party planning abilities.

The party was fantastic, surrounded by their closest friends and family, a table stacked full of gifts, the most delicious cake that had ever touched Kristen's palate, though she was surprised that the cake didn't incorporate the big gender reveal that Stacy had mentioned. The gathering was coming to a close—with full bellies, gifts opened, and games completed, however they still had not done any sort of big announcement. A few guests had asked whether they were having a boy or a girl, and Alec responded with "you'll just have to wait and see, we have something planned!" But the truth was, neither of the two knew what they were in for.

"Okay everyone!" Stacy clasped her hands together, her cheeks turning pink with excitement. "We have something special planned before you all go," she said giddily as she motioned to the entrance doors and called for Alec's uncle to bring the surprise inside. Kristen felt her stomach drop and her brow begin to sweat as she saw what her mother-in-law had put together. A large balloon arch surrounded an acrylic sign displaying the words '*what will baby be?*' in large lettering. The sign was on wheels, making it easy to transport the whole contraption into the room. Six of the round latex objects were white, mixed in with the rest which were berry colored, right-on theme with everything else.

"So, here's how this works," Stacy began, "there are six white balloons, three on each side. Alec will stand on one side and Kristen on the other." She handed her son two sewing needles and continued her instructions, ignoring the panic on her daughter-in-law's face. "Two of the balloons on each side are empty, and the third will have either blue or pink confetti once it's popped!" Stacy clapped her hands in a short, rhythmic movement, clearly very pleased with herself.

Kristen started to feel dizzy and knew she needed to sit down quickly. She struggled to catch her breath as she restlessly grasped around with her hands to grip something before she fell to the floor. Her hands felt the synthetic, cold plastic of the tablecloths and she lowered herself into a chair.

"I can't... I can't do this," Kristen choked out the words with her eyes closed. She knew she was causing a scene. She could *feel* one hundred glaring eyes boring into her face as she struggled to decide on her next move.

"Well, the party is practically over, Kris. What's the big deal? I'll just do it myself, then." Kristen tried to yell. She tried to tell her no with every fighting fiber in her body. But the piercing sound of a balloon bursting filled her eardrums, causing her to lose touch with all five of her senses. Before she knew it, she was on the cold hard floor of the party venue with guests piled around her, arguing over who had more experience with CPR.

Kristen woke up in a hospital bed in the labor & delivery unit. Her fall had caused a placental abruption, meaning the baby had to be delivered early. They named her Daisy, keeping the floral theme that they had started with Lilly. Daisy was spending time in the neonatal intensive care unit since she was born prematurely, though her doctors said she was doing wonderful and would likely only need a short stay.

"So, are we going to talk about this?" She asked Alec who was sitting in the appointed 'dad' chair, the one all of the new dads-to-be napped in while their wives were fighting for their lives in a sterile hospital bed lined with puppy pads while wearing an ugly green gown that felt like it was made from fifty-percent cotton and fifty-percent sandpaper.

"About what?" He retorted. Kristen rolled her eyes just as the nurse came in with a cup of ice for her to snack on.

"Kristen? Are you up for visitors? There's someone here to see you!" The nurse smiled at her before setting the Styrofoam cup onto the small bedside table. Stacy poked her head into the room, giving a gentle knock even though the door was wide open. She smiled apologetically at her daughter-in-law, failing to acknowledge her son in the chair beside her.

"Hey honey. I just wanted to say I am *so* incredibly sorry. I still don't understand..." She trailed off, folding her hands together and placing them in her lap, sulking. Kristen couldn't configure whether this was a genuine apology, or if Stacy was saving face. "It's okay, let's just put this behind us for right now. The most important thing is that the baby is here, and she's okay. I would say you could go visit her, but she isn't allowed any visitors other than mom & dad. Did Alec tell you? We're calling her Daisy."

Stacy's eyes lit up. "What a beautiful name! That reminds me, I have something for you. Let me run out and grab it." The woman returned minutes later with a bouquet of flowers. "I got you these." Kristen felt a warmth invading her heart, something she had never felt for Stacy before. She thanked her and took the flowers, placing them on the bedside table.

"Oh, there's something else, too. I left it in the hallway for now. Would you like me to go grab it?" She asked politely. Stacy barely gave Kristen any time to answer before she was giddily exiting the room, obviously excited about her next gift to the couple.

Kristen lost her breath at the sight. The monitors she was hooked up to showed her heart rate increasing, because in the doorway stood her mother-in-law with a second, larger bouquet complete with a 'get well soon' balloon sticking out of the top.

"*Get out!* Get the *fuck* out!" She screamed at the older woman and flailed her arms to the side, sending the first bouquet of flowers crashing to the ground. The monitors started screaming, but Kristen was too wrapped up to check on them. It wouldn't be long before the nurses came rushing in to see what all the commotion was about, anyway, so Kristen let herself lose her cool. It felt good to yell at her husband's mom, who had wasted no time exiting the room. "She's trying to *kill* me, Alec! Why is she doing this? What did I *do?*" Kristen sobbed to her husband who was at her side of the hospital bed, caressing her arm and reminding her to breathe.

"She is *not,* Kris, that's ridiculous."

"She *is,* and I am going to prove it to you."

Kristen, in fact, could *not* prove that her mother-in-law

was trying to kill her. She didn't need proof, though. She had had enough. The countless nights where her sleep was broken by the strange sound of a loud *pop*, the balloons at the party, the get well soon gift. Kristen even considered the day she had been at the coffee shop with Elise, remembering the little boy behind her excitedly discussing his birthday plans, and wondered if someone had *planted* him there. She could picture Stacy giving the boy a candy bar in exchange for the topic of a made-believe party, or offering his mother cold, hard cash. What bothered Kris the most were the popping sounds at night, though. Where could they have been coming from? She knew she wasn't imagining things. It was almost as if the sounds were emanating from the whole room, echoing off the walls loud enough to startle Kristen out of even the deepest sleep. She knew she wasn't crazy, and it was time to do something about that.

Stacy awoke to a strange sensation in her hands. She identified the feeling as pins and needles, her limbs falling asleep. She tried to move her arms but soon realized they were stuck in place, bound to her bed with something she couldn't quite pinpoint. Upon this realization, she tried to scream, but the wad of cloth in her mouth muffled the sound. Her tongue grazed the soft object that had been forced into her mouth. She realized it must have been a washcloth or something similar as she felt the fibers of the material and gagged.

Kristen sat at the foot of the bed staring down at her. As she noticed her mother-in-law's eyes opening, she smiled menacingly at her. "Well, hello!" She exclaimed, clasping her hands together in front of herself excitedly. "I would have killed you already, but since you've made me suffer for *months*, making me think I'm insane, it just didn't seem fair unless you suffer, too."

Stacy's heart began racing as she jerked her arms wildly,

unable to break the restraints. She yelled for help although her cries came out muffled. Hot tears trekked down her face and Kristen laughed at her display of fright. It was almost as if she regretted her actions now that she was about to face the repercussions, but that didn't matter. It was too late. Kristen grabbed a ball peen hammer from the foot of the bed that Stacy hadn't even realized was there.

"I figured since you like 'popping' so much, I'd try to recreate the sound." Kristen swung the hammer at Stacy's kneecap, causing a sickening crack followed by more muffled screams emanating from her body.

"Hmm, that was more like a 'crack.' We'll have to try again until we get it right." She swung again at the other kneecap, repeating the action on either side until she was sure they were both completely shattered.

"This just isn't doing the trick," Kristen said with a smile. She moved closer to the screaming woman, this time swinging the hammer down on her jaw. "There we go! That's what I'm talking about!" She cried gleefully as Stacy's jaw *popped*. The sound was different from that of a balloon, though, and she found herself enjoying it. She brought the hammer down against her jaw a total of four more times before stepping back to admire her work.

"My daughter choked on a balloon, remember? Her little face was blue. She couldn't breathe. I know you think it's funny, like it's some little *game*. 'How far can we push Kristen? How much can she take?' But this isn't just about *me*, Stacy. My baby girl couldn't breathe." Kristen wrapped both of her hands around the woman's neck. Her strength was running low after delivering several blows with the hammer, but she was sure she could finish the job this way. "Now you can't breathe, either, and you'll *never* be able to put me through this again." Kristen could feel the life draining from her mother-in-law beneath her grasp until something knocked the wind out of her from behind, sending her crashing to the floor, incapacitating her.

Alec clutched his woman's hand as they walked into the assisted living facility together, months after the incident. He carried his daughter, Daisy, with his other arm. She was two months old now and growing perfectly, her height and weight both hovering in the sixtieth percentile. She looked a lot like her mom, with auburn hair poking through and pale skin.

Daisy cooed at the receptionist, who smiled back at the happy baby.

"It's so good to see you all again!" The woman behind the desk exclaimed. "She's in good spirits today. I told her y'all would be taking her for an outing. I hope I'm not over-stepping, but I think it's so nice of you folks to visit her. Especially given the, you know, *situation*." She looked from Alec to his significant other with sympathy in her eyes. "That little girl has the sweetest family, and such a strong momma."

The three of them signed into the guest book, Alec signing for his daughter. The receptionist led them to the patient's room and gave them their privacy to visit.

Kristen sat propped up in the bed, unable to speak or move from the neck down. She stared blankly at the three visitors standing at the foot of her bed. She wanted nothing more than to lunge at the woman who she once confided in, now standing beside her husband with his arm around her waist. The most frustrating part of her condition was that mentally, she was all there, and week after week she had to sit in the company of the people who betrayed her, unable to yell or scream or warn one of her nurses.

"Kristen, we have to tell you something. A few things, actually. First of all, I quit my job. Elise finally broke the news to Isaiah, so I figured it would be best if I found somewhere else to work. You know, to keep the peace. I don't want any drama." Alec turned to Elise, who he had been seeing illicitly since just after Lilly's funeral. Elise comforted him in that devastating time, whereas his wife had just shut down, becoming a shell of herself.

"And the next thing. I've taken a new job outside of town. We'll be moving at the end of the month. Elise, Daisy and I." Kristen's heart shattered. They were taking her baby girl away. It wasn't enough that she had already lost one daughter, now they were depriving her of seeing the only thing she had kept holding on for. The couple were playing house with *her* little girl.

"But don't worry, I know it's inhumane to leave you here like this." Alec walked around the side of the bed, taking a seat on it beside Kristen. "So, we're going on an outing today. I've rented us a hot air balloon at the state fair!"

Kristen felt tears welling up in her eyes. How did it end up like this? She thought about her mother-in-law with regret. She should have known Stacy wasn't capable of all those things. Stacy could be uptight, sure, but she wasn't a monster.

The group of four arrived at the state fair after signing Kristen out of the facility for the day. Alec and Elise helped each other get Kristen into the basket of the hot air balloon before loading up themselves along with baby Daisy.

"Alrighty, folks, have ya ever been in one of these before?" The pilot asked. "I can take the reins, or I can show one of you how."

"No need, sir, I've done this before," Alec stated, and the pilot dismissed himself.

"Sure. You have two hours to return it."

Elise enjoyed the view, coasting over the fairgrounds and watching children running around eating corn dogs with their parents trailing behind them, begging them to slow down. She wore a baby carrier with Daisy snug inside, sleeping peacefully. Elise always wanted children, but Isaiah was totally against the idea, using work as an excuse. *I work too much*, he'd say. *I don't have time.*

"I have a confession to make, Kris, though I'm sure you've figured some things out on your own by now." Alec tried hard to hold back the smirk that was creeping upon his lips. "I planted a Bluetooth speaker in the vents of the house. I searched 'popping sounds' on YouTube and played that through the speaker." He laughed in a Machiavellian way as he combed through the memories. "I told my mom to get those balloons for the party. I said it was part of your healing. *Exposure therapy,* they call it. Healing from trauma by facing it head-on. The first set of flowers in the hospital were from her, the second set with the balloon? I had those sent anonymously. She was just the middleman, caught at an unlucky time. They must have been delivered right as she showed up and she offered to bring them in."

"I found your journal, Kris. We read the whole thing, Elise and me. I know you thought my mom was behind all of this. I know you were going to kill her. I showed up five seconds..." Alex trailed off, his voice cracking as he tried hard not to cry. "Five seconds too late. So, congratulations," he continued.

"I was going to leave you that day. I brought you coffee to lighten a heavy situation. I was ready to break the news and be with Elise, but then you told me you were pregnant. I couldn't leave you; things would have gotten messy. And I wanted my baby in my life. Elise will take good care of her, don't worry." He stood up and grabbed Kristen by the waist, lifting her easily since she couldn't move on her own free will. With a gentle push, Alec heaved his former wife over the edge of the basket, sending her careening downward from eight hundred feet in the air. They were over the river now, and he was sure she would land swiftly into the water, but knew she would drown due to her paralysis.

The new family sat together peacefully and enjoyed the rest of their ride, knowing it would be easy to pin Kristen's death on a horrific accident. *She wanted to see the view,* they would say, *so we helped her to the edge. We lost control as the winds got stronger.*

"Hey, what about the kid? She wrote in her journal that she thought your mom bribed a kid the day we had coffee together. Was that you? Did you really set that boy up in the coffee shop?" Elise asked. Alex was amused at the accusation.

"Wasn't me," he smirked at his lover, "that... that was just fate."

3

VELOXROTAPHOBIA

BY JOSEPH MURNANE

I am five years old, and my hands sweat as I grip the railing. I have to reach up to grasp it. I struggle against tears in my eyes, proof of my weakness. The line is moving, and I feel a stern hand on my back, pushing me along. My fear is precisely why I'm in this line. I'm supposed to learn a lesson, but all I can think about is trying not to vomit on my Scooby-Doo shoes.

I love Scooby because he's like me; perpetually afraid. However, the gang loves him anyway, and that's where our experiences split. Dad says I'll never be a man if I'm always afraid, but I'm so small that it feels all I can do is cower and brace against a world that seems too cruel, too indifferent for me to ever understand. I know I am weak because he tells me so, and I am so sorry.

As the line moves, inching us closer to my important lesson, I feel the eyes of surrounding strangers burning into me. Later, I will come to understand that they aren't looking at me. They're looking at him, wondering why he's forcing his small son through this, but I don't know that now. Hot shame burns my cheeks, because they all know that I'm a coward.

He tells me that I'll be okay, but there is no kindness or encouragement in his voice. Instead, it feels like he's making fun of me. My heart pounds in my chest and I wish I was in my room where the world can't see me.

But they can all see me clearly as we reach the end of the queue. I wonder if adults can smell fear as he pushes me along and into the car. Not just any car, but the one at the very front of the train. The coaster operator gives me a look, asks if I'm sure, and my father answers for me, tells the man to mind his business. Reluctantly, the man lowers the restraint bar over my lap, and I've never felt so trapped. I'm breathing so fast, and yet I'm suffocating. A warning alert chimes, and the train begins to roll forward on its track.

That's when I start to scream.

I buck against the bar, against his vice-like grip on my shoulder. I sob and beg and now I'm not breathing at all. I wonder if I'm dying. I can't go up that hill. If I do, I know I'll never make it back down. Why won't he listen to me? Why won't *anybody* listen to me.

I'm dying.

I'm dying.

I'm dying.

But now the train is stopping, reversing, and I can feel every eye on me, derisive, disgusted. An embarrassing worm holding up everybody else's day at the park.

My legs feel like jelly as they release the bar, and I fall out of the cart. I look up at my father, but he won't look at me. I buckle over and my shame spills from my body, ruining my shoes after all.

He laughs, and I feel even smaller than ever. I've never had a panic attack before.

But I'll never stop having them.

�

Now I am ten years old, watching through the wooden bars at the top of the stairs as he holds a flame beneath a glass pipe, sending acrid chemical fumes throughout the house. He doesn't know I'm here—or maybe he's forgotten I exist altogether—so I watch him until I can't bear the smell anymore. I retreat to my room, careful not to make a sound.

Creedence Clearwater Revival drifts up the stairs, dancing with the smoke, and I try to ignore it as I hold council with my inanimate friends. I tell them about my day at school, surrounded by other kids and yet so alone. I tell them about the movies I want to see. Shrek is coming out next week and I hope it's funny. I like the donkey in the preview. I ask my friends questions. There are no answers to be found in their plastic eyes and cotton stuffing. I wonder why he hates me so much.

I do not know that soon he will crash into my room in the middle of the night, gathering my friends into plastic bags and hauling them out to the curb. He will say it's time for me to grow up, but the older I get, the younger I feel. I don't know what's wrong with me, but in this moment, I am not alone. Not yet.

ᗄᗄᗄᗄᗄᗄᗄ

I am thirteen, and despite my weakness, a girl likes me. She thinks that I'm funny and kind. She tells me that it's okay to be afraid sometimes. Her name is Madeline, and I don't yet know it, but she will be my first kiss. She gets off the bus with me and I'm nervous for him to meet her, as though I can hold this person up to him and say "you see? There's nothing wrong with me."

"Hmm," he grunts. "Thought you were a faggot."

I am humiliated even though I don't know what a faggot is. I've heard the word on the playground but never directed at me. Nobody else seems to see me, at least not until now. Madeline explains it to me and I'm only more confused. I don't think it sounds like such a bad thing to be. I don't know what I am, but I know that I like her. I don't see why it matters, but maybe that's enough.

ᗯᗯᗯᗯᗯᗯ

I am eighteen. Despite it all, I've made it to my high school graduation. Tonight, he will punch me in the mouth and throw a random assortment of my things out into the yard. He will tell me not to come back as I lay on my back wishing for the stars in my eyes to swallow me whole.

But for now, a smile and a foreign sense of pride is keeping me warm as I hold my diploma. Madeline squeezes my hand, because right now, neither of us know that tomorrow I will tell her that I'm a curse, that she needs to give up on me. Neither of us know that she will listen, that I'll never see her again. I will tell myself that she's better off, and over time, I'll come to believe it.

I'll hope that she does, too, but right now, it's all right there in front of us. I still think I might be able to get off the tracks before it's too late.

ᗯᗯᗯᗯᗯᗯ

It is my twenty-first birthday. I am strung out at a truck stop somewhere in Virginia. Police come and herd me away. It begins to rain, and I take cover beneath an overpass. They say life is short, but it feels oh so fucking long to me. I drift off to sleep and hope I don't wake up, as I do most nights. My dreams are a never-ending ascent. Miles and miles of endless, rickety track, always waiting for the drop that never comes. I wake up screaming in terror and failure. The three cigarettes I have left have slipped from my pocket and now lay wet and ruined on the pavement. I crush them with my foot as I walk away. I am a living razorblade, poised to cut into anybody foolish enough to come too close. I leave the road and follow the train tracks beneath my feet and up my arms, praying for the drop.

🦷🦷🦷🦷🦷🦷

I am twenty-three, waking up handcuffed to a hospital bed. I rage and scream because I'm not supposed to be here anymore. It's supposed to be over and how fucking dare they take that away from me? A nurse comes to calm me down and I sink my teeth into her comforting hand. Orderlies fill the room and flip me over. I feel the prick of a needle in my ass-cheek, and everything goes black.

I will spend the next few weeks trembling, clutching the rim of a toilet as I dry out, the crashing roar of the coaster ringing in my ears. They will call my father, but he won't come. I will practically see the spit flying from his mouth around the word junkie, so loud through the phone both the nurse and I flinch. I will wonder if he sees the irony in it all.

🦷🦷🦷🦷🦷🦷

I am thirty-one, the oldest in my graduating class of brand-new engineers. I am sober, and for the first time, there is a foreshadowing of success to come in my life. But I am still an empty man. I did not do this to succeed, but rather to take the first steps in my plan of retribution. I have accepted a paid internship at the park where it all started. My only purpose is to harness my fear. To conquer it.

To weaponize it.

☙ 🦷🦷🦷🦷🦷🦷 ❧

I am forty-five when I retire early as the foremost coaster designer in the world. My rides have instilled terror and joy in millions across the planet, and I hate them all. Every single smiling face. I purchase ninety acres in the desert because I need flat ground to build. For the next five years, the only other people I see will be contractors hired to do the work that I can't. They do not understand what they are building, but knowing isn't part of their job description. They are naught but ants in my hill, and the work will be done, but I cannot risk them catching on. All it would take is for one of them to see the same online video I once did, for them to understand what this is.

Therefore, I change crews every few months, building in pieces, never letting any of them see the full picture. Most of the workers think of me as a standard millionaire building my own playground, because that's what I want them to think. It isn't until I bring the last group on for final assembly that the secret can't be hidden any longer, but I pay them millions for their silence. I won't need the money for much longer anyway. None of those men need to work again any time soon, and me? Well, it's almost over.

🦷🦷🦷🦷🦷🦷

I have just turned fifty when I charter a plane to a local airfield, then a helicopter, landing beside the hospice center where my father luckily still persists. It would have been a shame if the work hadn't been finished in time. But of course, I never would have allowed that.

I have not seen him in decades, despite paying for all of his care. The nurses and doctors advise against me taking him, but when your checkbook is bottomless, it tends to shut mouths and turn eyes away. He is a nearly empty shell, but I am made of blistering hatred and bitter resolve. There is no turning back. I watch him stare out the window as we fly away.

I can barely contain my excitement as I roll his chair across the rocky ground toward the boarding station back on my compound.

"Look," I say. "Look what I made for you."

He mutters something unintelligible and grasps weakly over his shoulder at my hand. I jerk it away. He doesn't get to touch me anymore. Not without my say-so.

"I'm sure you've seen some of my designs over the years, but sadly, I can't take credit for this one."

He doesn't respond, so I continue:

"What you see here, what you're about to test for me, was designed by a Lithuanian PhD candidate way back in 2010. Until now, the design has only been hypothetical, but I built it for you. For *us*. Allow me to introduce you to my opus. Are you ready to ride the euthanasia coaster?"

He doesn't understand. The hulking paragon of abuse has shrunk into himself, too frail to rightly fear the destiny I've built for him.

"Are you listening?" I ask, and I can hear him struggling to speak. I lean in close enough to hear.

"P-p-please, son." He says, and repeats the words, the only two he can find.

"P-p-p-*please*," I mimic, furious at his weakness. That which he hated so much in me, is now all he is, and it isn't fair. I smack the back of his wrinkled head, as he must have done to me 1000 times over the years. He slumps in his chair, and I have to catch him to prevent him from spilling out onto the ground.

I wrap around the chair so I'm standing in front of him, and I slap him in the face to make sure he's paying attention.

"Are you familiar with the term, 'prolonged cerebral hypoxia'?" I ask. "All things considered, it's far more merciful than you deserve."

More mumbles for me to ignore.

"Here's what's going to happen," I continue. "We're going to get in that cart—I specially designed it so you won't even have to get out of that chair— and it will take us 2000 feet up into the sky. In our descent, we will reach a speed of 220 miles per hour, and ten Gs of force are going to melt that cruel fucking head of yours. Once we reach terminal velocity, we will enter the first of seven loops. Don't worry. You'll be unconscious by the time we hit the second one, maybe even before that, as delicate as you've become in your old age."

This doesn't feel right. The man I knew was a living demon, propelled by animosity and crack pipe ferocity. He isn't supposed to be so...*goddamn feeble*.

But I can't stop now, can I? Not after all I've done, how far I've come just to land right back in the same place: at the foot of my own greatest terror alongside my father. Only it's different now.

He seems to have fallen asleep as we reach the boarding station. I wheel him into his specialized cart, eyeing my own seat at his side. He snores softly. The doubt growing in my chest feels as heavy as the remote in my pocket. The controller has only one button. Once engaged, there will be no stopping.

No kill switch.

Because I am the kill switch.

And I've already been rolling up this hill for so many years that he won't even understand the justice that I spent my life engineering for him. It's been so long that vengeance has changed colors, donned a new coat that's more akin to mercy.

And I hate him for that, too.

Nevertheless, I continue. Once he's strapped in, his wheels locked into the clamps I had installed, I hop the tracks and circle to the other side, where I take my seat and lower the restraint bar.

This is where we were supposed to talk. Where he was to understand all he's done to me that brought us here. But he's lost the ability to speak, maybe even to hear, so we sit in silence for a time, his head slumped forward, me listening to his snores.

I think of Madeline, and I feel a great shame. She was the only one that ever saw me, and I wonder what she'd say if she saw what I'm doing now. Would she think I'm a monster? Would she try to stop me? Would I allow her to? Could this all have gone differently? Is there a world in which I was ever happy? Did I build my own tracks as metaphorically as I have literally?

There are too many questions and no time to dig for answers. I look over at the husk beside me, trying to come up with the right words to bring him to awareness, to light him up like Scooby-doo shoes and see my own terror reflected back from his eyes.

But he isn't snoring anymore.

There's a new stillness to his form and before I reach out and shake him, I already know.

I'm too late. He's left without me and I'm alone here under the watchful eye of the desert sun.

But maybe that's my own doing.

And maybe it never mattered whose fault it was.

All my plans, all my resentments, I can see them now as the holes I carved out of my own heart, juxtaposed against a sudden, inexplicable urge to *live*. To atone. To forgive. I decide that I do not want to take this ride.

I turn in my seat and throw my arms around the dead old man who made me, telling him I'm not angry, that I know he was just another broken person like so many of us.

And my hip bumps against the side of the cart, engaging the button in my pocket.

"No," I whisper, then scream. I wail against the ironic safety bar, but it doesn't budge because I designed it not to.

No kill switch.

The ground is already retreating beneath us as the cart ascends.

Click.

Click.

Click.

I know the ride up into the sky will take around five minutes and I tear at my restraints the entire way, animal panic coursing through my veins like a coyote caught in a snare trap.

I beg a God I've never spoken to for rescue, and even the limp corpse at my side, but neither respond.

The top of the hill is getting closer, and I can't breathe. I am as small and afraid as any child has ever been.

Through tears, I wonder how long it will take somebody to find us out here. How many months?

Could it be years?

The fear in my gut boils over and spills out of me, the wind and angle of ascent pushing it back into my own eyes.

I squeeze them shut and try to take my last breaths whole instead of in jagged pieces.

Rage never built anything worth its own materials, and I only know this now that it's far too late.

At the top, the cart stops for a moment, suspended as though it might change its mind.

There is an instant of blessed silence, and I hear bird-song through my own screams.

Then we begin our final ascent, and I feel speed and terror rip through my body in equal measure, my lungs devoid of oxygen, my machine working perfectly as we enter the first loop.

I'm dying.

I'm dying.

I'm—

4

CACOPHOBIA

BY MATTHEW LUTTON

The entire office hummed with a false sunlight that painted the room more than it actually lit it. Brian scratched the tip of his nose, stopping abruptly at the sharp sting as his fingernail sliced through the paper-like skin of his nostril.

"God damn it," he uttered under his breath, pulling a tissue from his sleeve and quickly sopping up the trickle of blood.

"This is the type of shit I'm talking about!" He yelled, throwing the bloody tissue across the large wooden desk. The tissue missed its target, instead landing among the many awards and certificates that adorned the table. Dr. Mansfield eyed the bloody rag as if his stare alone could make the thing disintegrate into nothing. He finally lifted his gaze to meet Brian's.

"I told you we would hit the wall, Brian. This..." he said, pinching the bloody tissue between his thumb and forefinger as he lifted it, "...is the wall." He tossed the tissue into the wastebasket and squirted a large glob of hand sanitizer, rubbing it in with the cadence of an experienced surgeon.

"I pay you to ignore the walls and to keep me looking young and pretty. Not make excuses."

Brian would have huffed in frustration, but he thought better of it in fear of his nose flying clean off. Dr. Mansfield opened the drawer to his right and produced a thin golden box. He placed it on the desk, unclasping it and withdrawing a single cigarette pausing to offer one to Brian who looked on in horror.

"Are you nuts? Do you have any idea what cigarettes do to your skin?"

Mansfield lit the cigarette and then inhaled the smoke deep into his chest, leaning back into his chair to finally release the long cloud of smoke like some awakened Dragon.

"I'm more concerned with what they do to my lungs, but we choose what kills us and make peace with it, don't we?" He tapped the ash on the glass candy dish that seemed to be more of a decoration than actual communal feeding trough.

"Don't people eat those?" Brian asked, pointing to the now apocalyptic looking pile of skittles.

Mansfield smiled, tapping the ash once again after a long drag atop the candy.

"Only the really fat ones and let's be honest, if they are across that desk they are going to eat them because they know I'm going to fix them. That somehow, I'm going to scoop out all of their insecurities and chisel away at the grotesquery that their parents or high fructose corn syrup bestowed upon them."

Brian nodded, brushing the feeling of being insulted off his shoulders.

"How much?"

Mansfield smiled, shaking his head and sliding his tongue across his perfect porcelain teeth.

It had been like this for as long as he could remember.

ᗡᗡᗡᗡᗡᗡ

Years ago

The cold seeped into Brian's bones, rattling him awake from the merciful little sleep he had managed to get. His legs jerked against the bare mattress creating friction and pain along the wrinkled skin. He welcomed the heat it created, ignoring the sharp burn that followed in a merry-go-round of pleasure and pain. His long-chipped nails wove their way into the broken fabric of the blanket, pulling it up to his crooked chin in a desperate attempt to stave off any further chill. It was no use though, and his body shook in protest desperately trying to warm itself. Brian's tears felt good, rolling across his sunken cheeks in a warm escape from the milky pools that he dared to even call eyes. He covered his mouth with the blanket trying to snuff out the whimpers that, despite his best efforts, continued to escape through the harelip he desperately tried to cover.

The door slammed open, fooling Brian's senses of salvation as heat poured in from the kitchen above. His body realized the danger when the creak of footsteps entered his dumbo-like ears. His body tensed like a corded knot at the sound, steeling itself in some ancient response of neither fight nor flight, but the coward's de-evolution of playing dead. His body dared not even breathe in its attempt to hide from the horror that was making its way down the steps.

"I told you to stay quiet down here!" The steps quickened as his mother's hand grasped the rail at the bottom of the stairs.

He tried to brush the lock of hair from his face in an attempt to "clean up" before his mother saw him, but it was no use. The flashlight highlighted all of his hideousness in a perfectly illuminated ball, like a moon crafted from all things made ugly displayed perfectly against the darkness.

"I'm so...sor...sorry, mama. I'm just so co...cold." Brian's teeth chattered, the rows of sharp and misaligned calcium dug into his cheeks and gums like a jackhammer tearing up a sidewalk.

His mother grasped the blanket with her other hand, tossing it to the damp floor beside her in a fit of annoyance. The steam escaped her nostrils billowing up her cheeks and into the air like an angry bull ready to gore his way through a crowd.

"Lucky I keep you at all—looking the way you do."

Brian shuddered, this time from his mother's words and not the frigid air. She came closer, only inches away from his horrific visage. She flared her nostrils and inhaled sharply, turning away in disgust.

"You smell as bad as you look."

She wasn't wrong. He was covered in his own waste, filling the basement with a dry cold stench as if someone had shit in a freezer. A cruel grin crept across his mother's face.

"You need a bath."

She walked over to the sink where the mounds of Brian's food bowls had become a permanent fixture across the porcelain. She turned the handle and cusped one of the bowls as the pipes of the sink moaned in protest against the cold. Water sprayed from every opening along the old sink, but a solid stream finally made its way out of the faucet. His mother dropped the bowl from the shock the freezing water gave her, and she laughed as the bowl shattered across the cold concrete. She grabbed another of the bowls filling it to the moldy rim and walked it over to the bed where Brian lay. She lifted the bowl above Brian and without warning tipped the bowl over slowly.

Brian's body contorted in a futile attempt to escape the freezing water. The cold stabbed at him like a swarm of angry bees making his skin tighten around him. He tried to scream but his lungs betrayed him, sucking in air, trapping it in the prison of his rib cage. His mother dropped the bowl shattering it on the cold hard concrete and walked back to the sink to retrieve another.

Brian was finally able to push the scream out through his chattering teeth.

"Ple...please...da...don't, mom."

The last thing Brian saw before the darkness overtook him was a bowl flying at his face.

ꟺꟺꟺꟺꟺꟺ

The beep of the machine shook Brian awake. He was warm, that was the first thing he noticed. The room was filled with machines that beeped and clicked various fluids into his arms. The nurse walked into the room and pressed the alarm button on the machine to silence it.

"How are you feeling?" she asked, offering him a sip of water. Brian tried to hide his face in his shoulder.

"Are you alright?" She placed the cup down on the bedside table. He nodded but said nothing.

"Hey, you're safe now, ok?" she whispered as she patted his thigh in reassurance. Brian was only usually allowed out of the basement once a month to go grocery shopping with his mother.

"The thing about being so hideous is that people will

act like you don't exist," his mother had told him. She had been right, most people out of fear or some false sense of politeness barely looked his way, but this nurse was staring him dead in the eyes with no sense of being afraid of his hideousness.

"There was a fire, and the firemen found you in the basement. They have some questions for you." The nurse glanced at Brian's wrist where the handcuffs had left sores. He tried to cover them, and she quickly looked away and headed toward the door.

"You let me know if you need anything."

And with that he was finally alone. He saw his reflection in the black screen of the monitor. His face was badly burned on one side with the skin melted together in a malformed hunk of flesh. He started to weep and fell back asleep to the sound of his sobs muffled by the lumpy pillow.

"Brian." He was shaken awake by a large man in a grey suit. The small smile that creaked out the side of his mouth showed teeth stained from years of too much caffeine and cigarettes, but it was gentle, nonetheless. His hair was starting to thin, and he could tell that the man had a career that had put years on him at an accelerated pace.

"I'm Detective Hornsby. I'd like to talk about your mom and some things we found if that's alright with you?"

Brian looked away trying to disappear into the other side of the bed.

"She can't hurt you anymore Brian. She's in custody and going away for a long time."

He looked back over his shoulder at the detective. He was nodding in reassurance.

"What do you want to know?"

ᗐᗐᗐᗐᗐᗐ

Brian told the detective what he thought he wanted to hear: how his mother had become enraged when his father left them, how she blamed him for it—blamed him for his looks —and how she locked him in the basement as punishment. The detective did his best to reassure Brian, telling him that his father's departure wasn't his fault and that his mother must have been struggling with something to treat him that way. But deep down, Brian knew better. He knew exactly what he looked like, and ever since he was a child, his mother had made sure to remind him at every opportunity.

Weeks passed, and Brian continued to beg doctors to fix his face, but they always brushed him off, insisting it was unnecessary. He wrote to insurance companies over and over, but each response was the same: "Not medically necessary." Those words ate at him, and each day, he could feel his ugliness growing—festering—manifesting itself in new wrinkles, boils, and moles.

Brian was beginning to become a problem for the hospital. He had stopped eating-refusing meals to ward off gaining any more weight to his already obese frame, but the nurses and doctors kept insisting that he needed to eat. It wasn't that he didn't appreciate their concern, he simply didn't deserve it. Nothing so ugly deserved something as beautiful as kindness.

He had made his way through almost all of the nursing staff when he had finally met Brittney. She always came in and never said a word, unlike the other nurses who couldn't stop asking him questions about how he looked. They would make condescending comments about how he should be proud of his features-that he was perfect just how he was. Brittney, however, didn't lie to him. Her silence said more truth than any amount of bullshit the others spewed his way, even if she did ignore any attempt he made at conversation. Brittney looked like a skeleton had put on makeup and sometimes Brian truly marveled at how someone's hip bones could stick out as far as they did without causing some type of damage, but she had a beauty to her weakness. Like a sick kitten who needed to be nursed. Brian straightened just before she made her rounds for the day. He had brushed his hair back ignoring the grease and flakes of dead skin that haloed his hospital gown and smiled, hoping his yellow teeth didn't scare her off. Brittney walked in stopping abruptly at the disturbing grin Brian threw her way and then continued on checking the various tubes that stuck out of him.

"How are you?" Brian pushed the words out in nervous pants like a dog almost out of breath. She smiled at him but continued on without acknowledging.

"What time do you end your shift?" Brian asked, raising a brow toward the clock with his one functional eye. She picked up the chart and thumbed through it. Brian knew this was how she ended her nights: Checked his fluids, read his chart and then left, never saying as much as hello. Rage started to fill his stomach as she turned and headed toward the door.

"Fat bitch."

The words shocked Brian as much as they had halted Brittney mid-step. His mind raced. Should he apologize? Or should he double down, hoping she retreated never to return so he didn't have to face his embarrassment. He tried to speak. What he tried to say he didn't know but nothing came out, instead he just stammered like a buffoon. Brittney turned her head looking over her shoulder slowly as if she was too afraid to look back at Brian.

"What did you say?" she whimpered. Brian raced through his head trying to come up with what to say

"You're fat...and a bitch." He couldn't have told you

why he had said it, but it felt good. She turned and faced him.

"Ya, well you're ugly!"

They both looked each other over until finally a smile crept across her lips. They both started to giggle until eventually they were filling the hospital room with laughter. She walked over to the edge of the bed and sat down.

"They told me if I don't go back to counseling, I'll lose my job here." She fidgeted with her wristwatch trying to not look at him. Brian didn't know what to say to that so he said the most obvious thing he could think of.

"You're not fat though," he said, like it should clear all of her problems away somehow. Brittney lifted her shirt. Her abdomen retreated into her stomach as she ran her fingers across her rib cage. She settled her hand on her hip and pinched the skin between her forefinger and thumb. Her face scrunched up in disgust as if she was smelling baby shit.

"I could tell you you're not ugly and that wouldn't matter, so don't tell me I'm not fat."

Brian nodded in solemn agreement.

"Do you want to see my favorite room here?" Brittney asked, perking up. Brian nodded again, not sure what she meant. A different hospital room? She grabbed his chart and motioned for him to follow. They walked down the hallway and down to the elevator. Nobody paid him much attention besides the passing glances and courteous smiles. He hated them all for being so fucking fake.

"Always carry a clipboard," Brittney said, tapping it with her pen. "People always think you're working on something and never question it."

Brian nodded in agreement. The doors opened to the highest floor of the hospital. As they exited, Brian noticed that it looked more like a furnished apartment than a hospital. The colors were brighter, more comforting than the standard green that muddied the room he had been in. Actual paintings adorned the various walls and fresh flowers sat on elegant marble tables.

"Cassandra?" Brittney called to the silhouette on the other side of the silk curtain.

"Come in dear," a warm husky voice trilled. Brittney pressed a button on the wall and the curtain pulled back to reveal one of the nicest beds Brian had ever seen. The woman was hooked up to an IV with a bandage around her nose. She nodded toward Brian.

"Who's your handsome friend dear?" she asked.

Brian looked away ashamed at her comment, whether she meant offense or not.

"Cassandra, this is Brian. Brian, this Cassandra. She and I have become friends since she visits us so much."

Cassandra held out her hand for Brian to kiss it. He took it and placed his lips on it trying not to drool all over it. Cassandra sat back and folded her hands in her lap.

"How are we on calories today? Have you been cheating at all?"

Brittney shook her head.

"Nope, only at 300. Dinner should be another 200," she said, patting her belly button. Cassandra smiled, reaching out and patting the same spot.

"Good for you. my dear. And you, what procedure are you here for?"

Brian looked away again trying to shy his face from her peering stare. Brittney handed the clipboard to Cassandra who snapped her fingers until Brittney grabbed her glasses and placed them into her hand. She scanned the page holding the spectacles out before her eyes.

"Oh, I see," she said, looking Brian over like a cat eyeing a mouse.

"Come closer child." She lifted a bony finger and bid him to her. Brian inched forward, placing his chin into her cupped hand. He didn't know why, but he felt comfortable in her grasp.

"You're hideous." Brian's blood ran cold. He tried to back away, but she gripped his chin tighter.

"That's not an insult. Lucky for you I have a soft spot for broken and ugly things," she said looking from Brian to Brittney and back at Brian in an almost loving manner.

"Do you have a place to stay?"

He didn't know how to respond. He hadn't given that any thought. Now that his mother was gone, he didn't really have anywhere to go. He shook his head no and she nodded.

"Well, you do now," she said, like it was already done. Brian was about to interject but something about the woman and the way she presented herself said that nothing was ever up for debate once she had decided on a matter. Within a couple of days, Cassandra had moved Brian into her luxurious home. His room was three times the size of the basement and he often thought how wasteful he actually considered it being just him occupying the space. The room was a haven with every form of entertainment Brian could ever want. Food was always within reach. Cassandra had commissioned a shawl that was dark enough to hide Brian's hideous features while giving him the confidence to interact with the staff.

Brian had noticed that the room was filled with everything he would ever need, except for one outlier—the bed. He had slept on an uncomfortable mattress in the basement, but this was something else entirely. In the center of the fantastical room was a bed no larger than a footrest. It was adorned with a tiny pillow and even a set of sheets. At first, Brian had thought it was a joke or perhaps even that of a doll play set, but he could tell from the look on Cassandra and the servants faces that this was indeed no joke. The first night was unbearable and quickly he found himself lying on the floor. The next couple nights he tried various positions all of which ended up in one muscle being pulled the wrong way leaving him in pain the next morning.

Brian rubbed his strained neck, hardly able to stomach any of the poached egg that was plated in front of him.

"You know dear, you can always climb into bed with me." Cassandra let the idea linger, winking at him as she placed the remainder of the egg into her recently filled lips. Brian winced underneath his veil. He couldn't believe that the Doctor had agreed to fill her lips even more. She was now on her third lip filler appointment, and it had only been two weeks. She must have paid the Doctor to agree to it. An idea shook Brian from his disgusted bewilderment.

"Could you have your doctor fix my face?" he asked, trying not to let the excitement of such a possibility betray his calm demeanor. Cassandra swallowed her egg and leaned her chin onto her fist. Her long-crooked elbow scooted the tablecloth as she leaned on to it.

"We can start with some...adjustments. But these doctors are very expensive, Brian," she said, pouting her lips —as much as she could—to show a sad expression.

"I would need something in return...some companionship." She fiddled with the fork on the table sliding a finger along the shaft. Brian swallowed hard as he lifted his veil.

"Why would you want this anywhere near you?" he asked, holding a hand beneath his chin. Cassandra climbed onto the table, losing her balance as she crawled toward Brian in a broken display of seduction. She placed a cold fragile hand behind his head and licked the milky residue at the corner of her lips.

"I told you; I enjoy broken things."

🦷🦷🦷🦷🦷🦷

Brian was healing nicely despite Cassandra's constant bitching about him becoming obsessed. Over the years he had undergone sixty-seven surgeries. Each one brought him closer to something resembling normal. Cassandra crept her way into the room, wheeling an oxygen tank behind her. Her hair was thin and brittle, filling her scalp in patches. Her once manicured nails were yellow and cracked. Her spine was curved from the constant hunching over to drag the machine giving her the cadence of an old crone. She disgusted Brian almost as much as he disgusted himself.

"You need to stop this," she moaned. Gasping between each word. Brian lowered the hand mirror he had been admiring his latest eye lift in and faced her.

"I'm finally on my way to being normal and you want to stop me?" Brian said, sounding wounded. She raised her bony fingers to touch his newly implanted cheeks, but he scoffed out of her reach.

"You're chiseling the statue into dust," she gasped, placing the mask over her mouth. Brian reached up pulling the mask down before she was able to suck in the sweet oxygen.

"I will not be ugly any longer!" he shouted, throwing the mask to the ground as he brushed past her. His shoulders bounced against her gigantic implants, sending her fragile pale frame falling to the ground. Her body exploded on the bedroom floor sending shivers of agony everywhere her nerve endings were still able to respond. Brian knelt down beside her and stroked her wrinkled sunken cheek. She lifted her hand, shaking from the pain and exhaustion, but still able to stroke the bandage that adorned Brian's swollen face. Her strength betrayed her, and her hand came crashing down to the floor but not before she gripped the bloody bandage strap in her shriveled fingers.

Brian scowled but his features were not able to show it. His lips looked as if they had been sliced off, replaced with thin strands of flesh representing more of a tight labia than anything kissable. His forehead had been stretched back tight, leaving a sheen against his large forehead that almost reflected like a polished mirror. He looked featureless as if turning into a Grey Alien.

"You're ruining it," Cassandra wheezed, laughing into a fit of wet coughs. Brian smirked even though nobody could see it.

"I'm finally starting to look normal, and you mock me for it. You adopt me, bring me here and force me to fuck your shriveled corpse, only allowing me a couple procedures when you can see I desperately need them!"

Brian walked over to Cassandra's dresser and lifted the large pearl handled mirror to his face, admiring the work of the newest surgeon who had agreed to fix him.

"Middle drawer, under the false bottom," Cassandra laughed.

Brian glanced to his left at the ornate drawer handle and then back to his face. He placed the mirror down with careful consideration and opened it, dancing his fingers along the bottom of the wood until he felt the lip of the drawer. He lifted it and pulled out a manilla envelope.

"What is this?" Brian tore it open pulling out a stack of papers.

"When she brought you to me, I could tell something was wrong with you. She never brought me anyone that I couldn't fix."

Brian glanced through the papers—his hospital file from when they had found him with his mother.

"I'd donated my money to charity cases like yourself

before, fixing the things that were broken and ugly. Jagged teeth here, some lopsided breasts there, but you I could tell that you were going to need some real work."

The pages were all standard listing his weight, his blood type, and injuries he had sustained while being kept in the basement.

"I thought I could keep you for my own if I fed into your delusion and maybe even improve upon what was already glorious."

Brian finally got the last page of the file.

"But in my sickness, I haven't been able to save you from yourself. You and Dr. Mansfield have ruined my beautiful toy."

The letters in a capital font standing out among the medical lingo.

DIAGNOSIS: BODY DYSMORPHIC DISORDER

1. PATIENT SHOWS EXTREME DELUSIONS THAT VARY FROM HIS ACTUAL APPEARANCE.
2. HIS APPEARANCE CHANGES FROM DAY-TO-DAY WITH DIFFERENT DEGREES OF WHAT HE FINDS TO BE UGLY.
3. THESE RANGE FROM MISSING BODY PARTS COMPLETELY, HARELIP, CROOKED EYES, DENTAL ISSUES, ETC.
4. PATIENT REFUSES MEDICATION AND BECOMES ENRAGED WHEN NURSES AND THERAPIST TRY TO EXPLAIN THE SITUATION TO HIM; THAT HE IS ACTUALLY QUITE ATTRACTIVE

ACCORDING TO MODERN BEAUTY STANDARDS.

Brian threw the file, and the pages scattered around the room like some sort of clinical confetti. He lifted the heavy mirror by the pearled handle and walked over to where Cassandra was lying with a smug look on her face.

"I knew when you told me to slow down on the surgeries that you were one of them. That you wanted me to stay this ugly so I would never be one of you, be loved like you," Brian stood over her sickly frame and ran his fingers along the mirror.

"I told Mansfield you wouldn't pay for the surgeries anymore, that you told me I needed to slow down and to heal, but he understood. He sees me and wants to fix me. So, he gave me a way to get rid of you."

Cassandra's eyes widened thinking of all the times Brian had insisted she eat and when she wouldn't, the IV bags he would have Dr. Mansfield hook up to her.

"I was wrong," Cassandra said, staring up into Brian's cold dark eyes.

"You are truly hideous."

Brian raised the heavy mirror with both hands above his head.

"I know, but I'm working on it."

5

ORNITHOPHOBIA

BY JULES TERRY

*S*he stood by the sink, fixated on the parting of the curtain at the window. Abril's pulse gradually elevated with each passing moment. Shadows wavered beyond the glass. Panic consumed her, amplifying the sound of her breathing. Her heart. The sound of blood pumping through her veins or the air moving in and out of her lungs was a vague recollection of the noise wings made as they cut through the air.

Whoosh. Swoosh. Whoosh. Swoosh.

Shattering glass pulled her from the trance, and she took the moment to pull the curtain tightly shut before turning to explore the sound.

A large, admittedly very overweight tabby sat on her counter where a glass of water previously existed. Against her better judgement, her eyes fell to the floor to find the blue and green shards of her favorite glass just below the glaring beast.

"You are a truly vapid and useless animal some days, Goose."

Her late grandmother named the cat for his uncanny

tendency to hiss and emit an ungodly honking noise—that no cat should never make—nearly anytime someone tried to pick him up or show him affection. The irony was not lost on her.

While she knelt to clean up the broken shards of glass, the cat peered over the edge of the counter. Occasionally, his large paw would make its way into the messy bun knotted on the top of her head. Abril swatted back and cursed the cat.

"I will foil these counters, and then we will see how tough you are." She punctuated the threat with a hiss of her own, tossing the pieces of glass into the trash bin.

Satisfied, she turned to look at the window again. Her grandmother's dying wish for Abril had been that her granddaughter would finally spend a full day outside and get over her fears. Of course, that was so everyone would be able to attend the funeral.

Guilt churned Abril's stomach. A familiar sensation now. She couldn't even fulfill that one last wish.

It wasn't as simple as agoraphobia. Simple wasn't the right word. She was being dismissive again, as her therapist often pointed out these days. It was a valid fear. Yet she felt if it were something like that, she could move to a smaller town, maybe in Wyoming or Kansas, and gradually reintegrate into society. Medication would be more effective. Behavioral therapy would be easier. For fucks sake, she was a person. She could be around other people and deal with social situations just fine.

Even other mammals were easier for her to cope with. Goose, as much of a nuisance as the cat could be, was consistent. He stuck to the same basic routine and existed in a realm of predictability. Dogs? They evolved next to humans and even made similar facial expressions.

"Gosh, what I wouldn't give to trade you in for a

golden retriever..." she mumbled to the glaring cat. She never would. Her grandmother loved this little varmint fiercely and he was good to the old woman in her last few years.

No. It wasn't fear of people, or open spaces, or even the big blue with the clouds.

It was fucking birds.

If there was anything about this world, it was that it was covered in the avian freaks. The way they turned their heads to look at someone made her skin crawl. Predator or prey, they tilt and swivel in a way that no natural creature should be able to do. Any noise coming from a beak would send her into a spiral. All she could think of were demons crawling from the pits of hell when she heard a caw, chirp, or squawk. She couldn't even think about the scaley feet in combination with feathers.

Fuh-reaks.

A reminder dinged, announcing that her therapy appointment was only fifteen minutes away now. She murmured a stressed *fuck* under her breath, filling a new glass of water before jogging to the living room to settle in on the couch. A golden eye, the folded ear from a lancing situation gone bad just above that glaring orb twitch, peaked out around the corner from the kitchen.

Abril flipped the bird at the cat. The eye narrowed and sunk back behind the lip of the wall. One corner of her mouth turned up in an amused smile, for once entertained by this small twist of irony.

Her phone pinged with the five-minute warning. Time for her usual ritual. Prepare the pillow cocoon. Light the calming candles with scents of bergamot, lavender, and jasmine. Get the phone on the stand and the link opened. Breathe. Slowly. In. Out. One, two, three...

The therapist's homely face with her signature mauve

lips filled the screen right on cue. The tightly pulled bun always caused Arbil's head to start aching when she saw it.

"Abril, lovely to see you. How has the last week been for you?"

"Hey, Dr. Lewis. I kept the panic attacks under control. I cracked the curtains this week, too." She watched the woman's eyebrow peak briefly, before she jotted a note on her legal pad.

"Excellent. Let's dive into it then. Can you get through the story without stopping, you think?"

Nails bit painfully into her left palm. She'd forgotten her stress ball. She breathed in through her nose, and out through her mouth. She flexed her hands and stared at the red crescents left on the one hand.

"Miss Hernandez, please focus. You only have 45 minutes left of our session this week and you've made tremendous progress," Dr. Lewis was staring at her with the stern expression she reserved when Abril attempted to disassociate. While the woman's tone was supportive, the telltale clicking of her pen could be heard somewhere off screen.

The younger woman nodded, somewhat defeated while trying to rally her defenses, "Where to start..."

"From the beginning, please."

With a nod, Abril leapt in.

"When I was thirteen, my nana had a friend who needed help. The woman was quite elderly, and having recently fallen and broken her hip, she needed help moving around her house. Cleaning up. Taking care of..."

The therapist continued to stare at her, not saving her from this despite knowing the story.

"...Of her-her pets. Birds."

A click of the pen and a nod, another note scribbled, "Continue, please."

"Miss Lydia was lively, but infirm. While I was at

school, her nephew should've been checking on her. Especially the week I was *sick*." The word was said with venom. She felt her face contort as she remembered the dead-beat boy who cared only about getting to Hollywood and partying.

She looked at her psychologist, and the woman's eyebrow pulled up again.

"I apologize. You're right. Forgiveness helps healing." She said it, but still did not accept it.

"Anyway, I went over first thing on Sunday after feeling better to check in. I loved listening to her stories and wanted to ensure she had all she needed. When she didn't answer the door, I thought perhaps she had slept in. She had no way to get to church anymore. Her doctor's encouraged her to rest more when she could.

I checked the back door. It was also locked. So, I went to the... bird feeder... where the spare key was. Her living room was right there when you opened the door. It was transformed into an atrium for her animals. The cages were never locked. They could roam all they wanted- "

Dr. Lewis cut her off, "It is ok to pause. Maybe take a drink of water."

It wasn't a question. It was a command. Abril had not realized that she was nearly hyperventilating. Swiping the water glasses from the table, she took three chugs and took a breath between each one until her pulse began to stabilize. An errant drop dribbled down her chin, which she wiped away with the back of her hand. She heard the pen scratching again, before realizing the woman had seen the crescents.

"I forgot my stress ball."

"As long as we aren't regressing, Abril. We have a good plan in place for self-harm. Continue. You're doing exceptionally well, and we are down to 25 minutes."

She nodded and replaced the glass on the table.

"Lydia was in her favorite chair. Covered in *them*. None of the lights were on, which was a little odd, but it is usually sunny in San Diego. I thought she was enjoying the natural lighting. There were no curtains in the living room. Birds are diurnal. She wanted them to live as naturally as they could.

Then one that was on her shoulder moved, and I saw her face.

What thirteen-year-old can immediately reconcile that? I thought it was a sick prank that her nephew convinced her to play. Then I realized her chest was only moving because of the animals. Her nephew had not come to check on her.

Miss Lydia died alone. The doctors later said she had a stroke. Not uncommon after hip surgery, especially if she was stagnant for so long. Maybe it was already hiding somewhere and would have happened anyway."

Abril paused, her vision narrowing at the edges for a moment. She pressed her knuckles to her eyes, taking a deep breath, "Sorry, I need just a moment before this next part."

She couldn't see the therapist's curt nod but could hear the rapid pen clicking. Short scribbles. Was she drawing a fucking picture? *Calm down, Abril. She's helping you.* One more deep, shaking breath, and she continued.

"Okay, so, like any animal without a food source, they went for what was available. The nephew did not come by or feed the birds. So, they went for Miss Lydia. The thing about a lot of birds, they love seeds and fruit and shit, but they will eat anything if they are starving.

The one that still haunts me, though, is Strawberry and that eye."

"Tell me more about Strawberry, Abril."

She grabbed the water once again, knowing the sadistic

woman wouldn't let her end there, and took another long pull of the liquid before replacing it on the table.

"Strawberry was her prized Scarlet Macaw. He was a beautiful bird, and honestly, a menace. He loved Miss Lydia and tolerated everyone else. He was maybe five at the time and she loved to tell people he would outlive her."

Did she imagine the fleeting smile on Dr. Lewis's lips just then? Abril continued.

"The other birds certainly did damage, but seeing one of Miss Lydia's hazel eyes in that beak, the optic nerve dangling..." the room tilted momentarily, "Well, I ran from the house. Screaming, of course. It broke me." She let the silence follow for a few moments. It was the good doctor's turn. She got through it, and she'd be damned if she didn't get a minute.

Dr. Lewis cleared her throat, "Abril, what still worries you now? We have about seven minutes, by the way."

Frustration consumed her, and she pulled her knees up under her. Her hands were punctuating each word.

"I left the door open! That fucking bird is out there, doctor!" Abril was going to rip that insufferable eyebrow off that woman's face if she ever got the chance. If it went any higher, it would become one with her hairline.

"Parrots are all over San 'Diego. *I'll* never forget that demonic animal, but some random animal control agent? Strawberry could be living with a murder of crows down the street for all I know." She sat back against her pillow fort, lip jutting out defiantly, and arms crossed over her chest.

"I believe you are ready. If we need a prescription for an SSRI, we can explore that, too. However, this was an excellent session. You didn't vasovagal at all." *You mean you get paid for a full session.* Abril sighed heavily, nodding.

"You're right. It only took ten years. I will consider opening the curtains fully."

"Consider leaving the house. Let's discuss it next week. If it doesn't go well, we can talk about medication that can help mute the anxiety. Take care." The woman didn't wait for any returned sentiment before disconnecting the call.

Like a petulant child, Abril stuck her tongue out at the phone before thrusting her foot out to knock the stand over. She left her foot resting on the coffee table and sunk further into the mound of pillows, pulling one into her arms to hug.

She squeezed the life out of that pillow like it was Strawberry, pretending that she had some control in her life again. The worst part of the whole event was not that she lived inside. She had a social life and overall enjoyed this little bubble. She kept things limited to nighttime to avoid the vapid animals.

The theft of her childhood, that wonder of the world, was what left her feeling the angriest. Between Strawberry, whom she had admired despite how intimidating the bird was, and the worthless nephew, she had lost the ability to enjoy the remaining precious years of her youth. Now at 23, left alone with a cat named after one of the most terrifying birds ever, she buried her face into the proverbially murdered pillow and cried.

🦷🦷🦷🦷🦷🦷

The sun streaming through the window assaulted her rousing senses. She sat up, rubbing the sleep from her eyes, trying to remember when she had stumbled to bed. Also, when the fuck was the last time she woke up to sunlight?

Peeking with just one eye, she saw her black out curtains were missing from the rod entirely. The edges of her vision began to narrow, her pulse jumping. *No, no, no. Breathe. I must've got into the wine and listened to Dr. Lewis.*

She scooted to the edge of her bed, eyes shut, and breathing deeply until her feet dangled from the edge of the bed. Slowly, she let her feet fall to the ground. Her world slowly leveled out again. She opened her eyes to look at the shadow her body cast against the wall from the light shining through the window. No other shadows joined her own.

A deep breath, and she pushed herself from the bed with the exhale.

She could do this. Today she would reclaim her life, her fucking childhood, and do something for herself. She was going to fucking Sea World.

Before she could change her mind, she grabbed her phone off the charger. Swipe. Tap. Uber order. She tossed the phone back on her bed.

The bathroom was a quick jog down the hallway, but something nagged at the edge of her brain. Picking away at it with clawed tips. Her eyes darted towards the living room, taking in the familiar setting. Her grandmother's old floral couch, which reminded her of pepperoni pizza. The pillows from the night before. The water glass, almost empty on the table and its shadow.

The shadow.

There was light streaming into the living room. Creeping towards the living room on the tips of her toes, she peaked around the corner to see all the thick curtains gone. Her body melded into the wall, shrinking back from the vicious photons that would undoubtedly contain *them*. She was a child whose comfort blanket was removed.

No. She thought firmly to herself. The mission would be accomplished.

Abril edged backwards until she felt the edge of the open door and flicked on the light. She nearly pissed herself when a *honk* followed by a most disconcerting growl responded to the intrusion.

"Fuck off, Goose," she grumbled at the animal staring at her from the toilet seat. The feline's gold eyes were narrowed to reproachful slits as he dismounted the porcelain throne, swiping at her ankle as he waddled by, his primordial pouch swinging. "No one is a morning beast. Find a better place to pass out next time."

Her life had digressed to insulting cats. One cat, in fact. She may well order a few more, get the club robe, and call herself a crazy cat lady. Abril chuckled at that as she turned on the relieved her bladder and reached over to turn on the shower.

Routine was her friend; this is how she'd get through this day. Focus on what she could control and then add something new. Afterwards she could reward herself with another bottle of wine, watch an old 80's movie, and pass out on the couch. Maybe Goose would grace her lap with his bountiful gut.

The rest of the morning passed in a blur. She stuck to the areas of her home that allowed the least visibility to the outside world, using her wavy, raven mane to shield her view of the outside world when necessary. Despite the warmer temperatures for spring, Abril covered herself in an oversized sweater and jeans. Less attention, and comfort. Focus on what you can control. When life is turning upside-down, grab it by the *cajónes*... or dress comfortably and discreetly.

A notification from her bedroom caught her attention.

With a hand over her eyes, she grabbed her phone. If she looked outside her window at that moment, a 2023 Toyota Prius with an Uber light in the windshield would greet her. A simple "Be right there" was shot back to the driver.

Leaving her house during the day in the past was accompanied by her nana and a strong dose of Valium. Today, Abril grabbed the umbrella by the door and the darkest pair of sunglasses she could locate.

ᗰᗰᗰᗰᗰᗰ

For an Uber driver, the young man—maybe 18 years old—was absolutely delighted to allow Abril to feign a migraine and hide her face for the duration of the ride. He earned an extra tip, despite not being able to drop her off right at the park's entrance.

As soon as she was out of the car's interior shield, her umbrella popped open in an instant, the shrieking call of the gulls ricocheted through her nervous system.

Not one of the white, feathered demons appeared in her line of sight directly, but she could hear them. She could see their shadows.

Across the street stood the entrance to the park. She simply had to walk to the pedestrian button, press it, and cross the street. A small fair to pay to see orcas, sea lions, sharks, and dolphins and get on a few rides. Of course, Abril would avoid the penguins. They may be flightless birds but could still brutalize anyone with those beaks. Especially the big ones.

"Abril!"

Her eyes blinked rapidly. A car must've screeched or a surf breaking... Again...

"Ab-RIL!" This more urgent call pulled her head to the right. An older woman sat on a bench next to a palm tree. Not far from her there were a handful of pigeons and seagulls. *Fucking rats of the sky. Vermin, all of them...*

She watched as the woman tossed what appeared to be seed or bread on the ground. A couple of the birds flocked towards her. Abril was frozen in her stupor. Here was a simple woman, in old age, feeding these beasts of hate and violence. She understood these were her own thoughts, so she squeezed her eyes shut. Tight. As tightly as humanly possible. She focused on what she could control at this moment.

Her breathing, of course. She listened to the sound of the waves coming in and receding from the coast. Cars drove past her. Even the breeze was a small comfort. Not only could she hear the breeze, but she could feel it. There was one sound that pulled her brows together in contemplation, the dancing palm shadows causing visions beyond her closed lids.

There was a squelching.

Someone's wet shoe might squelch. Maybe a sea lion was near her on the lawn. A Rolodex of sounds played through her mind that might *squelch*.

"Abriiil..."

She opened her eyes.

Red greeted her vision. A beak digging into the palm of the old woman's hand for seeds. No. Not seeds. Flesh. Tendon. Bone.

The woman looked at Abril, a graceful Mona Lisa smile on her lips while her dangling eyes swayed in the breeze. Her empty hand rose in a friendly waive. Frozen to the spot, unable to turn her wide eyes, Abril's hands tightened on the metal rod of her umbrella.

An eye, like a flamingo, black in the center with a starburst of red and yellow—a demon's eye—turned towards Abril.

She would not let this happen again. She couldn't. It was in her control this time. The worthless nephew was off living his glamorous life, but Abril could save this woman.

She took a small step, despite the world shifting, and then another.

"Hey, Strawberry! You beaked freak!"

Every head in the flock turned toward her. It was a breathless moment. The woman's mouth turned down in a frown.

"Abril, why must you hold a grudge?" The blood red bird squawked before taking flight, in her direction.

She screamed and screamed. It would not stop.

Until, finally, the old woman was shaking her, her face and body unmarred from the avian attack.

"Dear girl, are you alright? Should I call someone?" A homely face peered down at Abril; concern written across the features.

She flinched from the unharmed visage, attempting to process the situation. Abril looked over one shoulder, then the other. She made brief eye contact with the woman before rising from an unconscious crouch. "I'm so sorry, did you see that bird?"

The woman's wrinkles deepened. Abril simply waved her off and turned toward the beach.

It was a short walk. She didn't realize that the public beach was so close to the entrance of SeaWorld. The logic should've made sense considering the ocean was required for the animals who lived there.

Abril planted her bottom in a spot near a populated area. There were not only plenty of umbrellas, but people. She'd read online that wild birds did not particularly enjoy the company of humans.

Sure, the food was nice, but the acquaintance of mammals was not a regular occurrence.

With the umbrella planted firmly in the sand—the excrement of parrot fish and other animals, if her research proved to be correct—she leaned back in the sand.

The sounds of the waves breaking brought her comfort for some time. When was the last time she ventured out into the world to get vitamin D or just a bit of Dopamine? Serotonin? Life would be simple if she could just step outside for a few minutes, instead of getting her fix from a bottle.

While there was absolutely nothing wrong with her daily dose of sunshine in a bottle, she wished it could come naturally for once.

Abril lay on the sand with her eyes closed, letting her fingers trace patterns in the warm grains. Her umbrella stuck in the sand to block out the view of the sky, she focused on what she could feel, smell, and hear. The sand and the warmth. An ocean breeze with its briny undertone. Waves crashing, the cars from the nearby highway, and...

Squelch. Squelch. Squelch.

Eyebrows drawn tight together, she focused on the sound, determining whether it grew closer or further. It did not. It existed in a static location not far from her location on the sand. A few other beach goers were posted nearby when she'd settled. Sunscreen. Slurping on a drink. Walking through wet sand...

She was curiosity's prey. One eye cracked, and with nothing in front of her to determine the source of the sound, she ever so slightly tilted her head toward her left. Flashes of white over a beach towel of crimson and blue. The eye squeezed shut again.

"Abriiil..." a mocking voice hissed, a symphony or gull calling, joining in to highlight the single lyric, "We saved you some, Abril."

Violent shaking consumed her world, a single word became her mantra: no.

"Come see what we made for you," the voice, so close to her ear, so familiar, whispered. Her eyes shot open, while her entire body turned to defend from the demonic bird. Empty space greeted her directly to her left. Beyond that a few feet away were the birds. Strawberry hovered a few feet above the flock, a long rope dangling from his beak.

Not a rope. Her eyes traveled to the rest of the birds—white feathers now pink from the fluids of their meal. A childlike face protruded from one end of the flock, grinning in her direction.

The macaw let the coiled innards drop, the sudden impact making the most awful noise Abril's mind could manifest. Surprised, the rest of the birds scattered momentarily, revealing their gruesome work. The beach towel blackened with blood and scattered with gore.

"It's all for you, Abril!" The crimson animal screeched before diving in her direction.

Her own flight instincts kicked into overdrive, saving her for once, but not before she earned a mouthful of sand. Others walking along the shore stared at her in confusion, greeting Strawberry as if he were a friend. The beating of the wings grew louder, her breath matching the staccato sound.

It was far too late for her to realize the mistake of her ways. Fighting off the bird with her umbrella may have saved her. Instead, she ran back toward the park and the busy road before it. The suburban barreling down the highway had no time to stop.

Her therapist often talked about the third fear response, stating Abril suffered from it more than she realized. The younger woman often rolled her eyes at this statement, muttering only deer did. However, at that moment, she was frozen. Fight, flight, freeze.

"We won't let you go to waste, Abriiil..."

The impact took the scream from her lungs. She heard

the glass shatter. The wheels emitted a screeching noise. It repeated...

Her Dead-Strawberry pillow flew across the living room when her body came forward from the couch cushions. She gasped to bring oxygen to her tired brain.

The alarm on her phone continued to ring, screeching at her to get up and start the day.

"Oh... oh, thank fuck." She fell back against the pillows, making eye contact with Goose. The feline perched at the edge of the coffee table, licking one of his too-small paws. He cracked a single, indignant eye to glare at her before resuming his mission.

Against her better judgement, Abril leaned forward to find a pink and green glass shattered on the tile floor of the living room.

"Alright, you cobra chicken wannabe. We're getting plastic," she paused, grabbing her phone from where it had landed earlier, "but from Amazon. I'll leave the house in thirty years when I know that bastard bird is dead."

6

UROPHOBIA

BY JAY BOWER

I push open the bathroom door. The leftover funk of a previous occupant's bowel movement permeated my nostrils. It was just another reason I shouldn't have been there.

My heart raced and my breathing grew rapid. I had to tell myself to keep it together.

It's just a bathroom. It's only a bathroom. You have nothing to fear.

I stepped up to the urinal. A bead of sweat dribbled down my forehead. I wiped it away with the back of my hand, then unzipped my pants.

Looking down into the porcelain basin, I was greeted with an almost orangish liquid that carried a putrid stench of piss. I almost couldn't get started.

There were two urinals and two stalls in the rest stop bathroom. My wife Lydia and I had been traveling overnight while returning from vacation. It was close to two in the morning and there was only one other car in the lot when we pulled in. Lydia waited in the car after we had a massive blowout regarding what I was doing right then: pissing.

Well, almost pissing. I still couldn't will my body to obey. Maybe it was the smells? Maybe it was the fear I'd had ever since I was a child of using a urinal. What happened when I was a teen only exasperated the phobia.

I was way too young when I was watching a horror movie late one night. I don't recall the name, but there was one scene where the killer crept behind the victim—a teenage boy–while he was standing at a urinal with no cares in the world. With this back to the killer, he gleefully released his bladder, whistling as he did so. Moments later, the killer shoved a ten-inch-long knife through his back. The boy died with his dick sticking out of his pants.

I remember thinking that while the killer was behind him, all he needed to do was smash the kid's head into the tile wall just inches from his head. The blow would be more than enough to crack his skull and kill him.

Not now. Not now. Just let it out and get the hell out of here!

I looked down at my flaccid penis in my right hand and willed it to work. The pain in my bladder was powerful. Blinding. Yet my body froze, a statue that should be spouting water. Or piss.

The noxious funk of some stranger's moments in the bathroom burned my nostrils. Everything I was experiencing was a giant red flag telling me to get the hell out of there.

But my bladder. My poor, stricken, painful bladder. Filled with Diet Coke and coffee and two bottles of water. It was a miracle that I hadn't pissed my pants in the car. My eyes were swimming by the time I agreed to Lydia's demand that we stop. She knows my fears and sometimes gives me slack. Tonight was not one of those nights.

I turned my head to each side. Surely there was someone behind me. There's *always* someone behind me. Like the killer in the movie. Or the man from the bathroom at the restaurant.

No, not here. Not now. It's just me. If you don't hurry, someone will *come in and then what? How are you going to handle it then?*

I swallowed hard, tasting the lingering funk, and wished...prayed...for my body to follow orders.

The moment a slow dribble escaped the tip, the door flung open, and my stream cut off like a dam had been instantly erected within me.

My heart tried to punch through my ribs. I let out a gasp.

"Hey," the man said to me as he sidled up to the next urinal. He was a large trucker with a blue plaid shirt and dingy red cap with a Mack Trucks logo emblazoned on the front. He smelled like cigarettes.

In no time he was pissing, making loud splashing sounds as he did so.

"Ahh," he said, as a fart escaped him. "Oops."

Stage fright had taken over. My legs shook. How was I supposed to relieve myself with this oaf of a man next to me?

When he was done, he shook his dick and tucked it back in his pants, zipping it home. He didn't bother to flush.

He washed his hands and used the air dryer, the sound deafening. It did stir the air and no longer was the stale stench of shit in my nose. The dryer turned off and he lumbered out of the door.

The entire time my anxiety had been through the roof. I couldn't perform the simple act of relieving myself because I was too focused on the man next to me and the possibility that he might harm me.

I turned to face the ceramic tile wall just inches from my forehead. The dirty grout outlined three inch smooth and shiny squares. They were a light blue color, lighter than the sky. The grout was white once, but most had turned a dull gray. Splotches of a dark liquid dotted the grout and splayed out onto three tiles.

This is how I die. Someone is going to smash my head into the tile and my skull will be split open, my brains spilling out into the bowl of orangy piss in front of me. I've lived forty-five years and raised two sons only to have my life extinguished in a public bathroom along interstate 64. Death is coming, and yet my bladder is full.

I've seen it happen. I know it's a possibility.

I know I've been here too long. Lydia does too. My phone goes off in my pocket, the crystalline jingle of my ringtone set specifically for her filling the now empty bathroom with its tone. I can't answer it. Not yet. Not when I'm holding my dick in one hand and trying to muster the courage to let the urine flow.

You can do it. All you have to do is start again. It'll flow. Don't worry about any danger. Nothing will harm you. Nothing.

My pep talk falls flat, yet my aching bladder is screaming at me. I can't hold it off much longer, but I also can't expel my urine.

I'm at a standstill. A Mexican standoff. Someone needs to make the first move to relieve the pressure of the moment.

The door opens again and my heart thumps loudly in my chest. I can't take much more of this.

The man that enters is much smaller than the previous occupant. He's older too, maybe in his late sixties. He's got wire-rimmed glasses and thin, gray hair. He's vaguely familiar but I dismiss the notion. He shuffles next to me at the urinal. I try not to look in his direction, but out of the corner of my eye, I don't dare ignore him.

He might kill me.

It's a dumb thought. Yet, it won't leave my mind. Staring intently at the tiles threateningly close to my head, I say a quick prayer that God might spare my life and not let me die in the bathroom.

The man next to me grunts and groans. A barely audible fart escapes him.

"Oh dear," he says. He flushes the toilet but instead of zipping up and washing his hands, he shuffles to one of the stalls. He slams the door closed and drops down onto the black seat.

"Ahh," he says, after which the toilet water splashes from the projectiles coming out of the man. I close my eyes, knowing that soon I'll be engulfed in another grotesque funk.

Come on, damn it. Just piss already!

The frustration building within me as my body refuses to comply only makes the situation worse. I'm actively working against myself because of a stupid phobia earned when I was a child. People grow out of those things all the time. I should have ditched this asinine fear years ago.

But I didn't.

And now I cling to a primal dread, to the absurd notion that a stranger is going to kill me while I'm occupied. It's a powerful feeling of helplessness. I so badly want to deny the feeling. I want to smash it into nothingness, to make it explode into a thousand shards that can never be put back together again. I will it into being. Or at least I try.

I'm failing. My mind screams to let it go. A drill

sergeant roaring his commands. Like a petulant recruit, my bladder refuses.

It's the fear. I feel it traveling up and down my spine, curling around my vertebrae and tightening its grip. No python was ever wrapped as tightly around its prey as the fear is doing to me. It's suffocating. Demoralizing. Crippling.

It's hard to focus. My chest constricts. I'm aware that my breathing is picking up and I'm in danger of hyperventilating.

My concentration is broken by the man in the stall who lets out a pained grunt, followed by a splash.

"Good gravy, that feels good," the man says. The relief is evident in his tone. I instantly envision a toilet bowl filled with a soupy brown liquid with chunks of unknown origin floating gleefully amidst the muck. It's not something I want to think about, yet it's all I can think about. It's my mind's way of distracting me from what I should be doing.

His expression is familiar. Am I making connections when none exist? My mind is cracking. I have to relieve myself or face losing more of my sanity.

My phone goes off again. It startles me. Rips me from my thoughts once again. Maybe I should answer it and let Lydia know all is well.

But is it?

Well?

It would be a lie. Not the first one I've told her, either. I don't like to lie to her. She's done more for me over the years than I could have ever hoped for. She's brought me from the brink many times over.

"Aren't you gonna answer that?" a small, squeaky voice calls out from the stall. It's the man, taking a break from giving birth to a chunky baby.

"Hey fella, are you still there?"

"Yes," I quickly reply.

He grunts. Splashdown. How can one man hold so much waste?

My phone goes quiet. A new worry crawls into my brain. Lydia. She'll come in here. She's done it before. It's been years since she's had to resort to that, but the longer I take and the more I ignore her calls, the likelihood of her bursting into the bathroom goes up.

You have nothing to fear. There are no killers here. You are safe. Just let it flow. Water. Waterfalls. Rivers. A lake. Ocean waves crashing on a beach.

Small vignettes of water in motion flash through my head. An aquatic slideshow that does nothing to persuade my body to give in and let go.

Toilet paper unrolls. Several long pulls by the sound of it. Then a muffled wiping sound. Flush. The loud pull of the water down the toilet is soon followed by a zipper and then a belt being buckled back in place. The door unlocks and the man steps out.

"Hey buddy, are you ok? You've been there a long time."

He washes his hands, taking time to get soap in all the nooks and crannies.

Happy birthday to me. Happy birthday to me.

The song continues in my head. Twice. Precisely demarcating the amount of time needed to wash your hands. Yet the man takes it a little further, not stopping until I hit midway through the rendition.

He turns the sink off and yet I have not moved an inch.

"Are you, uh, ok?" he asks again. "Oh wait, you aren't... touching yourself, are you?" He wrinkles his face in disgust.

"No, it's not like that. It's...I'm gun-shy, that's all." My lie is well rehearsed.

"Ah, ok. I hate to hear that."

He turns to the automatic dryer and rubs his hands underneath as the air blows hot and loud. A few moments later, he leaves, offering a nod in my direction.

A burgeoning ache radiates out from my midsection. I know it's my bladder desperately wanting relief. I've been there far too long. I *have* to get things moving. Fear or no fear.

I close my eyes and tune out the world around me. I focus on a single point of light beaming in a world of black. It was my happy place. Created with help from my therapist to deal with situations like this. If I kept my attention aimed at that pinpoint of light, I learned how to keep all intrusive thoughts away. I bore down on that hole like a woman giving birth. Like the man that had just left sitting on the toilet.

Within a few moments, a trickle of urine slips out of me.

Yes, yes! That's it. Concentrate!

The pinpoint of light grows larger, its circumference widening and allowing more light to escape. As it did, more urine spills out of me. I was at the precipice. The dam was about to burst. Relief would soon be mine.

ꑭꑭꑭꑭꑭꑭ

When I was sixteen, my parents divorced. It was a messy affair. Accusations of infidelity. Drug use. Neglect. It had it all. My dad moved to Oklahoma while my mom and I stayed in Ohio. We did our best on the secretary wages she earned. My dad never paid child support, and I had to help out by working at Burgers-R-US, a local fast-food chain with eight locations in central Ohio.

One night when I was cleaning the restroom, a man walked in. His eyes were bloodshot, and he slurred when he cursed at me. Apparently, I was in his way and prevented him from using the urinal. Instead, he just pulled out his dick and pissed all over the floor. And me.

I grew furious at the man.

"What the hell, man?"

He laughed. "I needed to...to pi-piss. You didn't mo-oove."

I stood with my mouth agape, anger boiling within me. He turned to walk away, and I lost it, striking out and smashing his head against the cream-colored tile wall. His head split like a melon. It burst much easier than I expected. He crashed to the floor, landing in his own urine. Blood mixed in with it, turning a pinkish hue.

I ran out of the bathroom.

The story I told my manager, a man named William Crawshaw, was that a man had fallen and hit his head on the wall. The police believed me, especially since the man was a known drunk around town.

That was his last night alive. What I did killed him. I already had a fear of bathrooms; this took it to another level.

�

That event clung to me like the stench that was wafting over me now. I tried to forget it, to cast it aside, and never give it life. Yet every time I stopped at a public bathroom, the thoughts returned. Coupled with my remembrances of that movie scene, and my complicated relationship with bathrooms made more sense. At least to me. I could never disclose what I did in the past. Not to my therapist. Not to Lydia. No one.

A sweet sense of relief filled me as my stream of urine grew larger and more forceful. All the time spent holding it in seemed like such a waste. It was now bursting out of me and splashing in the porcelain urinal.

I sighed with relief. My head dipped down and I read the top of the metallic valve. *Royal Sloan USA*. A nearly universal combination of words known to all men when they used a urinal.

Slowly the intense pressure and pain in my mid-section dissipated. It was like I was pissing out the pain, which in a way, I was.

When the last dribble dropped from me, I gave it a shake to make sure all was clear. The urinal had filled almost to the lip, my bright yellow urine mixing with the orangish liquid already there to create an uninviting concoction.

I pulled my underwear over myself and zipped up. When I placed my hand on the handle, the door opened again, and it was the man who was just in there moments ago. But something was different about him. Something... off.

Worry jolted my senses awake, but they didn't move fast enough. The man lunged at me and smashed my forehead against the blue tile.

A burst of agony accompanied the brilliant white light that blinded me.

I was right!

The small voice inside of me screamed.

You should have been afraid!

I lost my balance and fell backwards, slamming the back of my head on the cold, hard floor. Another burst of pain tore through my head.

I thought I heard my phone ring again. The man fished it out of my pocket and threw it across the bathroom, shattering it on impact. He went to the door, locking it, then returned to me.

He hovered over me, peering down at me. My vision

was blurry. I could barely make out his facial features. Echoes of the impact from moments earlier tore through my skull.

He bent down within inches of my face.

"You don't remember me, do you?"

All I could think of was shit. This man was related to shit for some reason. Thoughts were difficult to form. I struggled just to remain conscious.

"I remember you," he snarled. He peered at me, and I felt like I had seen those eyes give me a death stare before, but for the life of me I couldn't place it.

Bursting through the fog enveloping my brain was sheer panic. All of my fears were realized in this one moment. The memory of what I did in the bathroom so many years ago screamed at me. They brought a sense of guilt and shame. My actions followed with countless lies were now front and center.

Then it dawned on me. The realization made my eyes bulge. The throbbing in my head grew more intense. It couldn't be, but yet, it was.

William Crawshaw. My old boss from Burgers-R-Us. But why? I hadn't seen the man in decades. I thought he was dead or still back in Ohio. We were in Illinois, and I wasn't in contact with anyone from back home. I severed that connection with no intent of ever having it back. How did he find me?

"William?" I croaked.

A smile crept across his face. "You do remember me after all."

"I thought–" I closed my eyes against the blinding pain. "I thought you were dead."

"You would like that, wouldn't you? Because of what you did, I lost everything. Everything!" Spit flew from his lips and landed on my cheek. "My job. My marriage. My home. All of it. Gone! Once you murdered Ralph, every-thing went to hell."

I spit up blood. I could feel it leaking out of my skull faster than the piss that left my dick. If I didn't get help soon, my worst fears would be realized. Lydia would be a widow, and our boys would be without a father.

"Do you know how long I've searched for you? It took a random post on Facebook for me to get the final clue as to where you lived. But now...oh, now I will have my revenge."

His mention of Ralph made my stomach twist. The man I had killed in the bathroom. My lie never wavered and not once did I contradict myself. How would anyone know it was me that did it? A tiny moment of anger had consumed me with grief and guilt. I ran away from that long ago. Or so I thought.

"You stupid kids always thought you could pull a fast one on me. But look who's got the last laugh now." He poked his chest. "I won't show you any more mercy than you did to Ralph. Did he deserve to die? Did he?" He pushed on my chest with both hands. "No, he didn't!"

My eyes went in and out of focus. A chill ran through my body. Blood ran down the sides of my face. I didn't think I could last much longer. I kept thinking that if I could move him to the side, I might stand a chance of breaking free from his grip. It would take all my will to make it happen, but I was facing death. If I failed to give it my all, these would be my last moments of life.

William stood and paced through my blood.

"I dreamed of this day. I searched for you. Following you across the country. And here you are."

I know I deserved this. The guilt had been ravaging me for years, but not now. Not when I've bettered myself. I'm not the same man anymore. My phobia was the last remnant of that dark time.

"William, please..."

He dropped next to me, seething.

"I've spent the better part of my life trying to get over all that you've done to me. I could never shake it. I don't care what happens to me now. Once I'm done with you, it doesn't matter anymore."

William grabbed my hair and pulled my head off the floor. I swore my scalp was about to rip off of my skull. The room was spinning, and I was growing weaker by the moment. He pulled me up to my feet and forced me to face the urinal, the object of my irrational fear.

"This was how you did it, wasn't it? You smashed his head against the wall."

He grabbed the back of my head and thrust forward.

My chance was now.

I shot a hand forward and stopped myself an inch from the tile wall. Pushing back, I broke his grip and cried out in pain as I twisted and grasped his head instead. He fought me. A well-placed punch to the gut forced the air out of me and I doubled over.

William grabbed me by the neck and forced my face into the urinal. Luckily the urine had all been flushed. I gurgled in the water then twisted my body enough to free myself.

"You deserve to die!" William screamed.

I almost let him. I had grown weak and now faced with my past; I wasn't so sure I should continue. Life was for the strong, and I was far from that.

Yet something sparked inside of me. A flicker of hope. A spark of life. I wanted to live. For my family. I didn't deserve them, but they were all I had.

William and I wrestled in the bathroom, both of us losing strength rapidly. William because he was much older, me because I had lost so much blood.

"You ruined me!" he snarled.

I had no response.

We grappled with one another, twisting and spinning. Slamming each other against the walls. I got a favorable bit of leverage and thrust forward. William's head smacked against the valve at the top of the urinal. A sickening crunch sounded, and his blood flowed out, obscuring the Royal Sloan lettering. His mouth moved like a fish out of water and then went still. His entire body slumped, and he slid down until he was a heap of a bloody mess on the floor.

I bent over, resting on my knees. The pain of my own wounds came roaring back, the adrenaline that had fueled me leaving just as quickly as it had come on.

"I never meant to kill him. Or you," I whispered. "Never."

I closed my eyes and cried softly. How was I going to explain this to Lydia? How was I getting out of this? I was doomed. There was no way I was leaving a free man. I had condemned myself by killing William.

You can't think like that. You did nothing wrong. It was self defense. He was the one that tried to kill you.

I spat blood onto William's body, then wiped my mouth with my hand.

I had every right to be afraid of the urinal. A man with a knife didn't come to stab me, but a lunatic with a grudge did come for me. I glanced at the porcelain now stained with blood–Wiliam's blood–and knew I could never, ever use one again. With my back to potential dangers and vulnerable to attack, I knew it was impossible.

But what I needed to do was get the hell out of there and hope I don't get caught.

I couldn't hide the body or the blood. My best bet was to just flee.

I cleaned up as best I could, scrubbing off blood and organic matter. I gave one last look at my attacker, then left.

A man headed toward the bathroom, and I stopped him.

"I wouldn't go in there if I were you. It's awful." I placed my hand over my stomach to indicate a digestive issue. "Maybe try the ladies room."

"Hey, thanks pal."

I hurried out into the darkness toward Lydia where I knew I'd get a lecture. At least I'm still alive and my bladder is empty. My head is spinning with everything that just happened. It was an insane encounter that rendered me speechless.

All I knew was that from now on, I am always sitting down to pee. Who knows if there's another William out there.

7

APOTEMNOPHOBIA

BY LISA BREANNE

*I*t had been years since we had taken a family vacation. I think Aiden was three or four the last one we took, now that toddler I was fondly recalling; will be double digits next month, my daughter Ava only a few years behind.

I watched my wife lovingly carry our youngest on her hip as our family of five walked down the gangway to board the airplane.

"I get the window!" Aiden yelled, unable to contain his excitement over taking his first ride.

"We know Aiden, we discussed seating arrangements in the car on our way here, but you're going to need to help keep Addy entertained and not just be on your devices the whole time," my out of breath wife reminded him as she switched our two-year-old to her other hip.

"Do you want me to take her?" I asked.

"I'm fine!" she snapped back. I could tell by her tone it was best not to push the issue, hoping it was just the stress of traveling with kids and not something I did that made her temper short. We have been doing so well lately, our marriage seemed to be on the mend, but every abrupt response or furrowed brow in my direction still made my stomach queasy.

Addy had been a surprise three years ago, when our marriage had become nothing more than roommates who happened to share two kids. We were on the cusp of divorce when those little stick's positive results glared back at us. At that moment my mind whirled trying to remember the last time we had even had sex, while hers couldn't wrap around the thought of being stuck in this rut another eighteen years. Simultaneously we voiced what was on our minds.

"It can't be mine."

"I want a divorce."

Those confessions seemed like a lifetime ago as we took our seats to spend the next five hours in a cramped sardine can; before we reached the sunny beaches of Puerto Vallarta, Mexico.

꧁꧂꧁꧂꧁꧂

We stepped off the plane to a blast of hot air, I was already drenched in sweat carrying a sleeping toddler as we trudged up the ramp to head to customs. Ava was clinging to her mothers' leg for dear life, she had just been woken up from her nap to deboard and was clearly over-stimulated by her new surroundings. Aiden was bouncing around like a pinball who'd downed a quad shot espresso, firing off another question before we could even answer, pointing out everything new he saw.

"Daddy!... Daddy!... Look!" Aiden squealed.

"Hold on buddy, I'm trying to get your sisters situated." My wife and I dug through our bags for everyone's passports while wrangling the girls that were holding onto us like we were life preservers on a sinking ship.

"Daddy! Look!" Aiden said again, pointing toward a sign ahead of us that read *Se Busca Informacion*. "It's you!?" he proclaimed loudly with a big grin.

I glanced at what he was so animated about and came face to face with my own on a wanted poster. "You don't have a mustache," my wife casually pointed out.

"No, but I gotta admit the resemblance is uncanny." I said, as I read the poster's details.

Eduardo Emiliano Becerra Cabral
Wanted for:
Drug Trafficking
Resisting arrest resulting in the death of a minor
Human Trafficking
Aiding and abetting known cartel associates
Evading arrest
Obtaining illegal firearms for distribution
Murder in the 2nd degree
Murder in the 1st degree
Multiple felony assault charges

And the list went on. "I hope they catch him," my wife muttered, "what a terrifying man."

"The world is full of terrifying men, luckily you got your prince charming by your side to keep you safe," I boasted, putting my arm around her to give her a squeeze, almost dropping my toddler. She rolled her eyes and playfully elbowed me, easing the rest of the anxiety I had felt earlier. We finally made it to the front of the que, all three kiddos complaining about the wait, plus the heat, my nerves were frayed, I was so anxious to just be relaxing in a beach chair listening to the ocean that when a voice said, "Welcome to Mexico, are you visiting for business or pleasure?" I practically shoved my son to the side to get this over with.

"Family vacation," I responded curtly as I thrust our passports at him. I wasn't trying to be as rude as I sounded but his demeanor immediately changed from inviting to disapproving. He didn't take the passports from my extended hand but stood up straighter.

"Sir, I will need to check these over individually before entry. Are these your children?" he asked, making direct eye contact with me, which I quickly broke once I noticed he was missing the ear on his left side.

Attempting to mask the shudder that violently shook me, causing a moment of dizziness and tunnel vision. I cleared my throat, "*Ahem*...yes, yes they are mine."

"And this is your wife I assume?" He asked, while looking at her with a glimmer in his eye that I found unsettling.

"Mmhmm, yup." I still couldn't bring myself to look at him. The image of his missing appendage burning a hole into my retinas and threatening to make the pretzels from the plane reappear. He finally took the passports from my hand and began flipping through them. Kneeling down, he looked at the one currently open in his hand and then at my son.

"You must be Aiden?"

"That's right," Aiden said with a big grin, "how come you speak English"?

"Aiden!" my wife chastised, "that was very rude of you, young man. I am so sorry..."

"Javier."

"Javier. We informed him he may encounter residents here that did not speak English and..."

"Oh no harm, ma'am," Javier said with a chuckle, standing back up. I could feel his eyes on me again, but I knew if I met them, the composure I was barely grasping would crumble. So, this must be Ava? And this... Adaline?"

"Yes, Addy for short." My wife responded, flashing her tired mom-of-three smile.

"Amy?" he asked, "that's a lot of *A* names."

"Just the four of us, my husband is Dylan... D," she said quietly, I could tell the weariness of the day was taking its hold on her.

"Is this going to take much longer?" I spoke up. "I just don't want to miss the shuttle to our destination," I half-heartedly followed up with.

"Dylan Rivera," he read off my passport, looking me up and down.

"That's right." I busied myself, hoisting the backpack back on and adjusting my squirmy toddler, anything to avoid looking at the empty spot where his ear should be.

"Are you Mexican yourself?" He inquired. I quickly glanced up, only long enough to acknowledge he was speaking to me before continuing to fuss with things, "Oh...*ahem*...no, my great-grandfather was from Spain."

"My apologies sir, I just assumed, tan skin, dark features, last name. I should not have just assumed."

"He looks just like the bad man in that picture over there." my son piped up, pointing at the wanted poster.

"Aiden!" my wife scolded.

The agent looked over at the poster and then back at me, I could feel him scrutinizing me, the anxiety building in my gut, making the facility feel like it had gone up several degrees. I finally made eye contact and slightly chuckled while shrugging my shoulders. *Was that hostility I detected in his eyes?* His body language gave off an air of examination before he finally broke the silence.

"So he does," he said. "You've got a very perceptive boy on your hands."

"Yup, gotta be careful around this one," I said, trying to

focus on the spot on the wall right behind him so I didn't see the missing appendage, but just thinking about it was triggering my gag reflex.

"Well, I think that just about does it," he said, handing the passports back to me. Where are you staying?"

My wife responded, "The Grand Maya Resort and Spa."

"Nice place, pricey." He whistled. "Just head through the archway and follow the signs to baggage claim, from there an attendant will direct you to the shuttle that will deliver you to your destination."

I nodded and smiled, ushering my kids forward.

"I hope you all enjoy your time here in Mexico," he called after us. And I couldn't tell you why but even in the balmy climate of the crowded building, it sent chills up my spine.

🦷🦷🦷🦷🦷🦷

"I think you're overreacting, I thought he was nice, that job has got to be pretty taxing, dealing with grouchy travelers all day."

"I'm telling you; something was off."

"You mean besides his ear?" my wife responded with a playful smirk.

"Not funny." I scowled. I admit, I had been extra on edge since that encounter, but something just wasn't sitting right with me. We arrived safely at the resort a few hours ago but this feeling persisted.

"Oh, don't be such a stick in the mud, look around you; we're in a beautiful country at one of the most exclusive resorts in the world, where we get to spend ten days being pampered and catered to, instead of the other way around and our children are getting along; knock on wood. So, please, take a breath, turn that brain of yours off and enjoy it," my wife instructed, as she sat next to me on the edge of the bed, leaning her head on my shoulder.

"You're right," I said and gave her my most convincing smile. And she was, I needed to just bury these apprehensions and enjoy this time with my family.

𝅒𝅒𝅒𝅒𝅒𝅒

The next few days passed in a blur of countless sunscreen applications, sticky hands and faces, sand removal from crevices we didn't know we had and nights under the stars with my wife after the kids had finally crashed. It was a bliss we hadn't known for a long time. The uneasiness had all but disappeared, chalked up to nerves and ultimately forgotten. The morning of the fourth day was off to a great start, the bigger kids were off at Kids Club doing arts and crafts, while our toddler dozed peacefully in between my wife's legs on the beach lounger. My wife was deep into the new Duncan Ralston novel, while I only half paid attention to the posts I scrolled past on my phone.

"You'd hate this book," she chuckled, a smile spreading across her face.

"What's that?"

"This." She gestured, wiggling the book without looking up.

"Yeah? Why's that?"

"So much dismemberment...body parts getting lopped off left and right," she said with a wave of her hand.

"Ugh, how can you read that? Just that brief detail makes my stomach lurch."

Setting the book open across her chest, she reached over and squeezed my hand. "Is the big brave firefighter scared of a little amputation, only three toes wiggling instead of five? Hmmm?" she teased me with a smirk.

"Oh, for fucks sake, Amy, yuck!" I exclaimed, gagging as I got up from my lounger, "I'm going to head up to the main lobby where the signal is better and check in with the chief."

"Dylan, come on, we're on vacation. Why do you need to call in?"

"I just like to keep tabs on what my teams got going, Rozz is about to be a dad again and Foreman is back from knee surgery, I'd like to know how he's holding up."

"Yeah, yeah, go. Do you want me to snag you a drink when they come around again?"

"Naw, I'll swing by the bar after the call, maybe check out the kids club place and see how the brats are faring."

"Oh, leave them be, let them enjoy their vacation a bit without dad breathing down their neck."

Putting my hands up in defeat, conceding to leave them be. "Be back shortly." But she was already nose deep in her grotesquerie again and only gave me a little three finger wave off. "Ass," I said, chuckling as I walked away.

ꓪꓪꓪꓪꓪꓪ

I walked into the lobby and welcomed the blast the cold AC blanketed me with. The smell of the orchids adorning the check-in desk immersed me in a nostalgic haze of memories in my grandmother's art studio, zooming my Hot Wheel cars over the crevasses that had formed in the hardwood over decades of use. My grandmother planted on her old blue stool, studying the canvas in front of her, a look of solemn anticipation on her soft wrinkles awaiting the tightly woven cloth to speak to her.

I had almost completely forgotten why I even walked in

here when I felt the vibration in my pocket, alerting me to several notifications I had missed for lack of signal. I began swiping away the mundane alerts from places like Amazon, Dick's Sporting Goods and Temu when a familiar chuckle caught my attention. I craned my neck to see around the wall and out toward the front of the resort where the laughter came from, there stood our butler, deep in conversation with another man in khaki shorts and black tank top. There was something off about their body language, the man in shorts had an almost threatening stance, our butler listening intently to whatever he was saying, with quick glances over his shoulder like he was nervous to get caught speaking to him. With his back to me I couldn't see the man, but a heavy feeling of dread took over in my chest as I watched their interaction. He began chuckling again and put his hand on our butler's shoulder. Our butler put his head down and nodded in understanding to whatever he had said, as he lifted his head up, our eyes made contact and for a brief second, I thought I caught fear there before he plastered on a smile and raised his hand at me. "Mr. Rivera," he called out, "my apologies for briefly stepping away to attend to a personal matter, was there something you needed?"

"No, I...uh...just came up to make a call," I said, waving my phone at him to corroborate my intention.

"Good, good. How about I have the bartender whip up a special concoction of mine, it's a crowd pleaser, and bring it to you to try once I finish up here?" he said with a grin that I could see was clearly forced. It felt more like a dismissal than an offer.

"That would be great," I smiled in return. I stood and slid my phone back into my pocket, too unnerved to make that call to check in at the station. *I'll do it later tonight after dinner*, I noted. Before leaving the lobby, I took one final glance back over my shoulder and caught them both watching me, a somber look on my butler's face but his buddy had a grin, one that immediately sent ice up my spine just like it had the first time I saw it several days ago.

♍♍♍♍♍♍

I rushed as fast as I could back to my wife, who still had her nose buried in the book, "Amy... Amy..." was all I could get out while trying to catch my breath.

"Hmm," she responded without taking her eyes off the page she was on.

"Our butler was with the agent from the airport," I finally got out.

"Mmm," was all she replied, I could tell she hadn't really heard what I said.

"Amy, did you hear me? I said the butler, our butler..."

"Victor."

"What?"

"Our butler's name is Victor," she replied.

"Yes, yes, Victor. Anyway, I just saw him, up in the lobby, talking to Javier!" I professed.

"Javier?" She looked at me and cocked an eyebrow.

"The TSA, or whatever agent he was, from the airport, the one in customs."

"Oh right. That's nice," she said, eyes returning to her book. "How's everyone at the station?"

"I didn't end up calling, I got distracted. But didn't you hear what I just said? I saw Victor, talking to Javier, right outside the lobby. Why would they be doing that?"

"I don't know, they were chatting while on break?"

"Javier doesn't work here, he works at the airport, and besides, he was in street clothes anyway."

"Dylan, I have no idea, maybe they're friends or something."

"It didn't look friendly. Victor almost looked intimidated, you should have seen it, and then when he noticed me watching their exchange, his pleasantry was definitely obligatory."

"Understandable, seeing as you were spying on them," she said with a chuckle.

"Plus, Victor is...what would you guess? Twenty-three? Twenty-five at most? Javier is at least forty. Why would they be friends?"

"I really have no idea Dylan...maybe you're mistaken, and it wasn't that agent at all, maybe it was Victor's dad or an off-duty coworker swinging by for his paycheck."

"It was him."

"Was he missing an ear?"

"Huh?"

"Well, if memory serves me, that agent was missing his ear."

"I didn't... I don't know... I didn't notice." A shiver ran through me as I recalled his missing appendage.

"Well, there you have it, it probably wasn't him. Just someone who looked similar."

"I guess... maybe," I conceded. But I didn't think so. In fact, I *knew* so, but I could tell Amy wasn't seeing it the same way I was. That even if it was Javier the customs agent, what did it matter; they were probably friends.

"Your beverages as promised," a voice announced behind us. I jumped at the sound of our butler's voice, how long had he been back there? Had he heard the concerns I voiced to Amy?

"Oh, how lovely!" my wife exclaimed. "What is it?"

"I call it The Lazy River, it's my own concoction I came

up with, widely popular with the guests." Victor winked as he handed the glasses to her.

"What's in it?" she asked, holding the drink in front of her eyes.

"Equal parts Vanilla Vodka, Chambord and Blue Curacao with a splash of Sprite."

"It looks sparkly almost, like the pictures you see of galaxies."

"That's the edible silver glitter I mix in, ma'am, gives the drink the illusion it's swirling, like the currents in a river."

"Well, it looks absolutely wonderful Victor, thank you," my wife said with a big smile as she handed me my glass.

"The pleasure is all mine. I'll leave you to it then and give you some privacy," he said.

I knew that the last bit was directed at me, I glanced up and sure enough he was staring directly at me, I lifted the drink and feigned a smile. My eyes followed him as he trudged along the beach back up to the main guest house. "Don't drink that," I said to my wife, setting mine down on the table between us. But she had already sucked down a third of it as I reached to take it from her.

"What? Why not?" she scowled, moving the beverage away from my outstretched hand.

"Because I don't trust it."

"Dylan, just stop, okay?"

"I just think that..."

"No. Dylan. Just no. I don't want to hear your weird paranoia fueled nonsense. This is the first time in years I have felt somewhat relaxed, somewhat normal..."

"But..."

"No, but nothing. These last several years have been harder on me than you can imagine, between Addy being born and having to leave my career to stay home with the kids now that there are three. Mom getting sick earlier this year and trying to juggle getting her to her appointments and the kids' schedules, Aiden's soccer practices, Ava's piano lessons, not to mention the strain in our marriage..."

"Strain? Things have been, we have been so much better, haven't we? Haven't you?" I was stunned to hear her add our marriage onto that list like it was a source of stress or burden she was bearing.

"Yes, yes, of course things between us have gotten much better. But, Dylan, hurt like that doesn't just go away, you accused me for months about Addy's paternity, going as far as demanding the post office assign us a new mailman. Your paranoia was out of control."

"I know, I know. And I'm sorry, I'm so fucking sorry, Amy. I don't know what more I can do to show you I'm better, that I'm trying, every day I'm trying to be the man you and the kids need me to be." I felt defeated, all the progress I thought we'd made had just crumbled beneath me, and I was right back to the night she kicked me out.

"Dylan... Dylan... look at me," her tone firm but softening as she lifted my chin to look her in the eyes. "I love you, I love our family, I love our life, but I'll be damned if I'm going to stick around while you take a sledgehammer to it again. Not this time."

I nodded, unsure what to say at this point. "I'm going to go get the kids from their activities and take them to dinner. I suggest you take some time for yourself this evening and sort your shit out. Tomorrow we'll start fresh, no more cockamamie conspiracies or paranoid theories regarding the locals, just us, enjoying our last couple days here in paradise as a family. Got it?" It came out as a question, but her demeanor said it was a statement. All I could do was nod in agreement.

"Good," she said as she scooped up a half-awake toddler

and started to make her way up the beach, leaving me sitting there, alone.

🦷🦷🦷🦷🦷🦷

Sleep eluded me for several hours. After Amy walked off with Addy, I wandered the grounds of the resort for a while. Not really paying much attention to where I was going, just letting my mind drift over the events of the last few days, Amy's words weighing heavily on me. She was right, of course she was right, why did my brain always have to jump to the most absurd conclusions? So the guy was missing an ear, so what? That was a me problem. I had always had an intense aversion to amputations of any kind, dating as far back as I can remember. My great uncle was missing his left hand. I was told it was the result of a farming accident, but in my child's mind, it was much more nefarious. I remember as a kid feeling queasy just having him in our house, like something awful would befall us, just by having him there.

I got back to our suite and poured myself a drink from the minibar and sat down on the couch to wait for my family to return from dinner. I owed them an apology and a promise to make the rest of our vacation amazing. I don't remember falling asleep, but I must have dozed off. I awoke with a jolt, barely able to catch my breath. Drenched in sweat but shivering, I frantically looked around unable to reconcile my surroundings with the perdition I narrowly escaped from.

A nightmare...

Whew... it was only a nightmare...

Rubbing my face, I sat up and reached for my phone, 12:17 AM, *fuuuuck* I thought, I tiptoed to the bedroom and quietly peeked in, all three were in bed with my wife and sound asleep. Aiden was laying at a horizontal angle, legs over half of Amy, Addy splayed across Amy's chest, feet pressed against Ava's back, who was curled up into a little ball in the fetal position. The picture in front me put a smile on my face but just as quickly was replaced with the hazy lingering images from the nightmare of my family crawling towards me, crying out for help, their legs nothing but bloody stumps, their bodies writhing on the floor in agony as they reached out for me...

"Daddy, help meeee, it hurts, daddyyyy..."

"Dylan! Why did you let this happen to us, you were supposed to protect us!"

"Where are my legs daddyyyy, I can feel my toes wiggling, but I don't know where they are! Please, carry me, daddy!"

The echo of Addy's plea to be held in the safety of my arms resounded in my skull like a gong letting me know my time had run out.

I felt hot tears searing their tracks into my flesh as they ran down my face. I knew come morning everything would be fine, back to normal, but right now I was anything but fine, the guilt of falling asleep without giving my apology coursing through me like a poison, like no matter if everything was okay come dawn, nothing would ever be the same.

I slowly closed the bedroom door and tiptoed over to the coffee table where I'd left my phone, wallet and keys, I needed some air.

The night air was muggy and sickly sweet with the scent of the various tropical flora, it did nothing to quell the unease in my stomach, I was already sweating by the time I made it to the path that led to the beach, debating on turning around and heading back to the comfort of our air-conditioned villa. It was at least another two hundred yards before I'd hit sand, however the lulling sound of the waves crashing in the distance beckoned me. My mouth suddenly felt full of cotton, my tongue doing less than nothing to moisten my lips, I stepped on to the dimly lit throughway, deciding to swing by the clubhouse bar to grab a drink before continuing to the beach.

A light humming sound broke through the stillness of my surroundings as a golf cart pulled up alongside me, "Unable to siesta Mr. Rivera?" My butler grinned back at me from the driver seat.

"No, unfortunately," I responded as I kept walking.

"Where are you heading to? I'm technically off the clock but I give you lift." His pearly white teeth a bright contrast in the shadows along the path, giving him the appearance of the Cheshire Cat from Alice in Wonderland.

"I'm just swinging by the bar and heading down to the water. I appreciate the offer, but I think I'm good, I could use the exercise after all the delicious food you guys have been feeding us," I said, patting my belly and issuing the best forced chuckle I could muster. Nothing of this encounter was off putting but it still felt wrong, I felt like a sitting target.

"Are you sure Mr. Rivera? I do not mind; it is on my way. Fast drive for me, still a long walk for you."

I looked down the path, then back at Victor. His grin never faltered. The idea of accepting the ride unnerved me but he was right, it was still a bit of a hike from here. My hesitation was all he needed. "Come, come, Mr. Rivera," he said, removing his backpack from the passenger seat.

I took one more glance ahead of us and climbed in.

"Please, call me Dylan." I said as he took his foot off the brake and eased us along the path.

"Dylan, yes sir, I can do that."

"So, Victor, how long have you been a butler here?" I asked him.

"About three months, sir."

"Oh, that's not long at all. Do you like it?"

His face took on a sour expression, "It's just on my way, a thing I have to do for right now."

"I get ya, pay the bills until something better comes along, we've all been there, starting out and finding our place."

"Yeah, something like that," he said in a tone that sounded like he was annoyed.

His mood had drastically shifted since we'd started off, the air between us felt thicker than it was outside the partially enclosed cart, maybe he was embarrassed about doing something menial like waiting on people and didn't like talking about it.

"What is your tattoo of?" I asked, pointing to the partially covered ink poking out of the rolled-up sleeve of his uniform, hopefully the change of subject would break the tension that had settled on us.

He glanced down at his arm and tugged the shirt up further, "It's a scorpion with a human skull as its head." His response was flat as he pulled his sleeve back down, covering the art entirely.

I nodded, the image of his tattoo nagging at me the rest of the ride, I recognized it... *where had I seen that rendering before*? I wondered.

A minute or two later Victor pulled up to the front of the building, the interior was pitch dark, the only light that shone was coming from the neon closed sign that hung in the window.

"Oh damn, they're closed up for the night it looks like," I said, looking around at the deserted surroundings.

"Yeah, they close at midnight," Victor responded.

"Well, why didn't you say that back..." I started to admonish as I caught a glimpse of the neon light reflecting off the needle before it plunged into my neck.

"I'm sorry about this, Mr. Rivera. I really am. But it's like you said, I need to earn my place," he said. And everything went black.

🦷🦷🦷🦷🦷🦷

Where am I...

"Welcome back, Mr. Rivera."

Why can't I move...

"Umphfff.... umphfff...." was all I was able to get out, the words felt heavy.

"No, no, no, don't try to talk. Just relax," the same voice instructed me.

"Wherumf... amp... I?"

What happened to me? Is this a hospital?

"Mr. Rivera, I need you to remain calm, your blood pressure is spiking."

I could hear the rhythmic beeping of machines. *This must be a hospital. Why can't I open my eyes?*

"Whhym...can...t...mooofff?" I forced my mouth to make the words, slow and steady, "Whafft happ'nd?"

"Mr. Rivera. My name is Dr. Somal, you are currently under my care." A heavily accented voice spoke. "I understand this must be very confusing for you, but if you will just remain calm for a little longer as we finish up, I will answer any questions you have."

"Canfft mooofff."

"Mr. Rivera, you cannot move because you are strapped down. Now, please give us just a moment," the doctor commanded.

Strapped down? Why am I strapped down? What the

hell is going on here? I could hear the footsteps of multiple bodies moving around the room, but something was covering my face. I couldn't see anything, I tried shaking my head in hopes whatever cloth cover was obstructing my vision would fall off.

"His vitals are improving; I believe the transplants have been successful, sir."

"Excellent, excellent."

Transplant? What are they talking about? God, everything hurts. I need to move, I need to know what's going on. I tried to move my body into a sitting position, but I couldn't get my arms to work to prop myself up.

"Sir, the donor is moving again."

Donor?

"Mr. Rivera, please. Ah hell, just remove the bag, let him see for himself, I think we're just about done here anyway," the doctor instructed someone in the room.

"But sir... he may..."

"Remove the hood," Dr. Somal snapped.

The blinding light pierced my retinas like someone had just dumped salt into them. I blinked repeatedly, my surroundings clearing with each flutter... *concrete walls, water stains, another patient in a bed next to me, people... nurses? With guns? Why were there men with guns? Blood, oh my god there is so much blood, who's blood, is it?*

"What the fuck!?" I screamed, "my legs! What the fuck have you done with my legs?! Where are my legs?!" I attempted to lunge toward the man standing next to the table I was strapped to.

"That won't do you any good, Mr. Rivera. As you may not have seen quite yet—you no longer have your arms either."

My eyes fell to the miasma of gore pumping from the orifices where my arms used to be, soaking the crudely wrapped linen, "What the fuck...what the fuck... What have you done to me?" My head was spinning, the edges of my vision blackening, my chest constricting with each gasp. *Why is this happening? This can't be real...*

"Dr. Somal, the patient is ready for transport."

"Good, Good. Call ahead and let Stefan know we'll be enroute shortly," the man stoically standing next to my table instructed.

"Now where were we? Ahh, yes, Mr. Rivera. You see, my client is a very powerful man, who is wanted for some unsavory dealings. Staying here in Mexico was no longer an option, but as you can imagine, he cannot just waltz into the Americas either."

I wasn't listening, I just kept staring at my legs or where they should be. I could feel them right below the kneecap where only bloody stumps now stared back at me.

"This isn't real, this isn't real, this isn't real." I reached toward them in desperation—denying what was in front of me. If I could just touch them everything would be ok, but I couldn't touch them. My gore covered bandages unwrapped at the desperate flailing until I fell hard to the floor with a sickening smack. The surrounding men all laughed, lifting me back onto the piss-stained sheets.

"They say you look like a turtle now flipped over on its little shell," Dr. Somal chuckled.

"Fix this, fix me, this... My wife. My children..."

"They will be perfectly fine, please calm yourself."

My panic lessened the slightest bit at the thought that Amy and the kids would be ok somehow.

"They will be looking for me! They'll know what you did to me, you sick fu..."

Dr. Somal's hand smacked across my face sending cold sweat flying across the room.

"They won't know anything until it's too late.

111

Tomorrow Mr. Cabral's dismembered torso... Your dismembered torso will be found in the water and pronounced dead. We have a lot of nasty animals in these waters you see." The Doctor smiled as he pulled the curtain back revealing what I could only assume was Mr. Cabral's unconscious body.

"Jesus...where...what have you done with his face?"

Dr. Somal took a pen light from his front pocket and checked the pupils making sure not to touch the open exposed flesh that lay before him.

"Well, we need them to find his face. Makes it much easier to identify him that way. Plus, how is he ever going to wear yours if he still has his?"

Dread crept inside me like a thousand tiny crabs made of ice.

"Amy will know. Amy will know it's not me," I pleaded.

"The bandages will hide enough and the fall you took on your late-night stroll last night will explain why you aren't so chatty on the plane ride home. As for what the conversation looks like after that...well...Mr. Cabral can be quite messy."

One of the two men beside me held my torso down while the other held the oxygen mask tight against my face.

"Count back from ten for me."

I screamed and bit at the thick plastic mask until my vision started to blur.

Nine.

I thought about Amy and how I'd never hold her again

Eight.

About how I would never see my children smile.

Seven.

About how Amy would be trapped in our home with a disgusting killer wearing my face.

Six.

And then I thought about how light my limbs felt.
Five.
How calm my head was starting to feel.
Four.
And how I swear I could feel my feet.
Three.
Buried in the wet sand.
Two.
Warm and safe.
One.

8

MYSOPHOBIA

BY JYL GLENN

The fluorescent lights of the Humboldt Meat Packing Plant hummed a sickly, monotonous tune, a counterpoint to the rhythmic thwack-thwack-thwack of the meat slicer. Al, his hands already raw from obsessive scrubbing, adjusted his gloves, the latex a thin barrier against the ever-present threat of...everything. The air hung thick and heavy, a miasma of blood, sweat, and the metallic tang of raw meat. It clung to the walls, the machinery, even to the hairs on his arms, a constant, suffocating reminder of his deepest fear: contamination.

Each movement was precise, ritualistic. He'd counted his hand washes that morning – precisely seventeen, each lasting a minimum of thirty seconds, the water temperature a scalding 110 degrees, the soap a harsh, antibacterial formula that stripped the oils from his skin, leaving it burning and raw. He didn't dare deviate. Not even by a second. Not even a drop. The thought of unseen parasites, microscopic horrors burrowing beneath his skin, sent shivers down his spine. He imagined them writhing, multiplying, consuming him from the inside out.

Al was distracted, thinking about his fight with his wife that morning, as he went through the motions of prepping the meat for packaging. They had gotten into another fight over some stupid MomTok video she'd posted on her social media. *So what if she thinks she's an influencer,* he told himself. *But I wish she'd stop spending money on a bunch of shit we don't need to do it.*

The slicer Al used was a beast of stainless steel. Its blades, honed to surgical sharpness, spun with a hypnotic blur. But today, the rhythmic thwack was punctuated by a sickening crunch, a sound that sliced through Al's meticulously constructed world like a butcher knife through flesh. A searing pain, sharp and intense, ripped through his left hand. He stared, mesmerized, as his fingers, severed cleanly, tumbled onto the conveyor belt, joining the endless stream of sliced meat.

The blood spurted, a horrifying cascade of maroon. His hand pulsed, a grotesque reminder of his own mortality, of his body's fragility in the face of this indifferent machine. *And the germs...* The smell of it, acrid and metallic, overwhelmed the other odors, a pungent testament to his sudden, violent injury. He felt a wave of nausea, not just from the blood, but from the horrifying thought of the countless unseen pathogens that might now invade his body through the open wound.

Panic clawed at his throat. He ripped off his glove, his movements clumsy and frantic, the slickness of the blood making his already raw skin sting. He could feel it, the sticky, warm residue clinging to his palm. He imagined the unseen creatures, invisible yet voracious, already making their way into his bloodstream.

He staggered back, his vision blurring, the metallic shriek of the slicer echoing in his ears. The cold, hard floor pressed against his knees as he collapsed, his breaths coming in ragged gasps, each one a painful reminder of the air he was desperate to keep clean, now fouled with the stench of his own blood. He felt a deep, primal fear, not just of infection, but of his own fallibility, of the inherent vulnerability of the human body. This wasn't just a cut; it was a violation, a breach in his carefully constructed defenses against the microscopic world he feared so intensely.

The shouts of his coworkers seemed distant, muffled by the roaring in his ears. He saw them rushing towards him, their faces blurred, their words indistinct. He could see the concern in their eyes, but all he could focus on was the gaping wound on his hand, the pulsing crimson stain, and the horrifying certainty of invisible horrors descending upon him.

🦷🦷🦷🦷🦷🦷

Al opened his eyes slowly, squinting against the harsh fluorescent lights of the hospital room. The sharp smell of antiseptic washed over him, seeming to scour his nostrils. It did little to comfort him. He tried to sit up, wincing at the sharp pain that radiated from his bandaged left hand.

The nurse, her rubber-soled shoes squeaking on the polished linoleum floor, appeared at his bedside. "Try not to move too much," she said gently. "You lost a lot of blood. The doctor will be in to see you soon. We tried to call your wife, but she hasn't called us back yet."

Al nodded weakly, laying back against the starched hospital pillows. "Yeah, Erin is always busy with something, can we try her again?" *Too busy for me or the kids, sometimes.* He felt light-headed and disoriented, his body heavy with the remnants of anesthesia.

He turned his head to look at his injured hand. It was tightly wrapped in gauze. He could see faint outlines of blood seeping through the layers of bandages. Revulsion and panic rose in his throat. The wound, still raw and open beneath the dressings, was a portal through which deadly pathogens could invade his body. He thought of bacteria breeding in the moist folds of skin, viruses slipping into his cells, parasites burrowing into tissue. A sob escaped his cracked lips.

The nurse placed a gentle hand on his shoulder. "I'll try your wife again and get you something for the pain," she said soothingly. "It's going to be okay."

Al shook his head, tears spilling down his cheeks. "It's not," he choked out. "It's contaminated now." *And I'll have to deal with Erin if she ever shows up.*

The nurse's brow furrowed. "The doctor cleaned and bandaged it thoroughly. We have you on strong antibiotics to prevent infection."

But Al was inconsolable, lost in a spiraling abyss of contamination fears. In his mind, he could see the microbes spreading through his bloodstream, could feel them crawling across his skin. The nurse's words were meaningless against the horrific scenarios playing out in his thoughts. And his wife. How would she react?

The nurse tried her best to reassure him, but he only grew more agitated, his breaths coming in panicked gasps. Finally, she quietly left the room, a look of pity and concern on her face.

Al clutched his wounded hand to his chest, rocking slowly back and forth. The brush of the bandages against his skin made him shudder. He imagined ripping them off, scrubbing the wound raw until not a single microbe remained.

☙ ☙ ☙ ☙ ☙ ☙

When the doctor arrived, his calm words and logical explanations did little to pierce the haze of obsessive fear clouding Al's mind. Al closed his eyes, taking a deep breath to try and calm his racing heart. He knew the doctor was right—the antibiotics and bandages were protecting him from infection. But a lifetime of obsessive fears could not be quieted so easily.

The image of his severed fingers tumbling onto the conveyor belt played over and over in his mind. He could still hear the sickening crunch as they were severed from his hand. Bile rose in his throat as he remembered the hot spill of blood, the exposed inner workings of his body revealed in an instant.

He had spent decades fortifying himself against such a breach. His elaborate cleaning rituals, the scalding showers, the endless hand washing until his skin cracked and bled. All of it was an attempt to protect his fragile shell from the unseen predators that lurked everywhere, waiting for a chance to invade.

In an instant, a split second of inattention, all those defenses had failed him. The thought made panic flare anew in his chest. What if the antibiotics weren't enough? What if the wound became infected despite the doctor's reassurances? He would be ravaged from within, consumed by the very microbes he had spent a lifetime trying to avoid.

Al's gaze darted around the room, looking for anything he could use to scrub away contaminants. On the bedside table sat a bottle of sterile water. *No, not enough.* Next to that, a small bottle of betadine. *That's a start.* He uncapped it and unwrapped his bandaged hand. He poured it liberally over his left hand, gritting his teeth against the stinging pain. But it wasn't enough. The wound had been there for hours now, allowing every pathogen and parasite into his bloodstream.

And then he spotted it. *There we go!* What looked like a stiff-bristled nail brush lay discarded on the bathroom sink. Al swung his legs over the side of the bed and stumbled to his feet, swaying unsteadily, his injured hand clutched to his chest. He crept across the room toward the sink, turned on the hot water, and reached for the nail brush with his good hand.

A sound at the door made him startle. A nurse entered; her arms loaded with bandages. "Time to change your band — What are you doing!?"

Al's heart began to race, his breath coming in panicked gasps. "No, please, leave it alone!" he begged, clutching his wounded hand to his chest.

An exasperated voice behind the nurse said, "Don't be such a little bitch about it. Get back in bed and let her do her job." Erin had finally arrived.

"What took you so long?" he asked, his voice tight. "I've been here for hours."

Erin flopped into the chair next to his bed, her hands propped on her generous belly. "Well, excuse me for not jumping every time you have one of your little accidents." She rolled her eyes, picking at her nails. "It's not like your hand was going anywhere," she drawled. "Besides, I had things to do."

Al gritted his teeth. *Things to do? Really?* He knew exactly what Erin's "things" were: lazing around in bed, scrolling endlessly through her social media feeds, snapping selfies and judging people online. Never lifting a finger to help with the kids, the chores, or anything else around the house.

Al gripped the bed sheets, his knuckles white with restraint. "Things? You mean posting selfies and complaining about your life to strangers on the internet?"

She rolled her eyes dramatically. "At least I'm not the one who can't even use a meat slicer."

"I could really use your support right now," he said quietly. "This injury is really going to take a toll on my fears —on us." He gestured helplessly to his bandaged hand.

Erin glanced at it dismissively. "Oh please, it's just a cut. You're acting like you lost the whole hand. The doctor said he reattached some of your fingers; you'll be fine. And you're a grown man; drop the act. You can't possibly be *that* afraid of a few teeny-tiny germs!"

Al stared at his wife of fifteen years, and not for the first time, he thought to himself, *what a self-absorbed bitch*. He imagined the parasites that must be living in her filthy fingernails, making their way onto his bandages to infest his wound. His heart raced anew with revulsion. He shook his head to get rid of the intrusive thoughts.

"Anyway, can we just get this over with so I can take you home and get back to real life? You know how busy I am. And hospitals give me migraines." She glanced at her phone, a bored expression on her face as she scrolled through an endless stream of selfies and meaningless updates.

"I already asked. They're not going to let me go today. I literally cut my fingers off and had them sewn back on this morning."

"But, don't you have to go to work tomorrow? We have bills to pay and..."

"Seriously, Erin!?"

"Ugh, fine. Can you at least try to give me some advance notice when it's time to come get you. I have to get back. The kids are going to be home soon." She picked up her knock-off Chanel bag—which she'd paid way too much for on the TikTok shop and was the reason for their fight— and headed for the door. She whirled around and locked eyes with Al. "Like, what am I even supposed to do about dinner? And I suppose you'll panic if you get home and there's even a speck of dirt in the house, so I'll have to take care of that, too. This is super inconvenient. You're gonna owe me for this." Then she sauntered out the door.

♘♘♘♘♘♘

After a week in the hospital, Al was thankful to finally go home. He'd really missed the kids, and Erin couldn't be bothered to visit, let alone bring them to see him.

"So, I'm really sorry for the other day. Turns out your little accident has made great content for my social media accounts. Someone even started a GoFundMe for me!" Erin prattled on about inconsequential nonsense, pausing only to take selfies at stoplights or respond to comments on her phone. Al couldn't help but notice the smears of grime on her screen, the crumbs on her shirt from where she'd absentmindedly double-tapped her way through lunch.

His stomach churned. *A GoFundMe for...her?*

As soon as the car pulled into their driveway, Al practically leaped out, desperate to escape the confines of the vehicle. He stumbled up the front steps and walked in the front door. The house was a disaster. Dishes were piled high in the overflowing sink, various pieces of laundry were strewn haphazardly across the floor, and the smell of spoiled food wafted from the kitchen. Al gritted his teeth, struggling to maintain an outward semblance of calm. *The germs, the germs, the germs. All of our food will have parasites in it.* Erin, oblivious to the mess, collapsed dramatically on the couch with her phone still glued to her hand.

"You said you'd clean up before I got home," he said. "And what's that smell?" He eyed the fridge warily.

Erin merely giggled in response, scrolling through her

121

social media feed. "I'm sooo stressed out right now, Al. And I don't smell anything. Can't you see I'm dealing with this huge tragedy the best I can? Besides, the kids should've taken care of it."

Al's jaw clenched as he fought to keep from snapping at her. "The kids?" It's our job to make sure the house is clean, and the kids are taken care of. I work my ass off at the plant every day, I clean, I cook, and I get the kids ready for school every morning, and this is the thanks I get?" He gestured around the filthy living room,

Erin finally looked up from her phone, her eyes narrowing. "Oh, you think I don't know what you do at that gross job of yours?" she spat. "And your stupid little OCD obsession. Hiding behind 'germs' and 'contamination', when in reality, you just can't stand to be around a *normal* person like me."

Al recoiled as if she'd physically struck him. "Normal? You call this normal?" he sputtered, gesturing around the messy house. "This is a breeding ground for God knows what kind of diseases and parasites!"

"Whatever," Erin said with a dismissive wave of her hand. "You're always finding something to complain about." She turned back to her phone, effectively dismissing him.

The mess was overwhelming, both literally and psychologically. He pictured bacteria swarming over every surface, viruses lingering in the stuffy air. This was no longer a safe haven, but a contaminated war zone. Squeezing his eyes shut, he tried to recall the deep breathing exercises his therapist had taught him. In through his nose, out through his mouth. In through his nose, out through his mouth. The familiar routine, while not erasing the mess before him, did manage to center him somewhat. He knew he had to be rational about this situation despite his rising anxiety.

"Erin, I need your help," he said evenly. "My injury means I can't do a lot of the cleaning and cooking right now. I know it's not your favorite thing, but I really need you to step up, just for a little while, until I recover."

Erin didn't look up from her phone. "Why can't you just get over your little germ thing? When we got married, you said you'd take care of me. Are you telling me that was a lie? What about the kids?"

"It's called mysophobia. It's a real mental health issue, though I know you don't understand it. But right now, I need your support, not judgment."

Erin rolled her eyes. "You and your issues. Not everything is about you, Al. You're apparently not even going to be working for a while, and God knows you loooove to clean. And anyway, the tax return money is gone, so the least you can do is help around the house while I grow my business."

"Yeah, because I sliced my fucking fingers off! And a business? You have a TikTok account, that is NOT a business!" He paused. "And what do you mean the tax return is GONE!?"

"Whatever, I can't do this right now. I'm going out. I need a break. There's some leftover Chinese food in the fridge. The kids should be home in an hour... I think." She pushed past Al and headed for the door, typing rapidly on her phone.

Al stared after her, stunned. *How could she treat me like this?* After everything he'd done to provide for their family over the years. After every obsessive ritual and sleepless night spent battling his contamination fears, all to keep them safe. And what about the kids? School would be letting out soon. *She thinks? What does that even mean?* Were they just supposed to fend for themselves because mommy was too busy chasing fame on social media? Is this what it was really like every day while he was gone to work?

Al sat down on the couch, his head in his good hand. *How did I not see it?* Slowly, a plan took shape in his mind. First, he would call his brother Mike, beg him to come over and help with the cleaning and the kids' dinner. And he would... *Shit, I don't know what I'm going to do. Maybe call a lawyer? But I can't live like this. Mike will know what to do.*

♔♔♔♔♔♔♔

Erin came barging through the door just after 11 PM. The house was spotless, just like before the accident. *I knew that lazy fuck could do it if I just gave him a little encouragement.* She beamed, pleased with herself. She wandered into the kitchen to grab a snack and found Al sitting at the table.

"Well, I see you decided to actually be useful," she drawled, dropping her ugly fucking purse onto the countertop. "You know, Al, if you weren't such a germaphobe, we might not be in this mess."

"My brother came over and helped. The kids are asleep; I made sure they did their homework and fed them PB&Js since your leftovers looked like E. coli's wet dream."

"Don't you dare talk to me like that," she snapped. "I was out networking, trying to provide a better future for this family and all I get is attitude? And what the hell is wrong with you, letting your brother, *the felon*, come over and be around the kids? What would people think of me if they knew..."

"You wouldn't understand," Al said, turning away from her.

"I'm tired, I had a really rough day," Erin said. "Let's just call it a night, and we can talk about this tomorrow."

"No, we won't," Al snapped, whirling around to face her. "I think it's time we had a long overdue conversation."

Erin recoiled at the venom in his voice. This was not the doormat she knew and manipulated...loved? She couldn't remember anymore. "Fine," she huffed, plopping down on the couch. "But make it quick; I am exhausted."

"You don't support me or the kids. You only care about yourself and your so-called 'influencer' nonsense. You don't even try anymore, Erin. You expect me to work my ass off at the plant, then come home and clean up your messes—literally and figuratively. I want out."

"But... but..." Erin stammered, at a loss for words for once. "Out? Like a divorce? Are you insane? What will people say? This is your fault too! You and your damn fear of germs! If you didn't have your stupid issues, maybe your life wouldn't look so bad. I help so many people on the internet, and you don't even recognize how much that takes out of me. And all you do all day is stand there and run a meat slicer. We can't get divorced, that would ruin my platform!" she shrieked. "You're giving me a migraine; I'm going to bed."

"Erin, I know my 'issues' aren't the easiest to deal with. And you're right, I am finally seeing that maybe my fear of germs and parasites is a little irrational."

"Now we're getting somewhere."

"But where I really failed myself, and the kids, is taking so long to realize YOU are the scariest and worst parasite of them all. And you know I can't handle parasites in my home." Al pulled something out from under the table.

Erin's eyes widened in disbelief as Al, the man she once knew as meek and submissive, aimed a gun at her face. The gun she had bought for a "how to protect your kids" video months ago.

"After you left to go out, I remembered you'd bought this for one of your MomTok videos." The weight of the cold steel in his hand was foreign yet reassuring. It was a symbol of the control he had been so desperately craving.

"Al," Erin stammered, slowly raising her hands in a pacifying gesture. "What are you doing? This is insane! You've never used a gun, put that down. We can talk about this!"

"No, Erin," he said, his voice colder than she'd ever heard it. "You've given me no choice. Me and the kids have put up with your behavior for too long, and it stops now."

"Al, please!" she screamed as Al squeezed his eyes shut and pulled the trigger. The shot rang out like thunder in the silent house, echoing off the pristine walls that now seemed to mock them both. The bullet found its mark, tearing through the center of her face. Erin crumpled to the floor, her lifeless body settling into a heap on the floor, her brains and skull fragments splattered across the spotless wall. The silence that followed was deafening, broken only by the sound of the bathroom door hinges squeaking as his brother stepped out.

"Fuck, man, I didn't think you had it in you. I never liked that bitch," Mike said. "Good thing the kids are at my place. Why don't you go get cleaned up as best you can, and I'll take care of this mess."

"Thanks, little brother. I owe you one."

"More like one...million."

He stepped into the bathroom to clean up, the cool tiles beneath his feet grounding him as he approached the sink. The soft hum of the overhead light filled the room as he turned on the faucet, watching the water cascade down in a clear, steady stream. Gazing into the mirror, he noticed his need to meticulously clean himself was still there, but less nagging.

Al washed the blood from his hands, the warm water carrying not only the physical evidence of what just happened down the drain, but also a part of the man he once was. He stared at his reflection in the mirror, searching for some sign of remorse, but he found none. Only a man who had been pushed to the brink and had finally snapped. A man who, for the first time in his life, had taken control of his fear.

9

MOTTEPHOBIA

BY ANGEL RAMON

*I*t was a beautiful morning in Moca, Puerto Rico. Moca was a mountainous town in the northwestern portion of the island. During the winter, temperatures would get close to the upper fifties at night. However, as spring approached, the residents started preparing for warmer nights.

Orlando lived in a barrio, otherwise known as a village. Low to middle-class residents inhabited these barrios. Despite the humble nature of the town, it was a place where everybody knew each other. Neighbors helped and visited each other often. The holidays were especially wonderful with large gatherings.

A young boy named Orlando looked forward to finishing school for the year. He was eleven years old and an average student. He lived with his parents and didn't have any siblings. While that meant he was a lonely child, it also meant his parents dedicated all their attention to them. Orlando enjoyed the extra attention except for the times when he brought home a poor report card. However, those times were few and far between.

Lush vegetation framed Moca's breathtaking waterfalls. The town also played host to frogs, iguanas, lizards, and snakes. Young Orlando enjoyed heading to the waterfall near his house. On a beautiful Saturday, he was ready to spend time drawing the animals he had found.

"*A donde tu va*?" Orlando's father asked him where he was going.

"*Yo voy a jugar afuera.*"

"*Primero, tu va a comer.*"

His father was strict about eating breakfast before doing anything. His son hated when he lectured about the importance of a nutritious breakfast, but he did it out of love. Orlando's mother was sick, so she couldn't cook breakfast. Orlando didn't want to eat, but the smell of his father's cooking made him hungry.

Orlando's plate contained pancakes, strawberries, and sobao bread, which was the signature bread in Puerto Rico. As much as he wanted to draw, he enjoyed his father's cooking. Besides, it was wise for Orlando to stay on his father's good side.

"It tastes good, right?"

"Si, papi. Muy bueno."

While his father was strict, he could cook a mean breakfast. As Orlando was eating, he saw something on the window. It was disturbing to him, as it had large and fluffy wings. The longer he looked at it, the more dread he felt. He started sweating on his head and his hands started shaking. What scared him was a large moth on the window.

Orlando's father tried to find out why his son was acting weird.

"I gotta go to the bathroom!"

"What's wrong? My pancakes aren't that bad, are they?"

Orlando rushed into the bathroom to escape from the

moth's sight. When he entered the bathroom, he peeked outside the window and felt relieved when the moth flew away from his house. It took a few minutes before his hands stopped shaking.

Moths were an irrational fear that he was ashamed of. He knew they were harmless by nature. The worst they would do was eating clothes left out at night. However, they never threatened humans or other animals. Yet Orlando believed they could eat him. Unlike butterflies, moths looked devilish in his mind.

His irrational fear was his biggest secret. Only his parents and best friend, Jose, knew about his moth phobia. His father looked outside and saw the moth fly away.

"Orlando...*la mariposa se fue*. I told you they don't bite. Now get out of there!"

Orlando left the bathroom and saw his father was upset at him. He knew it was an irrational fear but couldn't help himself. Moths were the bane of his existence. With the warmer weather arriving, more moths would arrive. It was the perfect climate for the insects to breed.

Despite his scare, Orlando was still determined to go outside and see some frogs. His father was content that his son would leave him alone to work on his car. It needed an oil change, but he was good with cars, so he did the change himself.

Orlando grabbed his sketchbook and pencil. With those things in his hand, he rushed outside. As soon as breathed fresh air in, he thought he saw another moth. To his relief, it was just a monarch butterfly. Unlike moths, he was ok with butterflies. That made his irrational fear more bizarre, since moths and butterflies were considered the same insect type.

He chased the butterfly until he landed on a berry bush. Orlando was careful not to scare it away. Its beauty was on full display as it spread its wings. He used his pencil to sketch the butterfly onto his notepad.

"Damn, I should have brought my colored pencils. Oh well, I'll color it in when I get home."

Butterflies were common in Moca, but a Monarch wasn't a species that arrived every day. It was something Orlando needed to draw. His aspiration was to be a cartoonist. All the drawings he did gave him the practice he needed to make that dream come true. While all the other kids played tag and baseball, he was busy building his portfolio.

Cartoonists were still in high demand despite the invention of the computer. There was still demand for hand-drawn art even in the 1980s. Once he finished drawing the butterfly, he admired what he had drawn.

"Oh man, this looks great! I know my parents will love it."

His parents were supportive of his dreams. It was his irrational fear of moths that concerned them. There was still plenty of paper left in his sketchbook. His next stop was Jose's house.

Jose was sitting outside of his house waiting for his friend to arrive.

"Orlando, I thought you got lost, hehe."

"Very funny. Nope, I just got this butterfly drawn."

"Oh man, I wish I had your talent. All I can draw is a stick figure."

"Sorry bud... but at least you can swing a bat."

"Hehe, that's true. Anyway, wanna go catch some frogs? And I mean catch them, not draw them!"

Orlando wanted to practice his craft, but Jose had a point as well. A person was only a child for a short time. Adulthood was much longer than one's childhood. So, he needed to enjoy some good times with his friend.

"Sure. Besides, I'm sure I could get a close-up with a frog in my hand."

"*Asi es! Vamos!*"

Jose was too excited to head to the waterfall. Catching frogs was his favorite pastime when he wasn't playing baseball in the local little baseball league in Moca.

Despite Jose being a jock and Orlando being more of the artist, the two got along well. The waterfall wasn't too far from where they were. All they had to do was carefully cross Route 111, which was the main highway connecting Moca to the other towns around it.

The boys already knew how to cross the highway, so they had no problem entering the park. When they entered, iguanas and frogs greeted them. Jose went to grab a frog. Orlando joined his friend as he dropped his sketchbook. A black moth landed on the book when Orlando wasn't watching.

Both boys had fun chasing the toads into the waterfall. The other park goers looked at the boys with disdain, thinking they were nuts. However, the kids didn't care what others thought of them. They knew in only a few years they would be adults. The mission was to just enjoy their childhood without getting into too much trouble.

These were normal green frogs that roamed around the island. Jose wanted to catch a crested toad because he had read that some were sand-colored. However, the crested toads were located in the southern part of the island. The boys admired the frogs in their hands as they stood next to the waterfall.

Recent rains caused the waterfall to have a higher-than-average cascade. It was a beautiful sight when there was enough water. Plenty of tourists came to see the natural wonder. Also, there were plenty of locals who arrived.

"Let me get my sketchbook and draw the frog."

"You and your drawings."

Jose couldn't help but laugh at Orlando. He made an effort to be more outgoing, but nothing would separate him from his drawings. The sight of the frog in his hands kept him distracted until Orlando came back.

Orlando rushed to regain his sketchbook. He was relieved to see the book was still there, along with his trusty pencil. However, he stopped when he saw a large black moth on top of the book. Its fluffy wings and horrid-looking face scared him to a pulp.

Sweat profusely dripped down his head. Suddenly, another moth flew by him and landed on the tree to his right. Seconds later, a tan-colored moth flew into his hand. He freaked out and screamed as if he had been bitten. The moths all flew in his direction. He ran away like a man running from mountain lions as his heart throbbed.

The last thing he wanted was a moth landing on him. Eventually, he outran the moths as he ran into the forest. However, when he looked down, his pants were wet.

"No, no, no! I can't let Jose see this. He won't let me hear the end of it."

His fear went from being 'eaten' by a moth to total ridicule from his friend. Orlando couldn't control his heart rate as much as he tried to calm himself down. He looked around to make sure no more moths were around.

A few seconds later, he saw himself surrounded by moths of varying types.

"No, leave me alone!"

The moths continued flying around him nonstop. Orlando had no response other than rolling himself into a ball and hoping for the best.

"Please don't hurt me!"

He kept himself in a ball for a couple of minutes. To his

relief, he wasn't bitten. Orlando slowly opened his eyes and felt relieved when he saw the forest without moths.

"I must have been dreaming... Oh no, I still have the piss stain. My father won't forgive me if I pissed on my pants again. I have to get wet!"

Orlando preferred getting in trouble for getting wet over pissing his pants because of his irrational fear. His father was nice, but he was a different man when dealing with his fear of moths.

Cono, hijo. Teiene que ase hombre. La mariposa no ase nada! Ese cosa tu tiene es de babe. Si te vuelves a orinar en los pantalones, yo voy ase hombre a ti por el bueno o por el malo.

His father warned him he would get him to 'man up' if the 'moths' caused him to piss on himself again. Upon getting on his feet, he saw the forest turn dark.

"Why is it dark? Please don't tell me it's night again, please! I gotta be imagining things."

The head of a moth appeared in front of him. It was a horrifying sight for Orlando. He tried moving his legs, but neither of them wanted to go anywhere. It was as if the moth's head had frozen him on the spot.

"Please let me go!"

You're scared of me! Look at you... those little legs of yours can't move because of your fear. I represent hate. I'm the moth of hate! Admit it, you're terrified of me and moths. Orlando is nothing more than a scared little child. I might be gone for now, but I'll be back to haunt you over and over! Look at you, pissing on yourself again.

"Oh no! Why am I pissing so much?"

The eyes of the moth only grew bigger, terrifying Orlando further. As the moth got bigger, he saw what looked to be small little fangs on the moth.

"No, not fangs!"

Haha, estas asustado mi nino!

"Get out of my head!"

Upon screaming loudly, the illusion of the moth's head disappeared. A man heard the screaming and approached Orlando.

"Are you ok, little kid?"

Everything and everyone terrified him. Orlando ran from the man and headed for the waterfall. Nothing mattered to him. All he wanted to do was get wet to cover up his urine-filled pants. It would be easier to justify to his father than pissing on himself because he saw a moth. Heck, explaining the large talking moth would prove impossible.

Jose saw his friend rushing toward the waterfall. He had no time to react as he saw Orlando jump into the water.

"I thought you were going to draw?"

"I changed my mind. Come on in!"

Jose knew this was strange coming from his friend. However, he jumped into the water, anyway. Orlando felt secure no moths were around the waterfall, as they hated the water. It did little to take away the sight of the moth head he saw. That alone was nightmare fuel.

The problem was he knew he couldn't stay in the water forever and Jose knew that.

"Dude, we've been in the water for an hour. Come on!"

Jose was right. Orlando had to go home, eventually. He slowly got out of the water, terrified another moth would fly by him.

"Did you see a moth?" Jose asked, trying to hide his laughter.

"No..."

"Are you sure? I think you did..."

"No, really. I just felt like getting wet."

"Well, I admit we had fun, but you didn't draw anything."

"It's ok. I just wanted to have fun."

Jose smiled as he saw that Orlando could have fun. The two boys walked together back to where Orlando's sketch-book was located. To Orlando's surprise, the book was there. Unlike before, there were no moths on it. When he opened it, he showed Jose the sketch of the butterfly.

His friend said he liked it but seemed to pay little attention. Orlando was used to Jose drifting off when he talked about his drawings and did the same when Jose boasted about his baseball stats.

The wind blew, which turned the page on his sketch-book. The next sheet had a drawing of a moth. Orlando's heart dropped when he saw the drawing. He didn't remember drawing the moth. It was well drawn, which took Jose off of his suspect's list. Orlando didn't know who drew the horrid moth in his book. Fear struck his head.

What if it was that moth who spoke to me? Maybe I wasn't imagining things. I gotta get rid of this picture.

He turned his head and saw a moth heading his way.

"Come on Jose, race you to the highway!"

"You're on!"

It wasn't a race against Jose. It was a race to escape the moth. His irrational fear had taken over his mind completely. He had lost Jose for a quick second. It was enough time for him to rip the picture of the moth and throw it away in the garbage can. While he ripped the paper, Orlando got a small paper cut.

"Wow, you came ready to race. You beat me silly. It was as if a moth was chasing you, hehe."

"Yeah..." Orlando said, trying to catch his breath.

"Yeah, what?"

"It was my lucky day. You'll beat me next time, I'm sure."

Orlando felt better now that the drawing of the moth

was in the trash. He still had no explanation for it. Perhaps he just had a bad day. Or at least that's what he hoped.

☙ ☙ ☙ ☙ ☙ ☙ ☙

Orlando and Jose carefully crossed the highway back toward their small neighborhood. Orlando checked his sketchbook to make sure no other moth sketches were there. There were none—to his relief.

"I don't know what happened to you. You actually were fun to be with, hehe. I guess you're not always a nerd."

"I just wanted to have fun. You always call me a geek. Now you see I can have fun as well."

Orlando felt guilty lying to Jose. However, he didn't want Jose to know. His friend wasn't the most supportive of his fear. Jose wasn't a bully, so to say, but he had fun at his friend's expense with his fear of moths.

The two walked through the shortcut back home. A few lizards greeted them. Orlando had lost most of the day, so he figured to get a few sketches in. Jose chuckled while watching his friend draw.

"You couldn't resist, hehe. I admit, your drawings are rad. You still want to draw cartoons when you're old?"

"Of course, just like you want to be a baseball player, right?"

The boys laughed as they talked about their futures. They were prepared to be scolded by their parents for being wet, but they didn't care. They were boys having fun.

Back at the trash can, the mysterious crumpled moth drawing was still in the trash. Suddenly, the paper started opening on its own. The picture of the moth was still there.

Poor fool, you think you're getting rid of me that easily. This isn't over. You fear my kind and you know it.

A black moth landed on the paper. It looked similar to the one that haunted Orlando.

Jose and Orlando continued walking back home. Orlando felt something weird on his neck. His heart started racing, wondering if anything was on him. He felt around him, but nothing was there.

Whew

He looked behind him and felt surprised when something flew in his direction. He wanted to panic, but Jose was next to him. Orlando couldn't tell what was heading toward him. Without hesitation, he ducked and panicked.

"It's only a bird! Ya, no es nada."

"Yo se."

Orlando felt embarrassed as he saw the green-colored bird fly toward the giant Ceiba tree. He couldn't believe that he thought he had seen a moth.

A part of the boy knew what he saw was only an illusion. Another part figured the illusion was all too real. Despite the bird flying harmlessly toward the tree, Orlando felt a sense of dread going down his body.

The black moth that was on the trash can started flying toward the young boy. However, it didn't get close to him. The moth watched Jose and Orlando walking toward their village. While it was free to fly toward the boys, it stood where it was. Its evil-looking eyes stared at Orlando.

Besides the eyes, there were fangs on the moth. Orlando wasn't just imagining things back at the waterfall.

Jose's mother wasn't thrilled to see her son all wet. She ordered him inside to change.

She waved happily toward Orlando. In her mind, her son had coerced him to jump into the waterfall. Orlando walked from Jose's house.

The black moth flew toward Jose's mother and harmlessly landed on her hand. She embraced the moth as the innocent creature it looked to be.

Orlando saw the sun going down for the day. He wasn't looking forward to getting home or the scolding he would get from his parents for getting wet. At least he had sketches of a Monarch butterfly and an iguana. Also, the picture of the moth was gone from his sketchbook.

Upon getting home, his father wasn't happy to see him wet.

"*Que paso? Porque esta mojado?*"

"I just wanted to have fun."

"Ughh... ok. Just go inside and change. At least you didn't piss on your pants this time."

Orlando walked upstairs and changed into his dry PJs. From there, he brushed his teeth before eating dinner. He turned to the window and saw what looked to be a moth. There was nothing there.

"Come on, stop thinking about that. It wasn't even real!"

He tried to convince himself that the talking moth he saw wasn't real. Upon looking outside, he saw nothing but purple. The boy struck his head, trying to knock the thoughts out of his head. He didn't know why these dark thoughts wouldn't leave his head. Orlando turned toward the door and saw what looked to be a moth. He sweated knowing he was trapped inside with a large tan moth.

"No, please don't hurt me! No!"

Despite not wanting to scream, the moth intimidated him.

"Help!"

His father rushed up the stairs to see what was wrong. He opened the door and saw his son terrified in the corner of the bathtub.

"Que estar pasado aqui? Cono, los vecinos puede oir. No hay nada!"

"Hay un mariposa aqui. Tengo mucho miedo, papa."

Shame filled his heart, knowing he couldn't hide what was scaring him.

"Por favor, yo no veo nada. Ese tu mente. Las maraiposas no hacer nada."

He wanted to believe his father that moths were harmless. His mind refused to leave him alone. Guilt surrounded him as his father was upset with him. His parents did the best they could to help him with his irrational fear. Orlando knew he needed to defeat this on his own. When Orlando opened his eyes, there was no moth or any flying insect in the bathroom. He wished his father were more understanding, but it was tough to expect him to deal with something that was irrational. While his father was upset, he didn't touch him. Orlando was grateful for that.

All he did was shout at him to stop thinking about that and go eat dinner. His father took dinner up to his wife, as she was still sick in bed. Orlando sat at the table, trying to eat his plate of fried pork chops with rice and beans. It was a staple food that he enjoyed eating. However, the illusion of being trapped with a giant moth destroyed his appetite.

His father, while angry, was more concerned about his son. He knew moths looked scary, but there was little he could do to convince his son otherwise. Disciplining him wouldn't work. His son wasn't eating his dinner, which struck him as alarming. Pork chops and rice were one of Orlando's favorite things to eat for dinner.

After roughly ten minutes of contemplating his meal, Orlando began eating. His father felt a sense of relief as his son finally engaged with his food. The initial bites were delightful for Orlando, allowing him to forget what had happened, even for a moment. Meanwhile, his father glanced at his sketchbook and admired the drawings. It wasn't merely an effort to cheer up his son, Orlando's father genuinely cherished his son's artwork.

The drawings were detailed and contained most of the animal's finer parts. He decided not to bother his son as he walked to the living room to watch the news.

Orlando was enjoying his dinner. As he started eating the second pork chop, he saw it turned into a large, cooked moth. It looked horrid with its large wings and ugly face. He dropped his fork and ran from the table.

"Oh no, I ate a moth!"

He started feeling flapping in his mouth. Orlando freaked out and rushed up to the bathroom. Being poisoned was another concern of his. He used mouthwash to gargle the moth out of his mouth. Panic had set in on the young boy, believing his father had put a moth for him to eat. As he spat out the mouthwash, it turned out that there was no moth in his mouth. The only thing that came out of his mouth was pork and rice stuck between his teeth.

Once again, his mind had gotten the best of him. It was one thing to see moths that weren't there, but now he was imagining eating one. Orlando rushed back down before his father suspected anything. Upon returning to the dining room table, he saw the pork chop was normal. His appetite was gone, though. Orlando grabbed the pork chop and threw it outside so his father wouldn't see it.

The backyard door was left open for a minute. Orlando wasted no time going outside and rushing back in. Despite that, the same black moth that had followed him had flown into the house.

Unbeknownst to him, the black moth was inside his house, ready to cause havoc.

♙♙♙♙♙♙

Orlando was unaware the black moth he ran from was inside his house. The moth flew into the living room while his father was unaware of its presence. The evil moth flew atop a standing lamp in the living room.

The coast was clear when Orlando closed the back door. He was quick to lock it because moths had a tendency to enter the house. His father always told him to close the door right away to prevent the critters from entering. However, his parents reasoned that moths loved eating their clothes. He couldn't argue, since he found holes in his clothes.

One day, he felt devastated when his favorite frog shirt had holes. He tried wearing it despite the holes, but they were too recognizable upon wearing it. That was just another reason he hated moths.

After locking the backyard door, Orlando started washing the dishes. That was always his job after dinner, even when his mother was feeling well. He decided he wanted to help around the house on his days off from school, which was appreciated by his folks. Washing the dishes was mostly uneventful until he reached the last plate. Usually, when he started onto the plate, he would see a reflection of himself.

At first, that's what he saw. A few minutes later, though, he saw the image of the giant moth head.

"No... it can't be!"

Orlando dropped the plate into the sink and backed away quickly.

"Don't tell me that moth is in here!"

He did his best not to panic, but those evil eyes did him no favors. Suddenly, he heard voices in his head.

Tu no puede escapar de mi! Yo soy tu dueno.

. . .

The moth told him he owned his life. Orlando knew this was all too real. The fact he didn't know where the moth was scared him further. He went to a corner to hide until his dread went down. There were no moths flying in the kitchen, to his relief. However, he was too scared to go upstairs.

"Am I seeing things? Or is this moth real?"

Orlando was unsure what to believe. All he knew was that he was scared shitless. Despite that, he knew staying in the corner would do him no favors. That might have been what the moth wanted him to do.

As much as he didn't want to bother his father, he felt safe around him. He got up and strolled around the kitchen. There was nothing there to his relief. Dread filled his body, but he fought it off. His eyes were constantly on the move.

His moth phobia might have been irrational, but it seemed it was no longer such. Upon walking into the living room, his feet stepped on something slimy.

"Eww, what did I just step on?"

Orlando looked forward and saw webbing and moth cocoons surrounding the living room. The sight triggered his irrational fear further.

"What happened? *Papi, donde estan*?"

"*Hijo, yo soy aqui*?"

Orlando felt shocked when he saw the black moth back in the forest next to his father. Also, his father's face had turned into a moth. Unlike an actual moth, his father had fangs ready to bite.

"Get away from me!"

"Get over here!"

Orlando was running from his father. The black moth

had turned his father against him. The black moth followed his father. His father grabbed him and tried to bite him. Orlando saw the horrid eyes up close. However, instead of begging for mercy, he did the unthinkable. He used his knees to strike the groin of his father.

"I'm sorry, papi, but you're not my father now."

His father screamed in pain. Orlando ran up the stairs to get away from the black moth. His heartbeat was rapid, as his greatest fear was in his house. The concrete structure was supposed to be a safe haven. On this day, it was the place where his worst fear was coming true. When he reached his mother's room, he saw the room covered in cocoons as well.

I'm coming for you, hijo!

The black moth was determined to haunt Orlando's life forever. The young boy knew he needed to deal with his fear. Running from it would do nothing but ruin his life and friendships. The black moth flew onto Orlando's arm and bit it.

"No, it bit me. I gotta get rid of it."

The cocoons in his mother's room started hatching. His breathing became heavier as he had trouble doing so. The large number of moths hatching triggered his fear to an extreme level. To make things worse, he was trapped in his house with a moth that bit him, contrary to science.

Not taking any chances, he rushed into his room and closed the door. The window in his room was open. Jumping out was an option, but it wasn't a great one. Running from the moth would only grant him temporary peace. Not to mention, the moth and its minions had invaded his house.

"Where's the bug spray when you need it?"

Orlando looked at his arm and saw the bite. While it was swollen and red, he was still alive. He also didn't feel any ill effects from the bite. Some moths were poisonous, but the key was that they were not venomous. They were only toxic if someone ate them. A moth couldn't poison anyone on its own.

That scientific fact was enough to convince Orlando that he could face his fear. After gaining some confidence, he searched his room and found his fly swatter. A moth was an insect, so a swatter was perfect for eradication.

He took a deep breath before opening the door to his room. Orlando was ready to face his irrational fear.

"Ok, moth, ready to meet your match!"

The moth flew around the hallway, trying to intimidate Orlando. However, it wasn't working. The young boy chased the moth and swiped at it.

What are you doing?

"It's simple. You used fear to control me. However, I realized that I don't fear you anymore!"

The moth realized it was in trouble. The one thing that could defeat him was happening. His victim no longer feared him.

Orlando swiped the moth and struck it. It fell onto the floor. The boy looked at the black evil moth with an evil grin. Unlike before, Orlando had the upper hand.

"How does it feel to be the one fearing for his life?"

Have mercy! You wouldn't crush a moth, would you? I'm harmless, I tell you.

"Perhaps all moths are harmless, but you're evil. No more will you eat my clothes or ruin my life."

Ok, I'll stay out of your closet!

"Not good enough. I win!"

Orlando stomped on the moth, killing it. All that was left was the crushed corpse of the evil insect.

"I did it... I fought my fear."

He checked his mother's room. All the moths that were

flying were dead on the floor. He rushed downstairs and saw his father on the floor. His face was back to normal, to his relief.

"Papi, you ok?"

"*Si, mi hijo*... I must have hit my head. Where are you going?"

"I have to clean mom's room, it's a mess. You just stay there."

His father nodded his head. Orlando grabbed the broom and dustpan. Upon going back to his mother's room, he swept all the dead moths from the room. At first, he felt icky about looking at all the dead moths. As he continued cleaning, his dread went down. He felt encouraged as he finally started conquering his irrational fear of moths.

Once he was done, he kissed his sleeping mother on the forehead. She had been unaware of what had taken place. After being kissed, she opened her eyes and smiled at her son.

"Buenas noches. Te quiero, mucho."

His mother told him she loved him. Once her room was clean, Orlando left. Next, he helped his father from the floor and escorted him to where his mother was.

"Go to bed, papi."

"I think that's a good idea, *hijo*. Good night."

After years of his fear taking him over, Orlando could finally rest in his room without all the night terrors about moths. Before he went to bed, a moth flew toward his window. Unlike before, he looked at it and had no reaction. When he turned off the light, the moth flew away harmlessly.

Orlando was able to drift off to sleep without the fear of moths invading his dreams.

The next day, he pulled out his sketchbook when he

saw a tan moth fly toward his window. At first, he felt tense, since he was still getting over his fear. Orlando knew the moth was on the outside part of the window, so it couldn't touch him.

A few minutes of looking at the moth caused him to appreciate the beauty of the insect. He carefully drew the moth into his notebook, making sure he had the finer details drawn. After ten minutes, his sketch was done. It was a thing of beauty. Despite that, it still scared him to even stare at it. Orlando knew he needed to fight his irrational fear. Drawing it out proved to be a great start.

Despite that, it would take him time to cleanse out the horrible experience he had with the 'black moth' of hate.

10

OMPHALOPHOBIA

BY DEREK THOMAS

"*I* know what I heard, and it spoke to me."

"Joshua, it doesn't have vocal cords, it cannot speak to you. In reality, it is just a scar that almost everyone has, present company excluded, of course. This is your childhood trauma manifesting in your mind, most likely because of stress. Is something worrying you right now? A new stressor of some kind?"

"The only thing stressing me out is the voice I heard when we were in bed the oth..."

The jarring bell of a kitchen timer blasts from the top of the faux-antique, mahogany desk that separates the doctor and patient. "OK, time's up for today. We'll pick this up next week. In the meantime, I am prescribing you 5mg of Diazepam, it's a mild sedative that will help calm you and improve your sleep. Take one whenever you two are going to have um, relations."

Joshua sits up on the chocolate-colored Aniline leather couch and exhales a breath. The back of his impeccably styled blondish hair now flattened against his head, causing a little poof to form at the top.

"Thanks Doc, I appreciate that."

He accepts the slip of paper that he hopes will provide tranquility and at least a decent night of sleep and walks toward the door.

"Oh, and Joshua."

Joshua turns back to face Dr. Burgess, "Yeah, Doc?"

"Maybe try some ear plugs?" she says with a shrug.

"Next week, Doc," he replies as he exits the office.

♔♔♔♔♔♔

Joshua picks up Astrid to go out for tacos at Catina Frida on North Beverly. She looks stunning as always. The former model turned actress is five-feet-ten, slender with alabaster skin, and shark-black eyes. Her blue/black hair is cut in a super-blunt straight bob just below her jawline. She dressed impeccably in Jimmy Choo. Joshua sees elegance and sex rolled flawlessly into the human form.

They arrive at the restaurant in Joshua's arctic grey Porsche 911 Turbo Cabriolet convertible. As they enjoy an expensive bottle of Pinot Gris on the patio they are approached by Eva Luna, the current "It" girl in Hollywood.

Joshua stands to greet her, and they perform the official greeting of the pretentious elite, the double-cheek kiss. Joshua introduces Astrid to Eva; each forcing a half-hearted smile to the other. "So sorry to be a bother on your date, Joshua, but I've decided I want the mid-century in Malibu."

"The Walker Estate?" he asks.

"Yes, the one on the cliff with the infinity pool and the Greek statues everywhere. When can I see it again?"

"That's great, Eva. How about Tuesday at three?"

"Perfect! I'll bring champagne so we can celebrate!" She

flashes him a coquettish smile, desire dancing in her deep green eyes, so dark that they remind him of seaweed.

"Great! It's a date!" She bends down, kisses his cheek and struts away, putting a little extra sway into her hips.

"Have you fucked her yet?" Astrid inquires.

"Her? No, and I have no plan to either." He scoffs as he grabs his glass.

"Why not? She's stunning and she obviously wants you. It's not like you & I are in a committed relationship."

"Eva does not want me; she has a husband and a kid. Even if she did, why would I want anyone other than the stunning woman sitting across from me?"

"Smooth response mister, but she obviously wants it. I bet she thinks about her hunky real estate agent when she fucks her sixty-something hubs tonight." She says with a playful smile.

"Great, now I'm being compared to some old man," he rolls his eyes, "thanks honey."

"Whatever old man, you want her."

The food arrives. "Phew saved by ceviche and langosta tacos."

��щᗩᗩᗩᗩ

"Why don't you make us some cocktails and meet me at the hot tub?" Astrid suggests at her bungalow in Beverly Grove.

He arrives in the garden with two glasses and a tumbler full of Grey Goose extra-dirty martinis. She is already in the spa.

She pushes a button on a small remote and GloRilla's "Yeah Glo" emanates from hidden speakers. "Strip for me old man!" She demands with a chuckle.

He moves his legs back and forth with all the rhythm a white man can muster as he rips his shirt open. Astrid shrieks with laughter. He turns his back to her, half squats and attempts to twerk, at least she thinks that's what he's doing. He looks more like a kangaroo drunk from too much tequila as he hops around, then looks over his shoulder at her, winks and slaps his ass. She loses it, chortling as she pretends to make it rain. When the performance is done, he removes his remaining clothes and lowers himself into the steaming hot water. She stands, tosses her entire martini down her throat, throws the glass onto the lawn, and approaches him. He admires her slender twenty-five-year-old body, her small, perfectly pert breasts, the chrome bars that penetrate and exit her dime-sized nipples, her miniscule waist, her flawless stomach with its diamond crown sat upon her navel.

They kiss and she descends onto his already erect penis. They begin to thrust, he upward and she pushes against him. As they are about to climax in unison, he hears what he thinks is a voice. Though it is muffled, as if underwater. His movements cease, but she continues to ride him, moaning louder as she increases her speed. He is still trying to make out what he hears, but it is difficult with her moans and the bubbling of the spa. Astrid rises high leaving just the tip in, her navel above the waterline, and he hears the voice with absolute clarity now.

"I'm drowning down here man," it says. He shudders in fear. She slams back down on his cock, screaming like a howler monkey. She rises again. Water spews from her belly-button into Joshua's face causing Joshua to wail. The voice yells, "Fuck you!" She crashes down onto his cock again, squeals with the pitch of new sneakers on a basketball court and collapses into him. They both spasm and tremble, all four legs quaking, she in ecstasy and he in abject terror.

"I need to go." He announces.

"What? Why?"

"I have an open house tomorrow," he lies. That Richard Requa Spanish Colonial in Beverly Hills. I'm anticipating a ton of interest. It's going to be crazy busy."

"Dammit, I wanted to go another round." She pouts.

"Not tonight, babe. Why don't you come to my place tomorrow night, and I'll make dinner for us? Something sensual, and then we can fuck until neither one of us can walk. Sound good?"

Still pouting, "fine, I'll see you tomorrow night."

ᗯᗯᗯᗯᗯᗯ

Joshua has three skills—selling ridiculously high-priced home to the wealthy, fucking, and creating gourmet meals. Since he isn't selling today and won't be fucking until tonight, he spends the day gathering ingredients at the Century City Farmer's Market and the Santa Monica Seafood Market.

Without bothering to knock, Astrid strides into his condo at seven, "hey old man, I'm here. What's for dinner? I'm famished."

"Hey babe, perfect timing, I'm just about to plate. There's a nice bottle of Albariño in the fridge."

"On it. It smells amazing, what are we having?"

"Tonight, I have prepared for you garlic-seared Chilean sea bass with lemon, smoked paprika, and a drizzle of Beurre Blanc on a bed of roasted asparagus. On the side, you will find fresh smoked oysters on rosemary crackers w/ honey-olive oil drizzle, sea salt, and a single drop of habanero pepper sauce."

He places the plates on the table. "Oh my god, this looks incredible. Thank you," she says excitedly.

As they dine, he tells her about dessert, which is panko crusted, fried bananas, dipped in chocolate, and frozen.

He makes after-dinner drinks and brings them to the living room where he finds Astrid lying naked on his couch.

"Old-fashioneds, you fancy." She laughs as she takes the drink.

"I figured since I had the smoker out for the oysters, might as well use it again."

He sits next to her, and she immediately begins to undress him.

"So, we're not watching a movie then?"

"I'd rather we make one," she says with a seductive smile and a wink. "I need to properly thank you for that delicious meal and if you have any more of those bananas in the freezer, we might need one or two before I'm finished."

He chuckles as she pulls his pants off and slides up his body. Before he knows it, he is inside her and she is riding him again. He tries not to look at or think about her bellybutton, but his anxiety is at a nine right now.

"I want to watch your ass, turn around," he tells her.

"Mmmm, reverse cowgirl it is then."

She spins around and they continue to fuck. They spend the next couple of hours, fucking, sucking, biting, squeezing, tugging, even a little slapping and spitting. Astrid has always liked it rough, and he has discovered with her that he likes it too.

He never hears the voice, and this time her bellybutton doesn't aquatically accost him.

They retire to bed and quickly fall asleep. Two hours later he wakes to a sound he can't place. *Are the palm trees outside whispering in a breeze? That can't be it, it's definitely coming from inside the bedroom. It sounds like someone rubbing on fabric?*

"Psst buddy. I'm over here."

He sits bolt upright and listens. "I'm down here, dude, under the covers. I need to tell you something." Fear and anxiety flow through his veins like heroin; making him nauseous and sweaty. Slowly, he lifts the comforter and looks underneath.

"I'm over here, on this hot bitch's tummy."

He can barely see in the shadow of darkness, but he can make out a glint off the diamond ornament lanced into her stomach.

"I've got something important to tell you, Joshie."

"It's Joshua, and how in the fuck do you know my name?" *Jesus Christ, I'm talking to her bellybutton. I've completely lost my mind."*

"Nah man, your brain is right inside that big ol' cranium of yours, just like it should be."

Is it reading my mind? Oh, hell no! This is not happening; this is not fucking happening!

"Dude, I know everything about you, I have for your entire life. I've experienced everything you've experienced. I am the bellybutton you were supposed to have but was violently taken from you. By the way, this chick right here ... nice job man, she's amazing."

He sees the reflection of the diamond moving when the voice speaks. *It's moving when he talks. I've got to get the fuck out of here.* Joshua gets up quickly, but realizes he is home. He has nowhere to go.

The voice screams, "stop, being a pussy! We need to talk." Astrid stirs but doesn't wake.

Panicked, he goes into the living room. His heart hammers in his chest, threatening to bust out. *What can I do, I have to do something, but what?* "A-HA!" He exclaims as he sees a solution.

He enters the bedroom with his Bluetooth Bose noise-cancelling headphones on his head. He gets into bed, grabs his phone and puts on a Spotify playlist of popular heavy metal songs.

"Finally, where'd ya go, bro? Can we talk now?" Joshua doesn't hear it. He rolls over with his back to her and her weird, fucked up bellybutton. He gets zero sleep the rest of the night, but he doesn't hear the voice as it rambles on for hours.

᳟᳟᳟᳟᳟᳟

Eva arrives at three sharp. She is dressed to impress, in a tight red pencil skirt to show off her best asset, along with a tight white blouse with two more buttons open that should be, and heels. He is near the tremendous fountain in the center of the massive entrance area, she honks as she drives into the covered drive-thru carport. He greets her and they perform the double cheek kiss, though her lips "accidentally" softly graze his as they switch sides.

"It's great to see you, Joshua."

"And a pleasure to see you, Eva. Shall I take you on another tour of your new home?"

"Please," she smiles from ear to ear and wraps her arm around the crook of his elbow, "lead the way,"

They enter through the immense, weighty wooden front doors and walk into the Italian marble foyer. Eva's smile vanishes. He is not unaware of Eva's motive to meet alone.

"You remember my associate, Amber."

"It's a pleasure to see you again, Ms. Luna," Amber extends her hand in greeting.

"Oh yes, I'm sorry I wasn't expecting you,' she says with a sneer.

Amber retracts her hand. "Oh sorry, I failed to mention that she would be here. I bring her on all showings where we expect an offer to be made. That way if the seller accepts, we can sign the initial paperwork today."

Eva is not impressed and mutters, "whatever," under her breath.

After touring the mansion, they go out back to the private pool and grounds. Rows of black sage, California buckwheat, and western jimson weed are tailored immaculately throughout the pathways. Along the paths there are life-size replicas of Greek statues. Venus de Milo and Aphrodite are among the dozens that can be found throughout the grounds.

Eva, someone who is used to getting her way, hasn't given up yet. "Let's take a walk along the paths, Joshua. Your assistant can stay here." She says with zero shame.

"Associate, and fine. We'll be back shortly, Amber."

Eva puts her arms around his waist. Since it is weird to walk with only one person's arm around the other, he returns the gesture. They approach an ornate cement bench, "let's take a break." She guides him to the bench and attempts to seduce him with her lips and hands. Women tend to want to sleep with him. He is tall and well-built, often compared to Liam Hemsworth. He knows he's a fuckboy, and if it will help close a sale; it's just good business. As she is unbuttoning his shirt and kissing his chest he stares at two small statues on pedestals across the path; they are the Minoan snake goddess figurines. He stares at them and sees movement on their exposed stomachs. *What the fuck, are they moving?* He squints and sees a snake on each one coming out of their navels, the snakeheads weave in circles, twisting around one another, and speak as one. "Jossssssshua. Come to ussssssss." Their yellow eyes shine bright in the shadows, their fangs drip with venom that sizzles as it lands on the gravel path.

He jumps up, throwing Eva to the ground in the process, "NO, NO, NO, NO, NO!" He shouts.

"What the actual fuck, asshole?" Eva scolds as she gets up off the ground.

"Don't you see that," he is pointing to the statues, "Don't you hear them? They're talking to me." He is shaking as he stands there, frozen in place.

She looks at the statues. "All I see and hear is a fucking lunatic!"

"Jossssssshua, we want to sssssspeak with you." The snakes stretch farther out of the figurines, and closer to their target.

Joshua snaps out of it and takes off running. Each statue he passes speaks to him, their navels opening and shutting like mouths. They say things like, "Don't leave us. We need to tell you something. Don't run away! Don't be such a PUSSY!"

The cacophony of voices, the movement of the statue's stomachs, eats at his brain. As he dashes through the house and past Amber like an antelope escaping a pride of lions, he sobs, and he squeals like a barn owl searching for a mate. The statues on the interior and out front speak to him through the moving holes in their stomachs, "Don't be a PUSSY! We need to tell you something!" Their eyes follow him as he passes.

Amber chases behind him, moving surprisingly fast in her stiletto heels, and jumps into the passenger seat of the Aston Martin DBX 700 as he floors it out of the carport.

Eva runs out front as he leaves, "You can take this fucking piece of shit house and shove it up your ass, you goddamn psycho!"

Amber stares at him, and only says, "Tell me what to take care of and it will get done."

"I need to see my shrink!"

"OK, drive us there, I'll take an Uber or Lyft back to the office. but please slow down or let me drive."

He mops the sweat that is dripping from his hair into his eyes with the back of his hand and slows the car to a reasonable speed.

ᗜᗜᗜᗜᗜᗜ

A disheveled Joshua pushes past the assistant and into Dr. Burgess' office, interrupting a session with a Real House-wife of Beverly Hills that he happens to know.

"You can't barge in here like that, Joshua!" The doctor scolds as she rises to her feet.

"This is an emergency!" He looks at the patient, "Hi Erica, I'll give you twenty-five thousand dollars right now to leave." She accepts his offer and vacates the office.

"What the actual fuck, Joshua? You can't do that."

"I'm sorry, I had to. I am losing my fucking mind."

"Sit down and tell me what happened, but if you ever interrupt me with a client again, I will drop you that very second. Is that clear?"

He nods, sits and tells her what happened in the hot tub, in his bedroom with Astrid and how the statues came to life at the Walker Estate. His breathing is erratic, sweat still pours from him like water through a colander. He clutches his chest, "I think I'm having a heart attack."

"You are not having a heart attack."

"Everything is tight, my hands are numb, doc! Help me!" He cries.

"Joshua, look at me, look at me." He looks her in the eye, he looks horror-stricken, lost, like a frightened little boy, "listen to me, and breathe." He exhales, unaware that he had stopped breathing.

"Breathe in through your nose – hold it – let it out through your mouth. Keep doing that and listen to me. You are not dying, this is a panic attack, caused by your hallucinations. You're fine. You're here, in my office, it's a safe space." She presses the intercom, "Becky, bring Mr. Slater some chamomile tea and a Xanax from your stash. I'll write you a script for more."

Joshua is beginning to calm down as Dr. Burgess continues to speak, "obviously statues don't come to life. These are hallucination, so I am going to order blood work and a prescribe some Haloperidol, it's an antipsychotic, that should help with the hallucinations until we know what's causing them." She buzzes her assistant, "Becky, cancel my next two appointments and hold all calls. Tell them I have an emergency and squeeze them into my schedule as soon as is good for them. Next session will be paid for by Mr. Slater"

"You might as well get your money's worth today. The next three hours are yours. Tell me again what the bellybuttons said to you."

"Basically, that he is the bellybutton I never had because of the surgery for bladder exstrophy I had at birth. He said he has experienced everything I have and that he needs to tell me something."

"Let's not call it a he. It is an it, OK?" He nods, "and when it spoke this afternoon, it was through the statues, so not a person's navel?"

"Yes, and he, er it, started as two snakes coming out of two small statues." Joshua looks as though he has seen the devil himself. His leg is pumping faster than a hummingbird's wings, he is still sweating, albeit less than when he arrived. His eyes are filled with terror.

"And you were bullied as a child because you don't have a bellybutton, right?"

"Yes, someone noticed in the locker room after gym class in fifth grade. It was all over the school by the next morning."

"It seems pretty obvious these hallucinations have roots in that experience, so I want you to tell me again, exactly what happened back then."

He takes a deep breath and gulps his tea. "When I got to school the next day, everyone was staring at me, some were whispering and giggling. The meaner kids were even laughing and pointing at me. I didn't understand why at first, but by the time P.E. started, I figured out that everyone knew I didn't have a belly button. We were outside and a bunch of us were playing kickball at the far end of the field. It was really hot that day too. About ten minutes before P.E. ended, a group of boys and a few girls approached me and formed a circle around me. There were ten of them, I think. Angie Foster, one of the popular girls, told me to show her my bellybutton. I said, 'no' and tried to walk toward the building, but the boys pushed me back to the center of the circle. Then she said, 'let me see it, look, I'll show you mine' and she lifted her shirt. Then all the other kids lifted their shirts too. I tried to leave again, but they didn't let me. They wrestled me to the ground and lifted my shirt. I was screaming and crying, but no one came to help me. The teachers either didn't see or didn't care. Then Big Rex stepped up. He was the fattest kid in school. He was a year older and probably weighed at least two hundred and fifty pounds."

Joshua is sobbing on the couch; salty tears cascade down his cheeks. "That's when two other boys picked me up and put me down on my knees. One of them stood on my calves and the other held my head still. Big Rex then pulled up his tee shirt and stuck his fat stomach right in front of my face and told me to lick it. The kids were all laughing and screaming, chanting 'lick it!' over and over. Mitch, the kid holding my head, pushed my face into Rex's sweaty belly. It was dripping in sweat and already growing hair. The kids continued to chant. I couldn't breathe with my face in his stomach, so I gave in and stuck my tongue in his belly button. It was disgusting, it felt gritty, like there was sand in there, and something fuzzy too. I can still smell and taste it. It was vile, like week old taco meat, salty and rancid. I'll never forget it."

His breath hitching now, "everyone laughed and began chanting, 'Joshie is a freak!' a name that stuck with me the rest of my adolescent life. Everyone I would pass in the hallway would lift their shirts and yell 'freak' at me for the rest of that school year."

"How did that make you feel?"

"Goddammit! How do you think it made me feel? My life was miserable. I never had a single friend after that. I never went on a date. Hell, I was a damn virgin until I was twenty-three!" He shouted.

"Do you think that is why you are promiscuous now?"

"Hell if I know, I think I sleep with a lot of women because a lot of women want to sleep with me."

"So, you won. Beautiful, wealthy women throw themselves at you and you're ultra wealthy yourself. You're even somewhat famous now, just for being around the Hollywood elite." Dr. Burgess smiles as she tries to show him how good his life has turned out. Joshua stares blankly at her.

"Have you told Astrid about what is going on?"

"Of course not, she'll think I'm insane." He scoffs, "we don't have that type of relationship anyway. It's more a superficial, good time sort of thing."

"OK, I want to see you again in two days. In the meantime, it would be best if you told her. She might surprise you. Take the new meds and try to relax."

"All easier said than done, doc."

"And try those ear buds, Joshua. I'm serious."

ᗣᗣᗣᗣᗣᗣ

"Hello Joshua, how are you today? Any more incidents?"

"Not good."

"Did you speak to Astrid?"

"Yeah."

"How did that go?"

"Not great."

"Please explain."

"I told her about how I was bullied as a kid. She was sympathetic about that. But then I told her about what I had seen or heard. She looked at me and said 'you think my bellybutton is speaking to you? And you think it purposely spit water on your face?' Then she busted out laughing. She actually fell to the couch, grabbed her stomach and laughed so hard she cried."

"What did you do?"

"I just stood there like a goddamn fool. When she finally calmed down, I guess she saw the look on my face and said 'oh god, you're serious. I thought you were joking.' Or some shit like that. She tried to hug me, but I pushed her away and went home. What am I going to do, Dr. Burgess? I feel like I've lost my mind. I can't just hide in my condo forever; I have an event to attend in two days. It's important I be there for my business, all the big players in Hollywood and Beverly Hills will be there, and it's a pool-side gala." He looks exhausted and the doctor can see the fear coursing through him.

"I want to try an experiment if you'll let me."

With zero confidence and a tremble in his voice he says, "OK."

"You have what is known as omphalophobia, a fear of bellybuttons. It is uncommon, but like any phobia it can be overcome. Yours is caused by the fact you have no navel and were bullied about it as a child, cruelly I might add. I want you to sit here and listen to music to help you relax. I'll return in a little bit to conduct the experiment. I need you to trust me, and we'll see if we can fix this."

"Yes. Anything to get over this."

She leaves the room and classical music, Handel's Concerto Grosso in B Minor, flows softly through the room and surrounds him. He begins to truly relax for the first time in weeks. Just as he is about to drift off, he hears the door open. Becky brings him another cup of tea and the doctor walks in behind her with a stack of paper in her hand.

"To overcome any phobia, you have to face it head on. If you're afraid of heights you climb a ladder, if you're afraid of spiders you expose yourself to spiders. You get the picture."

He nods.

"Are you feeling relaxed?"

"As much as I can be, I suppose."

"Good then we will begin. Becky, please shut the door." She softly shuts the door and comes over and sits in a chair to the side.

"I am going to give you pictures of beautiful women, one at a time. And since these episodes seem to happen when you are in a state of heightened sexuality, I asked Becky to print pictures of attractive women in different states of dress. We'll start with women who are fully clothed, then move to crop tops and midriff shirts, bikinis and finally varying styles of lingerie. Got it?"

"Yeah."

"I'd like to video this from two angles, so we have an accurate record, and I don't want to take notes while working with you. Camera One will be on my desk to record your physical reactions, Camera Two will be behind the couch to show the picture you are looking at each time. Do you give your consent for the recordings?"

"This will never be shared, right doc?"

"No, Joshua, this is a safe space," she touches his knee in an effort to comfort her patient. "Plus, I would lose my license to practice."

"What about Becky? She hasn't taken an oath. It's not that I don't trust you both, but the tabloids pay big dollars for shit, and it would ruin my career."

"True, Becky hasn't taken an oath, but she is working on her doctorate in Psychology and plans to have a practice herself one day. It would kill that opportunity if she leaked the footage. I trust her with everything. She knows more dirt on me than anyone alive, if that helps. Or I can ask her to leave if you like. It's your call, Joshua. You are in control here."

"No, she can stay. I'm good with everything if this helps me."

"Great."

Becky sets up their phones to record and once the cameras are rolling Dr. Burgess introduces all three of them, states the date, time and location, as well as a description of what the experiment entails. She sets the pictures face down on the table in front of them, they are all numbered with number one being on top.

"Let's begin. Joshua, pick up the picture on the top of the stack please. Turn it over and look at it," he does as instructed, "really study it, look at how beautiful she is and then focus on her stomach. I want you to spend about a minute on each picture."

He works his way through the stack of pictures without an issue. Some are clothed, some in swimwear, some in lingerie. The final picture is of Astrid in a lingerie ad, prompting Joshua to say, "really doc?"

"Really. Since two of the three incidents involved her, it only makes sense to end it with her. You seemed to make it through the forty-two pictures just fine, how did you feel? At any time did you feel that something awful would happen?"

"I felt nervous the entire time, just waiting for me to freak out again, I suppose."

"Would you like to take this to the next level?"

"What's the next level?" He asks.

"Exposure to a live human navel."

"I don't know, what if it talks to me?"

"Then we deal with it, Joshua. You are safe here. Safe physically and from embarrassment. This is the setting to try this. Becky graciously volunteered to be the variable in the experiment if we need her." She looks to her assistant, "are you still OK with that Becky?"

"Yes, I am, assuming that is OK with Mr. Slater."

Joshua has been interested in Becky since he's been seeing Dr. Burgess, so he agrees without hesitation. He wants to see the body under her professional attire. She is in her upper twenties, with fake blonde hair in a golden hue, and unlike the rest of the women in LA, her hair is the only thing that isn't natural. She has no obvious fillers, has large natural breasts, is of average height with hips and an ass most women would kill to have.

"Becky, please come over here and stand in front of Mr. Slater."

"Please ladies, you can both call me Joshua."

"Alright then Joshua, please sit up close to Becky. Are you still comfortable with this?" He nods and licks his lips.

"Becky, begin unbuttoning your blouse." She starts with the top button and moves down slowly. Once she is unbuttoned, the doctor asks Joshua if he is OK. He says that he is, but he can feel his heart rate increase and his temperature rise. He wears the look of a person waiting to be called back for a root canal at the dentist's office.

"Becky, please untuck your top and open it to expose your belly button. Still doing fine, Joshua?"

"Uh huh," he says weakly.

"Caress her stomach if you are able. It's fine if you're not comfortable." He reaches out and places his hand on her midriff. Becky lets out an almost inaudible moan. "Move your hand to her navel, touch it, place your fingertip inside."

Becky giggles. "I'm sorry, it tickled."

"That's alright Becky. Are you still fine Joshua?"

He feels his core temperature still rising, and feels fluttery, but he knows that is only because he is turned on from this intimate moment with Becky. "I'm fine, doc."

"Thank you, Becky. You may redress now. I can't explain why this is happening to you, Joshua. But hopefully this exercise has helped you. Go to your upcoming event, I think you'll be fine. Just try to not hook up with anyone. Maybe refrain from any intimate contact for a bit and go do your blood draw. I don't think you're suffering from anything physical, but I want to be sure."

He exits the doctor's office with Becky. "Becky, this thing I have Saturday night is a big charity event, you wouldn't want to go with, would ya?"

"You mean like a date?" She asks in surprise. "That wouldn't be appropriate, I can't socialize with clients but thank you."

"First off, I am not your client. And B, I've wanted to ask you out since I've been seeing Dr. Burgess, but haven't because I knew you would say no. And three, you can't deny there was a charge in there when I touched you. I know you felt it too. I heard the tiny moan."

"Yes, I felt something, but it would be unethical. Now,

can I put you down for your regular day and time next week?"

"Nope," he walks back to the doctor's door, "Doc, can you refer me to a new shrink?"

"Why? Is something wrong?"

"Nothing at all, and even though I'm crazier than a blind race car driver, you've been great, and helped me a lot. The issue is that Becky won't accept my invitation to a fancy soiree."

"Becky, come here please and shut the door."

A few minutes later Becky returns wearing a subtle smile, "Dr. Burgess will email you some referrals for another provider."

"Excellent, I'll pick you up at six."

"I don't have anything appropriate to wear."

"No worries. Amber, my associate, will be at your place at one o'clock on Saturday. She'll take you shopping and to get your hair done if you want, just let her know. I'll pick you up at six and we'll go hang out with all the snobs, you'll love it."

ㅂㅂㅂㅂㅂㅂ

Joshua goes home and plans a quiet night by himself. He makes dinner, a porterhouse, loaded baked potato and French beans. Then lies on the couch to read the latest horror masterpiece from Jay Bower.

Several hours later he wakes up on the couch and hears something coming from his bedroom. *Is someone talking in there?* He picks up his Ping nine iron from his golf bag that perpetually sits by the front door. With the golf club lofted up over his right shoulder, and feeling like he could puke at any moment, he creeps into the bedroom and flips the wall switch that illuminates his hula girl bedside lamp. Silence fills the room as he checks the closet, under the bed and behind the blackout drapes. He finds nothing, not a person, nor a single thing out of place. Letting out his breath with a large sigh he drops the club and goes to the kitchen for a bottle of Evian.

As he twists the cap, a shrill, blood-curdling shriek calls out his old nickname from school, "FREAK!" He drops the open bottle of water on the floor and runs to the bedroom. The hula girl lamp is dancing and laughing. He runs over, yanks it from the table, and unplugs it before throwing it across the room where it smashes into a painting on the wall.

"Joshie is a freak! Joshie is a freak!" The lamp continues to taunt him. He picks up the previously discarded golf club and smashes it to bits. As he stands over the busted pile of ceramic shards, catching his breath, the chant begins anew, this time in the living room.

"FUCK!" he shouts as he runs from the bedroom to find a nude painting above his fireplace heckling him. The woman's navel is smiling as it reminds him that he is a freak. He takes the art down, busts the frame over his knee and tosses it out his front door.

Now from the kitchen, the voice beckons him. His salt and pepper shakers, ceramic girls in bikinis, call his name, "Joshie come here, Joshie come here. We love freaks. Come play with us." As he approaches the shaker set, dark-purple tongues, split in the middle, emerge from their bellies. Black detritus drips onto the granite countertop. He grabs them and forces them down the drain and turns on the garbage disposal, grinding them into dust.

"Yoo-hoo! Over here, Freak," Joshua looks to the living room again. "I'm over here dumbass." He looks toward his coffee table. The navel of the woman on the cover of Health and Fitness magazine is speaking now, "Hiya, Freak!" It spits in his face as he leans down to pick up the periodical. He tosses it in the gas fireplace and engages the automatic starter. He runs through the condo looking for anything with an exposed stomach, the only thing left are his old porn magazines hidden in a drawer. The hundreds of navels on the covers and in the pages laugh, whistle, caterwaul, and grumble at him as he carries them to their death pyre.

𝅘𝅥𝅮𝅘𝅥𝅮𝅘𝅥𝅮𝅘𝅥𝅮𝅘𝅥𝅮𝅘𝅥𝅮

After the silent auction concludes Joshua and Becky join the numerous actors, producers and politicians near the jungle inspired pool in the backyard of the most powerful producer in Hollywood. He shmoozes with the elite, with Becky by his side.

Later they are alone at a table, finishing their last drinks. They are laughing and enjoying one another's company while drunk, famous people cavort in the pool. A few are in swimwear, but most are naked. He knows it's only a first date, but he feels some kind of way with Becky. He thinks he may be ready to settle down and that she is the perfect woman for him.

Then he hears it, the voice again. It sounds like a chorus of dozens. He looks toward the pool and sees all the women floating up out of the water, the bellybuttons chanting in unison, "Joshie is a freak," on repeat.

Becky screams, "what the fuck is happening?"

"You can see that?" He yells to Becky.

"Yes. I can hear them too."

The people float toward the couple, chanting and laughing. While terrified, Joshua has a sense of relief that someone else is experiencing this too. The couple stares at the approaching mass as it closes in on them, "Come on, we need to get the hell out of here." He grabs her hand and begins to run. He runs too fast though, and she trips in her heels and falls to the ground. Joshua doesn't stop and runs right into the thick foliage surrounding the backyard.

Becky calls to him, "Joshua, NO!"

He is falling and falling, until he isn't. He hits the solid ground with a sickening crunch and snapping of bone. The partygoers run to the edge of the cliff and look down from sixty feet above. They are crying and screaming, some of them vomit.

EMTs arrive and find him alive, but unconscious, and take him to the hospital where he is rushed into surgery. The doctors are able to save his shattered leg, but more surgeries will be required over the next several months.

ᗣᗣᗣᗣᗣᗣ

Eleven Months Later

Joshua wakes up in his bed, looks at the white world outside his window, and smiles as Becky brings him a cup of steaming, black coffee.

After multiple surgeries and months of physical therapy, he can walk again, albeit with a significant limp. He sold off his investment properties, condo and cars. He gave his business to Amber, who now sells primarily to men. He has enough money to live out his years in his new home, Kautokeino, Norway, north of the Arctic Circle. They live among the Sami people and their reindeer.

He will never see another belly button again.

He still doesn't know what his non-existent navel wants to tell him, and he doesn't care.

11

EPHEBIPHOBIA

BY ZAQ CASS

I can tell that it is time to wake up because the numbness from my knee is replaced by a thousand needles stabbing into my nerves. I stretch it out, trying to get the blood flowing back to wherever it needs to be. It pops loudly, making me gasp in relief, the pins dispersing slowly as I slide into a sitting position on the edge of my bed. I roll my shoulders back, small pops sounding from various parts of my spine and neck. A small headache is coming on, my nicotine-addicted body irked that I've been awake for two whole minutes without smoking.

The looks and physique of youth are long gone. Even with as active as I was, it refused to fade out slowly, hitting me like a Mack truck all at once—the smoking, the unhealthy diet, the overworking. Anytime I wasn't working in my thirties, I was on my ass, doing my best impersonation of a lump.

I work in a warehouse. I used to move inventory around with a pallet jack, stacking boxes and crates by hand, unloading tractor trailers, all of it—constantly on my feet and moving. One would think that would keep me rather healthy, but the fast food, beer, and smoking I consume worked against me. Plus, it isn't like I practiced the best ergonomics. My knee first gave out when I was twenty-two, my back right before I hit thirty. Now sitting at forty-five, I was glad I had managed to get a desk job, running inventory and routing deliveries. Sadly, sitting at the desk didn't help tendons and muscles abused by daily labor for so long.

Sleeping was worse. Whether I was in a fitful slumber and rolled around all night or stayed completely still, my joints would get restless and numb. It was common for me to wake up fully in the middle of the night just to shift my arm out from under me. The circulation would be cut off and it would feel like electricity constricting around my entire limb.

I grab my phone off the night table and check for texts from Janet. As always, I'm kidding myself. There's nothing there, an ever-present experience since she ran off with her spin instructor. I sigh to myself, not too terribly surprised. I wasn't the best husband. Janet gave and gave, and the only thing she ever wanted, I talked her out of. She wanted children, and I talked a big game on how we would save money and spend all of our time together, just the two of us. Once she was thoroughly convinced, I failed to keep up my end of the bargain. I can still hear her anger and sadness. Why work so much if I was just going to spend my money on fast food and alcohol? Why not have children if I was going to spend all of my time at the bar and not with her?

Like I said, I'm not surprised at the lack of a text.

I slip on my clothes and step outside to grab the newspaper. I grit my teeth when I see where the little brat who delivers it managed to land it. It'd be one thing if it was in the bushes. At least then it would be at the house, even if a little annoying. Instead, he barely made it onto the curb of the sidewalk, still off property. Kids these days don't have pride in their work. They'd rather have everything handed to them. I walk down the path, my slippers scratchy against the cement and bend down to scoop it up.

The hair on the back of my neck stands up. I catch something in my peripheral; something that wasn't there before. Newspaper in hand, I slowly stand back up, ignoring the creaks of my spine arguing with the effort of bending over.

Across the street stands a boy. Now when I say standing, I mean it, and nothing else. He's not busy, not in the process of doing something. He's standing inches from the curb, perfectly straight, just staring at me. An older teenager, jeans with a small rip in the knee. His hair is overgrown, brown bangs nearly poking him in the eye. His t-shirt is too tight and his overshirt too baggy. He has a delinquent look about him, only magnified by his eyes boring into me, a plastered grin on his face.

I look at him for a moment as he slowly lifts one arm, waving at me. I put on my best scowl and turn back to my house, making my way in as quickly as I can. I'm not too speedy when I first wake up. Back in my house, I peek around the curtain. He still stands there, staring at the spot where I was, his arm still outstretched in a wave.

It gives me the chills.

My gut feeling is to call the cops, but I shake it. Janet once told me I have a pretty bad reputation as the guy who wants kids to stay off his lawn. I don't need the added layer of calling cops on a teenager that's technically not doing anything. As much as that smile on his face disturbed me, he was just standing there.

Maybe I could say I thought I saw blood? Cops know how teenagers can be, how violent and impulsive they can be. No, no. Better to not even bother.

I've never liked teens, even when I was one. Probably

because I was one. I knew how they operated when they were among my so-called peers. Only thinking about themselves, not caring how their actions affected other people. Unchecked anger and emotion combined with some false sense of immortality. Conceited, vain, narcissistic. They were dangerous. People would say they were just being kids, and they'd practically get away with murder.

My own parents thought it odd that I didn't join in on shenanigans. Why not take up a sport? Why not go out to parties? It wasn't worth it. Teens are a disgusting species, always have been. It's even worse now with the internet constantly in their pocket.

When Janet said she wanted kids, I almost agreed with her. It was when I brought up teens that things got terse, and she would try to change the subject. She knew that she wouldn't win that argument with me. Imagine putting all of that time and effort into raising a respectable child only for them to turn thirteen and make your life an absolute hell. Kids are chaotic and destructive, but teenagers do it with spite. Kids cause accidents; teens premeditate.

I have a cup of coffee and a cigarette much to my lungs' joy before peeking out the window again. The boy is gone, and I can't help but breathe out a victorious sigh of relief. My achy bones creak, letting go of the tension they held, my shoulders finally able to relax. I shove my pack of smokes into my pocket alongside my lighter, grab my keys and make off for my truck, looking around to make sure he is really gone. I find myself looking in the rearview just to see if he will pop up again as I turn the ignition, a grinding sound in response rather than the start of the engine I was hoping for.

I curse and step out of the car. I was hoping for a lax weekend, but it was beginning to look like I would have to go grab some parts from the auto shop. Luckily, one of the pros to living within the town proper meant I could walk just about everywhere. My knee would have to forgive me.

Everything goes well for the first block, but as I walk past city hall, I notice some teens skateboarding on the steps. I can feel my face grow hot as my blood pressure rises. The sheer disrespect of these punk ass kids treating such a significant part of this town as their own personal playground gets to me. I start to walk my way toward them to tell them off and how I wish they had school seven days a week, when one steps off his board. He points to me and his friends form a semicircle around him. In tandem, the rest of them snap their heads toward me, smirks slowly stretching into smiles across their face.

I stop in my own tracks. A few of the others start taking slow steps toward me, their pace in lockstep, arms swinging at the same rate. I turn on my heel and continue toward the shop, checking over my shoulder as I ignore the throbbing in my knee as I quicken. With their slow, consistent gait, I create a bit of distance, facing forward just in time to see another group of three teenage girls walking toward me from that direction. They're all wearing the cheerleading uniform of the local high school, each of their hair styled with ringlets and pigtails.

Not delinquents like the skateboarders. Probably on their way to practice or a competition. I slow my pace, thinking I'll be able to slip past their group with no problems when the one in the center eyes me up and down. I can sense the judgement, the hate from her gaze. I'm about to remind her that she'll age one day too, when she slowly starts to smile. The girls on either side follow suit, their own teeth baring to me in unison.

I feel my stomach drop and I slip into the next business I pass, closing the door and holding it tight. The cheerleaders stand in front of the glass door, looking at me, only the thin pane separating us. They stay and smile and the skateboarders are soon standing behind them. I lock the door and back away slowly.

The group continues their stare down, but don't attempt to open the door. I back into a table, and it is only then that the smoky smell of meat hits my nostrils. I look around and realize where I ended up. Joe's Diner.

On a typical Saturday morning, Joe's would be filled to the brim with families, friends, couples, and an assortment of regulars sitting at the bar. Waitresses would be running around without breaking stride, delivering plates and receipts and wishing everyone to enjoy their weekend. As I look through the narrow restaurant now, I am taken aback of the absence of people. Every table is empty, every barstool lacking the ass of a regular customer. The television still plays above the expo station on mute, the captions a line or two behind whatever the newscaster was saying. The smells and sounds of cooking still emanate from the kitchen.

A boy steps out from behind the kitchen door, carrying two plates of food. Seeing him, I felt my chest tighten up around my heart before realizing that it was just Daniel, Joe's son. He has worked the grill since he was just a boy and was ready to become a partner when he turned eighteen in just a few months.

"Hey George, just in time," he said. "Breakfast is ready."

He sat the plates down on the bar between us and stared at me.

"Where's your dad, Daniel? In fact, where's all the customers?"

Daniel laughed a stilted, fake chuckle, "A bit slow so far today is all. Dad will be out in a bit now that you're here. Eat up."

He stared at me, eyes unblinking as I looked down at the plates and sat down. On one plate was a bowl of grits, butter already melting on top with a couple of sugar packets next to it. On the other was hashbrowns, an assortment of sausage links and strips of bacon, and two eggs over easy. My usual, for the most part. The only thing different was the slight blue tinge to the eggs.

"What's with this?" I say, pointing down.

Daniel smiled, a little too broad from a boy who inherited the casual smirk his father always had, "Oh, it's just new seasoning. Gives it a weird color but tastes delicious. Try it, George."

As much as I didn't mind if Daniel called me George, he usually only used it on greeting. He knew I was particular about how the youth should speak to their elders. I pick up the fork, every nerve in my body on alert, warning me against it. Just as I'm about to give in, another boy comes out from the kitchen. I look him over. He's about the same age as Daniel and has a lot of similar features. There's a familiarity I can't place.

"Heya, George," the boy says.

I bring back my scowl from earlier, "Son, I don't know you. I may tolerate Daniel calling me by my name, but not you. Show some respect when you speak to me." Even with the scowl, I only barely manage to stifle the quiver in my voice.

"Don't know me? We grew up together! You spent all your free time here when my dad owned the place," the boy says, his smile widening, matching Daniels.

Plates go flying as I push myself off the stool, away from the bar. I point at the newcomer, my gaze shifting between the two boys, nearly identical. I always used to tell Janet how much Daniel looked like Joe when he was younger.

"What? What's going on?" I all but holler. "Joe? How is this possible?"

"It's great, George," he says, slowly making his way down the counter toward the opening, never taking his eyes off of me, "With just a little bit of this new spice, you'll be feeling younger in no time. No more pain. No more aging."

It takes a second to register that Daniel spoke the end of the sentence at the exact same time as the teenage version of his father. Joe finally makes his way through the opening in the counter and begins walking toward me. I tighten my fist around the fork and thrust it out, holding it between us.

Joe's slow, methodical pace continues though. I keep the fork between us as he closes the gap, the prongs now poking into his shirt, causing a dent. He leans into it, and I feel the blunt cutlery push against him then the pop of pressure as it manages to poke through his shirt and skin. His eyes keep boring into me, his grin spread as watery blue liquid travels from the wound down the silver fork.

"I feel young again, George. I feel free. I don't have to share the restaurant. Daniel doesn't have to worry about aging or needing a steady job running this place. We can live the lives we want," he says confidently, his voice steady rather than the animated cadence I had grown accustomed to from the man.

"And we know so much," the same voice coming from Daniel. "We know what each of us knows. We learn what each of us learns."

He backs me up to the wall, my knuckles turning white still clutching the fork still pierced into Joe. The blue liquid keeps dripping from him, gathering into a small puddle on the floor. A pounding on the door snaps my attention away.

The head cheerleader slams a palm against the glass over and over, no emotion registering on her face. The thudding continues to make an echo into the near empty restaurant. Daniel hops the counted and makes his way to her, unlocking the door and letting the group of cheerleaders and skateboarders make their way inside.

I push into Joe, letting the fork go and slip around him. They slowly pace toward me, one phalanx of teenagers giving me almost no chase. I make my way through the kitchen and out the back exit, hearing them collectively chant at me.

"Join us, George."

"Be young again."

"We can be teens forever."

"No more pain."

"No more loneliness."

I come out into the alley behind the restaurant and turn toward the residential area, away from the shops. I knew that, as slow as they were being, I couldn't run for too long. My knee was already furious at me from all of the running around I was doing. I can feel it swelling, the pulsing flame of an overworked joint. It wouldn't hold up for much longer. My truck might be out of action, but there has to be a car somewhere I can access.

The first few houses have garages, vehicles shut behind their doors. I continue to the next block, seeing from a distance that driveways were actually occupied. I jog toward it, noticing how much slower I am getting.

I make my way toward a house with a red sedan in the drive, but as I approach, I notice a teenager standing on the porch. He tilts his head and smiles a broad smile at me, before holding out his hand. He jingles a keyring.

"Need to go somewhere, George?" he says, his grin deepening.

I continue to the next house, meeting the same result. These new kids come off their porches as I run past, joining in walking after me, the core group led by Joe closing the distance as my body groans against the constant movement that I'm forcing it to endure.

House after house, more teens join the mob, slowly walking after me as one hive, chanting over and over again at me to join them.

"You're weak."

"You're frail."

"We can fix that."

"Join us, George."

My body aches, but my mind doesn't give in. To be a teenager again. To feel distant and insecure was bad enough in my time. Having access to technology and the internet just to feel worse? I power through the pain, ignoring my haggard breathing and the ice cold burning of my lungs.

I turn down streets, mentally trying to keep tabs on where I have traveled to. I make my way toward a self-pump gas station that would only be a few blocks away, the mob growing house to house, waiting for me to finally drop.

I push through the pain and soon see that station in front of me. My lungs burn from a combination of going so long without a smoke and more physical exertion that it is used to. I swallow, the dry cotton that is my life, offering no help. I pant and wheeze, watching as the crowd grows around me before reaching for a pump.

I squeeze the trigger and put the latch in place before dropping it to the ground. I move to the next pump and repeat. I do all eight pumps before looking around for the horde of teenagers. They surround the gas station entirely, five or six rows deep. They all watch me with dead, cold eyes, smiles etched on their faces.

Joe steps forward, "You don't have to do this, George. Join us. Look at you. You're forty-five, but your body feels like you're ninety. You smoke like a chimney and are bitter and lonely."

"Screw you, buddy. I don't trust any of you. A bunch of bottom feeders, leeching off the success of their parents."

Joe shook his head, "No more parents. Just youth forever, George. No more worrying about bills and ex-wives and whether or not you'll be able to go up a flight of stairs without running out of breath. No more knee problems, pissing problems, or being too tired to work off the calories."

I hold up my lighter, "And be some sort of evil, violent teen?"

The head cheerleader steps up, "No George. We'll all be a collective. We'll all work together to make the world a better place. When we're all one mind, we don't lash out our insecurities on other people."

The boy from my house steps up on the other side of her, "And not just here, George. We want to spread out into the state. The country. Maybe even the world. When we're all thinking the same, think of the peace this place can finally have."

I look around, clocking in faces that look familiar. Some are teens that were already in town. Some are the younger faces of the adults I knew, some even as familiar as a memory from back in school.

My lungs still burn from the exertion. My knee shakes, ready to just give up altogether. My forehead and shirt are drenched in sweat. With each ragged breath, my ribs feel like they stab into me, and I feel my chest tighten.

I relax my shoulders, and the horde seems to react positively, now acting more individual. A few of them shout for me to join them. Some are just talking to each other loudly. A cheer goes up from the back and a path part between a few of them as Daniel walks up with a plate of food. Eggs, with an odd blue seasoning on top of it.

A collective chant rises from the crowd.

"EAT IT! EAT IT! EAT IT!"

I take the plate from him and the crowd starts closing in around me, eager for me to take a bite and join their ranks. Once I feel like they are close enough, I drop the plate, letting it shatter into pieces on the ground before reaching into my pocket.

"I'm never letting you fucks take me," I say before sparking the lighter and dropping it into the pool of gas, watching the world turn white.

🦷🦷🦷🦷🦷🦷

We enter the diner and head for the back booth like we normally do after swimming in the lake. The four of us decided that we could go for some grub, and there was nowhere better in town than Joe's.

Daniel came to our table with our plates immediately, having known we were on our way and what our usuals were like the professional he is. The bacon smells amazing and the eggs pulse with their blue spice, a sweet and savory mix of flavor that made everything taste better. It also had the added benefit of fixing up any injuries we had gotten since the last time we had some.

Maya comes into the diner and slides into the booth next to me. I throw my arm around her and give her a peck on the forehead. Apparently, she had been the local math teacher at the high school, but since we all share information, there was no need for that. She had missed being a cheerleader when she was younger and had the habit of wearing her old uniform around as much as possible, even when she was at the school manufacturing more spice.

It was her month to work on the spice. Mine was next. We take turns so that nobody would ever feel like they were in a dead-end job. None of us actually minded, however. Distributing the blue spice into the world was something all of us were passionate about. In just a month or two, we'll be ready to spread the blue spice to the rest of the state.

"Are we still going to the movies later?" Maya asks me. I know she's worried that conforming Janet when we spread would cause me to lose interest in her. I tighten my grip around her shoulders, trying to reassure her. I can sense her ease a bit.

"Yeah, of course. As soon as we're done skating, you and I are going to grab some snacks and check out that new flick you want to see."

She smiles at me brightly as Joe comes out to our table, a slight smirk on his face.

"Skating? You sure your knee can handle it, George?" he jokes.

We all join in at laughing with him. Except the occasional scrape, my knee was happily sound, no cartilage on joint problems waking me up in the middle of the night.

"Oh, yeah," I say, barely remembering the pain I had experienced for so long a few weeks ago even felt like. "It's never felt better."

12

ABLUTOPHOBIA

BY DAVID K. SLATER

The first thing he heard was her breathing. That's how it always started. Chris' nightmares had persisted for so long now, they were as much a part of him as the colour of his eyes.

The act of falling into each nightmare was more like awakening from the safety of reality. His heightened senses were on full alert—everything was razor sharp. There's something eerie about the beautifully bright colours of a nightmare, the icy cold clarity of her piercing eyes. Chris could sense them boring holes into him from the darkness. With his remaining senses beyond his reach, the only things he could experience were the dark and the dry wheezing of her laboured breath.

The panic spread through his chest, and he would reach out for a light switch, a door handle, a wall, anything to help him escape the black.

'Christopher...' her serpentine voice would whisper so closely behind him, he could feel the warmth of her rancid breath on his neck.

'Itsss tiiime....'

Light bled into the room like someone turning a dial to activate the sun. Then Chris would find himself at the end of a hallway, peering towards an open bathroom door. The light buzzed and crackled like a lampshade full of moths. A low and pathetic moan leaked from Christopher's throat as he shook his head from side to side.

'No...'

His arms hung by his sides like a statue made of lead.

'No, please...'

The magical invisible conveyor belt would spark into life and pull him towards the door.

'It'sss tiiime.' She sang.

Tears in his eyes, drool pooling in the corner of his mouth, Christopher pleaded with the unseen woman.

'Please, no...'

His body continued its forward motion at the same drudging pace. The light sputtering out just as he reached the threshold of the bathroom. Unseen bony hands would lurch against his back, forcing him through the doorway.

Chris stumbled into an average suburban bathroom, nothing out of the ordinary confronted him. There was nothing to fear here. Except maybe one thing.

The shower curtain was drawn.

Chris had been deathly afraid of a drawn shower curtain since he was a boy. Something about that thin veil standing between you and who knows what. A perfect hiding place for a monster or a murderer. All would become silent. Just the faint whooshing sound of the futile rush of blood coursing through Christopher's veins. His heart would not still. Here I am, it called. Here is the oil that powers this broken machine. Ready to be spilled across this filthy linoleum floor, warm and sticky at first. Quickly congealing to a glistening, oily puddle, a banquet for the flies. One giant setting scab.

'It'sss tiiime.'

Chris could just make out the barely human silhouette on the other side of the curtain.

Who is it?

What is it?

'It's time...'

The curtain bunched up, about chest height, near its edge, and an unseen hand would pull it downward, causing the curtain rings to ping off one by one.

Ping

'It's time...'

His heart in his throat.

Ping

'It's tiiime...' exhaled breath like cockroaches escaping from a broken drain. Freezing cold, skeletal fingers grasping at his insides.

Ping

'It's time... to wake up!'

Christopher woke with the start. Each morning held the same wake-up call. Reality washed over him like a bucket of cold water. He was forty-two, overweight, unemployed, divorced and laying in a puddle of his own urine. Daylight forced its daggers through the holes in his frayed blackout curtains. He rolled to the side of the bed, swung his feet outward. It took a concerted effort and a theatrical groan for Chris to get himself upright. He shook his head at the notion of the day ahead of him.

'Reeeown,' came the croaking, somewhat nasal call of Christopher's cat, Jim.

Jim was a stray that Chris had taken in one night when he was too drunk to make it home. The two of them slept on a bench in the bus station, using each other for warmth and much needed affection. There was a genuine romance between Chris and Jim when they first met. It took a while to coax Jim indoors after he had willingly followed Chris home. A tin of forty-nine pence worth of the best tuna that money can buy sealed the deal. For months, Jim avoided Chris most of the day, then snuck into his bed, under the cover of night, like some feline booty call. Sure enough, he would be gone before the sun came up, leaving nothing but a bunch of discarded ginger hair and the occasional whisker. Chris enjoyed finding a whisker so much in the early days that he took to stabbing them into a ball of Blu-Tack on his bedside table. Years had passed and now the whisker trophy now resembled one of those horsehair brushes that a barber uses to give you a wet shave. That same trophy that some people would probably refer to as "rank" was the only reminder of those happier days. If Chris was honest with himself, he couldn't stand that cat now, the fat ginger bastard.

'Reeeowww' There he was again.

If it was possible to get a divorce from your cat, Chris would do it in a heartbeat.

'Yes Jim, I'm coming,' he sighed, sounding absolutely defeated.

Jim brushed himself against Christopher's leg as he bunched up the wet bedding in his arms.

'I know, I know. You're not going to waste away...'

In an attempt to either get fed sooner or cause his untimely death, Jim weaved in and out of Chris' feet on every step of his journey from his bedroom to the kitchen.

'Fuck's sake, Jim!'

Chris stumbled and slipped on the exposed wood of the last step, where the carpet was worn through, which his knee protested. He got no sympathy from Jim, though.

The cat food had barely touched the bowl before Jim inhaled it. The loud smacking noises from his lips were not entirely unpleasant, and it triggered a sympathy hunger pain in Christopher's belly.

Should I eat?

Chris hated to eat early in the morning. Ever since he was in his early teens, he'd always chosen to forgo the pleasures of tea and toast with his family before school. Instead, he opted for the extra ten minutes in bed. After five or six months, his body stopped expecting food before noon. It's funny, the things you can get used to.

Today felt special, though. There was no tangible reason for that feeling, but Chris knew it was a beans on toast kind of day. He set four slices of medium white toast on the go and emptied a tin of off-brand baked beans into an orange-stained plastic bowl. Set the microwave for two minutes and forty seconds and hit the start button. Chris rubbed his face and let out a groaning sigh.

Should I have a drink? It's too early for that, surely.

The fridge called out to him. He could hardly recall what food he had in there, but he was certain of one thing he had: vodka. The dim yellow light of the refrigerator caused Chris to squint as he rooted for the booze. *It's always Happy Hour somewhere.*

Chris struggled to remember a full hour of happiness in the last decade.

The toaster popped, the microwave pinged, and the bottle glugged as Chris poured himself a vodka orange.

This is kind of a breakfast drink...

He held the glass up in the sunlight and saw that it was only a bit dirty, so he knew he'd picked a good one. Predictably, dishes piled high in the sink, caked in days-old food remnants. With one generous swig, Chris took his first drink of the day. The odd mixture of cold orange juice and the burn of the vodka made him feel alive. It was about the only thing that made him feel that way lately. He closed his eyes and exhaled deeply, enjoying the feeling of the cool liquid coursing through his system and dropping into his belly.

A wet smacking sound disturbed the relative quiet of the kitchen. Christopher's eyes popped open, and he looked around; half expecting to see someone standing in the kitchen with him, licking their cold grey lips with a rotten black tongue. Instead, he saw Jim standing on the counter, tucking into his beans on toast.

'Oi, me beans!' Chris yelled.

Jim fled, but not without a slice of toast in his mouth, slick with sugary tomato sauce. Chris considered if he could still eat food a cat licked. Images of Jim licking his arsehole flooded his mind. It didn't take too much effort to suppress those images, though.

Fuck it, I've had worse things in my mouth.

🦷🦷🦷🦷🦷🦷

Chris paced in the living room, phone in hand, debating if he should call the hospital.

His dad had been in there for weeks now. Although Chris was over the initial shock of seeing them cart him away in the ambulance, he didn't know if he could stomach visiting him yet. Most people dislike hospitals, there's not much to like about them, but Chris had seen enough people on life support to fill a lifetime. He wasn't ready to add more scars to the mural of emotional trauma etched on his brain.

'Fuck it.'

He dialled a number and put them on speaker.

'Good morning, you're through to James Cook University Hospital. Please be aware that calls may be recorded for training and monitoring purposes. Please state the name of the person or department you would like to contact.' A tinny recorded voice spoke.

'Ward Twelve.'

'I heard paediatrics. If this is correct, press one, if this is incorrect, press two.'

Beep

Chris upped the intensity of his pacing. It was a miracle he hadn't worn the carpet out over the last few years with all the times he'd been in this position.

'Please state the name of the person you would like to contact.'

'Ward, Twelve.'

'I heard paediatrics. If this is correct, press one, if this is incorrect, press two.'

Beep

Chris gave a frustrated half growl through his teeth.

'Please state the name of the person...'

'Ward Twelve!'

'Connecting to paediatrics...'

He hung up the phone and threw it on the sofa. Waves of anger rushed over him like a heavy rain.

'Deep breaths, deep breaths...'

Chris grabbed the phone again and checked his messages, hoping there would be something from his dad that would prevent him from having to call again. It was one thing to battle with the automated lines, but he would hate talking to the nurses even more when he finally got through.

'Why is nothing ever easy?' He sighed.

He drained the vodka and went to get another. Sunshine in a glass was the only answer to this problem. Everything else could wait.

🦷🦷🦷🦷🦷🦷

Daytime TV droned as Chris lay on his bed, nursing his fourth drink. The buzz cancelled out the stress he'd felt since opening his eyes this morning. His eyelids were just feeling heavy when he heard a *Clack... Clack... Clack...*

Something echoed from another room in the house. Chris got to his feet and staggered awkwardly from his bedroom, out onto the landing. Nothing was out of place. Maybe he'd imagined it. After all, there was no...

Clack... Clack... Clack...

'Shit...' he muttered under his breath.

The sound came from the bathroom. It sounded like someone tapping on the window with a piece of metal. Someone was trying to get his attention. The bathroom door was closed, and Chris did everything he could to convince himself that he didn't have to go look.

It's probably nothing. Probably a bird or...

Clack... Clack... Clack...

'Fuck's sake' he said, more annoyed than afraid, because he knew that no matter how scary this situation was, he couldn't just walk away and do nothing.

Chris took a deep breath and marched toward the door. He pushed it open with one swift motion and immediately saw the shape of a blackbird sitting on the outside window ledge. The bird's yellow beak was just visible through the frosted glass.

'I fucking knew it...'

Chris turned his head slightly and froze.

The shower curtain was drawn.

His breath was shaky as he slowly stepped backwards, hoping to slip out and act like it wasn't there. Deal with it later.

Screeeeeeee...

The sound of the rusty taps turning.

'It's ok, just walk away. You don't have to...'

'Uhhhhhh' a low guttural moan came from behind the curtain.

I'm dead.

'Ohhhhh' the voice moaned in pain. 'Chrissssstoper....'

Chris stood frozen, his head shaking from side to side. Denying the horrifying reality he found himself in.

'No...' he whispered.

'It'sss tiiime...'

The shower curtain tore from its railing as the unseen creature lurched from the bath and hurtled into Chris like a speeding car. Both he and the creature smashed into the wall, entangled in the curtain.

Chris screamed until he felt his voice disintegrate.

He woke in his saturated bed with a feeble yelp.

'Fuck my life!'

The piss-soaked duvet wrapped around Chris like some disgusting burrito as he rolled out of bed and ran his hands across the mattress. He hoped the damage wouldn't be too bad.

'Yep, ruined...'

Back to the kitchen he went, with another armful of drenched bedding. In a rare moment of fortuitousness, the dryer had finished its cycle now and there were clean sheets ready to go. He put the still warm sheets up against his face and gave them a smell test. They were technically clean but still had an acrid smell of ammonia.

I need to get more of those little dryer sheets. I fucking love those little dryer sheets.

Chris folded the sheets and stripped himself bare-arse naked in the kitchen. He threw his Cookie Monster pyjama bottoms and faded black t-shirt in the washer too. The stink was as much from him as it was from his clothes. Jim sat on the kitchen counter watching intently and hoping that this would somehow turn into a bonus mealtime.

'Jesus Christ, Jim. I am fucking honking.'

Jim averted his gaze in agreement. Chris then made his way back up the stairs. He was almost halfway to the top when he saw that the bathroom door was closed. A pang of concern rippled down his spine, but he didn't let it get the better of him this time. He marched right up to the door and swung it open. The shower curtain was bunched up at the far end of the bath, and aside from the place being a general shit-tip, nothing was out of pace. Nothing to fear here. Chris turned on the taps with a high-pitched squeal. They probably need some lubricant or a new washer or something. Chris wasn't the kind of man who knew about stuff like that. He wasn't any kind of man. There was just enough bubble bath in one of the many plastic bottles on the floor. He squeezed the lavender scented liquid in the hot water and stepped into the bath.

'Ow, fuck, fuck, fuck!'

The water was too hot, but he didn't want to get back out of the bath with wet feet, so he turned the cold tap on full blast and stood as close to the tiny area of cool water it provided as it filtered through to the rest of the bath. In minutes, there was enough cool water for him to ease beneath its surface without fear of making himself sterile by boiling his sprouts.

The warm water nursed every inch of his aching body, and he finally felt himself unclench for the first time in weeks. He felt like he had been walking around, braced for someone to punch him in the stomach. That slug would come soon enough, but maybe not today. He leaned over the side of the bath and grabbed a bottle from the floor. It was a mostly empty bottle of supermarket brand vodka.

One more drink to take the edge off. He thought.

The room temperature dregs of the bargain bin alcohol burned his throat like acid, but it hit the spot. Jim appeared in the doorway and rubbed his face against the door. He had an odd habit of watching Chris, on the rare occasion that he took baths. Jim would never fully enter the bathroom, though. Just quietly judge Chris from afar.

'Oh god Jim. What am I gonna do with myself?' Chris said. 'I need to call the hospital. See how my dad is doing...'

He doesn't want me there. Not after last time.

The steam from the bath fogged the windows and mirror which hung on the wall opposite. Chris took off his foggy glasses and let them drop to the floor. He closed his eyes and let out a sigh that carried all the weight of the world with it.

Eeeee... Eeeee... Eeeee...

Some strange squeaking sound forced Chris' eyes open with a snap. He looked around frantically for the source of the sound.

Eeeee... Eeeee... Eeeee...

He grabbed his glasses from the floor and rubbed the steam from the lenses. A golf-ball wedged itself in his throat when he glanced in the mirror.

Something was written in the steam, in thin streaks, as if by a bony, gnarled finger.

"Its"

The sound repeated as more letters were etched onto the glass.

"T. I. M. E."

The shower curtain rattled at the far end of the bath. Chris lay motionless, afraid to admit that this was even happening, as the curtain slid itself slowly along the rail, drawing closer and closer. He couldn't make a sound as the curtain surrounded the bath, obscuring everything but the black mould spotted ceiling above him.

The only sound was the gentle sloshing of the surrounding water.

Then the lights went out.

The sound of an icy wind filled his ears. Then, as though someone was turning up the sound on a TV in the next room, a high-pitched beep began. Chris lay in the cold water, blinking and trying to gain some sense of night vision. The curtain came into view as a wavering shadow. He reached up and tugged at it, pulling the thing down in one swift whooshing motion, a magician revealing his greatest trick. The moment the curtain hit the floor, Chris saw it was the divider from a bay on a darkened hospital ward. He clambered out of the bath and stood there, dripping on the slippery floor, shivering from the cold. The ward housed eight bays. One of them held his bath. There were six freshly made beds, and at the far corner of the room was a blue curtain divider suspended by a rail, attached to the ceiling. Beyond the curtain, he heard the beeping of a heart monitor and the mechanical wheezing of a ventilator. Chris approached the curtain, wincing at the sound of the machine, breathing on behalf of what was surely a ravaged slab of meat on the other side. He stood at arm's length from the curtain, and with tears in his eyes, he reached out to grasp it. He pulled back the curtain, and a wave of ice-cold water struck him. Chris awoke, flailing, in the half-empty bathtub. He tumbled out onto the floor, gasping.

🦷🦷🦷🦷🦷🦷

Christopher always loved his grandmother. She was only ever referred to as Nana. She was a wonderfully kind lady. Not only did she bake an exceptional cake, but her birthday cards also contained more money than anyone else's. Secretly, she would give him extra biscuits from a tin she hid from his grandad. A trip to Nana's house was always a good time. Then she got sick, and although Chris was too young to fully understand what was going on, she wasted away right in front of him. It was one particularly hot summer, the kind where no amount of open windows could cool you down. The fan just blew hot air like an oven. He had just turned six years old.

Chris was staying at his Nana's house while the family was there caring for her. He woke in the night to an awful smell. There's nothing worse than being woken up by something that smells so bad that it invades your dreams. He crawled out of bed in just his Incredible Hulk underpants and stepped out into the hallway, squinting in the dark.

'Hello?' He called out, hoping for an adult to come and tell him to go back to bed.

He took one step and felt something wet and sticky underfoot. He jumped back with a fright and glanced down to see a dark trail leading up the hall. On tiptoes, he followed the trail from his bedroom to the bathroom. The door was ajar, but there was no light inside the room, just the sound of rushing water. He pushed the door open slowly. Barely audible over the sound of the water, he could make out a faint sound, like crying. The curtain was drawn, and he could just make out the shape of someone on the other side. *People don't take showers in the dark.* Being too young to have any kind of better judgement, Chris approached the bath and drew back the shower curtain.

'Nana?'

There she was, but not how Christopher had always thought of her. No, his nana crouched, naked in the shower, crying gently to herself, a mixture of blood and faeces running down her legs and swirling the plughole. Her emaciated body, ravaged by time and disease, looked like a reanimated alien autopsy. She recoiled in horror when she saw him.

'Get out! What are you doing here? Get out!' She cried.

He ran back to his room, tears in his eyes, still able to hear her wailing from the bathroom. Things were never the same between them after that. She died two weeks later.

ᗡᗡᗡᗡᗡᗡ

Chris towelled his hair roughly as he thumbed through the contacts on his phone.

He stopped at "James Cook Hospital" before hitting the dial button and putting them on speaker.

'Good morning, you're through to James Cook University Hospital. Please be aware that calls may be recorded for training and monitoring purposes. Please state the name of the person or department you would like to contact.' A tinny recorded voice spoke.

'Ward Twelve.'

He waited with bated breath.

'Connecting to Ward Twelve.'

Halle-fucking-luyah.

'Hello Ward Twelve, how can I help?' A kind voiced lady spoke.

'Hello, yeah, thanks. I er, I just wanted to know if you can... Can I have an update on my dad, please?' He fumbled.

'Sure, what's his name?'

'It's Thomas... Thomas Wilton.'

'Let me just have a word with his nurse. I'll be one moment.'

Silence fell on the line, and Christopher saw the startling sight of his father lying alone and unvisited in a hospital bed.

'Why?' He said without moving his lips.

'Hello?' The lady came back on the line. 'Your dad is stable at the moment. We're trying him on some different antibiotics because he's got a bit of a stubborn infection, but he's comfortable.'

'Great,' he blurted out, not knowing what else to say.

'Is there anything else I can help with?'

'Yeah, when are visiting hours again?'

'You've just missed daytime visiting hours, but you can come over between six and eight tonight.'

'Ok, great. Thank you.'

'No problem, bye.' She hung up the phone first, no doubt having a million other jobs to do.

Chris sat on the bed and tried to gather his thoughts. Even though he felt like a terrible person, he didn't want to go to the hospital. He didn't want to be around it. He was afraid that he would go see his dad and it wouldn't be *him* anymore. It didn't seem fair to Chris that people spent their entire lives loving someone and creating beautiful memories, then the final years and months steamroll those memories, stripping away everything you loved about a person piece by piece. Until finally, you're left embracing a nightmare, hoping for it to die.

It's not important what I need though.

What's important is it's that man's last hours, and if Chris couldn't be there for him now. If he let his dad down; he would never have the chance to make it up to him.

I'm going to do the right thing. I should see him.

Getting dressed was a chore. He hadn't dressed properly in days. Everything was a stinking, crumpled heap on the bedroom floor. It took more effort than he would have liked, but Chris finally found some presentable looking clothes and threw them on. His mattress had even dried out mostly, so he turned on his console and battled zombies to kill the time while he waited for visiting hours to come around.

The alarm on his phone went off, letting him know it was time to get his shoes on and brave the outside world. Chris had never been good at keeping time, so he set alarms on his phone for almost everything. Otherwise, he would get nothing done. Come to think of it, even with the alarms, he couldn't get anything done.

He stepped out of his bedroom and felt a shudder when he saw the bathroom light was on. The darkened hallway suddenly felt cold, and he sensed eyes watching him. Faces leering at him from the yellowing wallpaper. He knew, being an adult, to turn off lights when not needed. Paying bills was already difficult for him. However, going into the bathroom to flip the switch wasn't something he wanted to do.

It's time.

Chris had little time to spare if he wanted to catch the bus and not miss visiting hours. He made a deal with himself that he wouldn't go all the way into the bathroom. He could just reach around the doorframe and hit the light switch. It seemed like the best plan of action was to get it over with quickly, rip off the Band-Aid. He set off towards the stairs and in one fluid motion; he swung his arm into the bathroom without breaking his pace.

A cold, wet hand grabbed his wrist and yanked him backwards into the bathroom. Chris fell into the arms of the rotten corpse of a woman. The vice-like grip of her skeletal fingers burrowed into his flesh.

'It's tiiiime...' she hissed through her grey, remaining teeth.

She was too close for him to fully make her out, but the glimpses he saw as she wrestled him towards the bathtub made his insides clench like a fist. She invoked a kind of fear normally reserved for things like plane crashes or nuclear attacks. Her skin resembled rotten brown paper bags, and her dehydrated, bruised lips looked like dead slugs resting on her face. The only sounds Christopher could make were pathetic moans of terror as they both plunged sideways into the bath. Their bodies entwined in the fall, causing Chris to smash his face into the taps. The pain was both a blunt trauma and a searing, sharp agony at once. Broken, rattled teeth hung from his gums, and blood poured from his nose and mouth. With a strength that far exceeded her appearance, the woman grabbed Chris by the face and pulled him to his feet, her fingers of jagged bone digging into his cheeks. They locked eyes, his wide and full of fear, hers black and full of swirling muddy water. Scalding water lashed down on them both as she pulled him in closer and licked at his cheek with her rotten tongue, as rough as sandpaper.

'It's time,' she hissed into his mouth, forcing the stench of thirty years of decomposition into his lungs.

'Please...' he wept.

'It's tiiiime...'

Chris felt his life fading, his heart fluttering like a tiny bird trapped in a snare. The creature's foul, fishy breath, like an ocean full of discarded corpses. He breathed in the stench of a beach full of dead bodies, washed up after a cruise ship had gone down. Her rough tongue, like tree bark, scraped at his face, drinking his blood like a... like a cat...

Christopher's eyes opened. He found Jim standing on his chest, breathing right up his nose. It was past midnight. Chris had pissed the bed again.

'Reeeowww.' Jim said. It's time to wake up.

13

ONUXOPHOBIA

BY STEPHANIE HUDDLE

*J*ane sat on the edge of the bed and sighed in the early morning light creeping through the curtains. Her husband, Jake, rolled toward her and pulled her close, sensing her anxiety.

"It's going to be okay. Everything will go off without a hitch, I'm sure," he murmured, moving his hand in calming circles across her inked skin.

Jane laughed. "Um, do you know Vivienne? I love her, she's my best friend, you love her, but you know she can get a bit...high strung. I just want today to be perfect for her. She deserves it after everything she's been through." She gazed down at her spouse.

He nodded his head, agreeing with her. "In that case, you'd better get your ass in the shower, so you aren't late for your 'girls-only' breakfast and spa day. You're all sweaty from your run." Jake leaned up and kissed her cheek before Jane slid off the bed.

"You're right. She has soooo much planned for us today. I don't know how she thinks we'll get it all done before the ceremony this afternoon. But I guess that's part of my job as matron of honor. What are you going to do all morning in this beachy paradise without me?" Jane flashed him a grin.

"I, my dear, will be lazing around on the beach and possibly day-drinking. Have you decided what you're going to do about the mani/pedi business?"

Jane narrowed her hazel eyes, her already-light skin paling even more. "You know how I feel about that. I love her, but she needs to understand that's something I can't do. Not even for her. She knows my history." She spun and walked into the bathroom, turning on the water in the shower as hot as she could stand it. Jake watched the doorway for a moment, then followed her in so he could brush his teeth.

ᗄᗄᗄᗄᗄᗄᗄ

Jane made her way toward the large primary suite of the massive, rented beach house, admiring the view of the white sand and sparkling ocean through the multiple windows. Vivienne and her fiancé, Sam, had saved for the last three years to afford a place like this for their wedding, foregoing any fun extras and getting jobs during their summer breaks when they weren't teaching. Jane could hear the 90s pop music as she approached the bedroom. She knocked on the door, letting herself in. Vivienne gave a shriek of happiness when she saw her best friend and dashed toward her.

"I'm getting married today! Can you believe it??" Vivienne was already beaming as she grabbed Jane in a fierce embrace. "I never would have had this day if it weren't for you." She sniffled.

"You can't get all sappy this early in the day! You know your eyes will get all puffy and fuck with your makeup application," Jane snickered.

Vivienne let her go and gave her a playful swat. "Shut it, beyotch! Let me have my moment. Actually, let me have all of them. This is my day! Well, my and Sam's day, of course. But I mean it. I wouldn't be anywhere without you, Janey."

As Vivienne hugged her again, Jane thought about their friendship. They had met the first day of kindergarten, and matching purple unicorn lunch boxes had made them instant best friends. Their bond only grew throughout the years. Viv supported her through her parents' contentious divorce, Jane kept her from flunking every math class she ever had to take, teenage angst, acne, the SATs. The little moments added up, but two defining events cemented it for life.

When her parents separated when she was twelve, Jane developed an aversion to nail polish—she never figured out why. It started out fairly mundane. She would see girls with painted nails, and it would freak her out a bit. She couldn't walk through the nail polish aisles at Wal-Mart, and she couldn't stand the thought of wearing polish, so she never did, even though Vivienne often wanted to have them paint each other's nails during sleepovers. After the divorce was finalized, Jane's disgust turned into a full-blown phobia. Anytime she saw nail polish, whether it was a commercial, in a bottle, or on someone's finger or toenails, her heartbeat would skyrocket, pour buckets of sweat, and have a full-blown panic attack if she couldn't get away from it. It got to the point that she could barely function outside her own home, and after she was sent to family court for physically attacking another girl in her class who swiped nail polish on her arm as a cruel prank, a sympathetic judge gave her diversion and ordered her to see a psychologist when she was fifteen. While Dr. Gardner didn't give her an exact diagnosis, as the closest approximation was Onuxophobia, the fear of fingernails, she completely validated Jane's terror and

worked on a comprehensive treatment plan. Jane under-
went cognitive behavioral and exposure therapies. After
close to two years, she got to the point where she could at
least be around or see nail polish without having a melt-
down, much to her best friend's delight, as she no longer
had to abstain from painting her nails. Jane still felt some
disgust, but it was nothing compared to the absolute freak-
outs and violent urges she used to have.

Vivienne, her biggest supporter and defender, was there
through it all. Because high school girls are a special brand
of cuntiness, once they realized Jane's fear, they were relent-
less. But Vivienne was always there, all 5'2"of her, threatening to beat their asses every day alongside Jane and
standing by her during her hearing and treatment. After the
assault, the bullies realized they were better off moving on
to their next poor target.

Once they were in college, Jane was able to repay Vivienne for being her rock. During their sophomore year, Viv
met Douglas, a beautiful boy with dimples and a wicked
smile. She was immediately smitten, and the two rushed
into a whirlwind relationship, moving in together after only
three weeks and discussing marriage after two months. Jane
was already living with Jake, whom she met while getting a
tattoo at the shop where he worked, and was excited her
friend found love, too, although she worried about it
moving so fast. More than that, she noticed something
seemed...off about Douglas. She began to see her friend less
and less. Eventually, after confronting Vivienne about the
bruises on her arms over dinner at Jane's, a rare treat in
seeing her bestie anymore, Viv confessed Douglas was
hitting her and controlled her every move. The two young
women wept, and Jane swore she would help get her out of
this. Jane did extensive research on safety planning, talked
to the local domestic and sexual violence program for

assistance, and started helping Viv stash money away so she would have something of her own to fall back on. When Vivienne managed to call her late one night, terrified that Douglas was finally going to kill her, Jane didn't think twice. She grabbed the Glock she had purchased since Jake worked nights so often and hauled ass across town to the small house Douglas owned. She used the key the women had copied in secret and stormed into the house, weapon drawn and ready to mow him down in a barrage of bullets if she had to.

What she saw made her trigger finger twitch. Vivienne was in a ball on the floor, her right eye swelled shut, her nose broken and bloody, with red marks around her neck. Seeing the terrified look in her friend's one working eye brought back all the rage Jane thought she had permanently suppressed.

"What do you think you're doing here, cunt?" Douglas sneered at her. "Get the fuck out of my house right now, unless you want to end up like that worthless bitch on the floor."

Jane looked at the pathetic excuse for a man and did something that surprised them all. She laughed.

Taking a step toward him, she brought the gun up and aimed it straight at Douglas's head, her finger on the trigger. "If you ever lay a hand on her again, I'll kill you. If you ever threaten her again, I'll kill you. If you ever come near her again, I'll kill you. If I ever see you again, I'll put a bullet in each of your knees, and then you know what will happen? That's right, say it with me. I'll kill you." Jane's smile was both sincere and crazed. Whatever Douglas saw in her eyes, he didn't challenge her. A predator knows when to back down and live to fight another day. That was the last time either woman saw Douglas Evans.

Fast forward through college graduation, Jane and

Jake's wedding, and Vivienne meeting Sam in grad school. Sam was amazing, the anti-Douglas in every way, and Jane adored him. It hit both women hard when Sam and Vivienne found teaching jobs in another state. After being together their whole lives, they had to somehow figure out how to navigate their friendship through adulthood. Lots of FaceTime calls and a mandatory girls' trip every year helped them stay solid. And now, here they finally were for Viv's dream beach wedding to a man who loved and respected her.

All of these thoughts flashed through Jane's mind in an instant. Letting go of her friend, she heard voices approaching down the hall and groaned inwardly to herself. As much as she loved Viv, she couldn't say the same about her two bridesmaids, Mary Beth ("Not Mary, Mary *Beth*") and Sarah ("I'm Sarah with an H!"), whom she had met for the first time last night. She didn't know what Vivienne saw in them, as they seemed uptight and came across as condescending and a bit rude. She could practically hear their judgmental thoughts as their eyes roamed over the numerous tattoos she and Jake had. Their smiles were stiff and never reached their eyes, at least not with her and her husband.

"VIVIENNE!" Mary Beth's squeal was shrill and instantly annoyed Jane.

"It's your wedding day, omigod!" shrieked Sarah. She flashed Jane a look. "Oh, you're already here. Morning."

"Good morning to you." *Bitch.*

"I'm so happy you're all here with me." Viv was looking glassy eyed again. Jane knew she needed to step up and be an adult for her best friend. She would do everything she could to make sure her day was perfect, even if that meant chumming it up with Tweedle Dum and Tweedle Dee.

Vivienne took a deep, calming breath and turned the

music off, wanting to be free from distractions. "Okay, ladies. Here's the plan for the day. Now that we're all here, we can start with breakfast." She gestured toward one wall of the room, where a table had been set up, laden with fruit, pastry, and a warming dish full of fluffy scrambled eggs. "After we eat, oh, and have mimosas, of course, we'll get all set up at the prep stations. We will each be getting our hair done, makeup applied, and my favorite—coordinating mani/pedis!"

Sarah and Mary Beth clapped their hands and jumped up and down. Jane gave her friend a sharp look. Vivienne glanced at her, a worried look in her eyes, and offered a small smile. "C'mon, Janey. It's my wedding day. We talked about this. Please, please do this for me."

"You know how I feel, Viv. I told you I didn't have a problem with you or the others getting their nails and toes done. I've been able to cope with that for years. You know that. But I can't have that stuff on me. No. My skin is crawling just thinking about it."

Mary Beth and Sarah peered at her. "What's going on?" Mary Beth asked. "What is it that you aren't willing to do for Vivienne? You're the matron of honor; it's your job to make sure she gets everything she wants. Unless you can't handle that?" Her tone was snide, and Jane could practically see her salivating at the chance to usurp her and be the maid of honor. Sarah glared at her.

"Look, Vivienne and I have already discussed this. I don't see the need to rehash it. I'm going to eat." Jane stalked across the room, piling a plate with strawberries, pineapple, a small cinnamon roll, a cream cheese Danish, and a generous mound of eggs, which she sprinkled with the tabasco sauce Vivienne had remembered to get for her. Pouring herself a mimosa that was heavy on the prosecco and light on the orange juice, she made her way out to the attached patio, where they would be enjoying their break-fast listening to the sound of the waves and smelling the salty air.

The other women joined her. Jane noticed the brides-maids had the tiniest servings of eggs and just a few pieces of fruit on their plates, with drinks that were far more orange than hers. Sarah looked at Jane's plate. "You want to be careful eating all that. You need to look good in your dress later."

Jane gave her a syrupy smile. "I have a good metabolism. And since I already ran ten miles this morning on the beach while you were still sleeping, I need the fuel." Sarah huffed and sat down, stabbing her eggs petulantly.

It didn't take a rocket scientist to feel the tension between the bridal party members, so Vivienne tried to distract them with wedding day talk. "For your hair, I'd like it if you would all do some type of updo. Elegant and simple, nothing too crazy. The same with the makeup. No bright colors; you're bridesmaids, not clowns!" The others all nodded in agreement, fine with whatever Vivienne wanted. She could have told them to style their hair in an 80s bouffant and wear blue eye shadow for all they cared. That was definitely the one thing they all agreed on.

Vivienne took a deep breath, side-eyeing Jane. "Now, for the mani/pedis. I was hoping to do coordinating colors in an ombré, so you'll all have lighter shades, and mine will be the darkest. They'll all be shades of purple, of course. Sarah, since you will be walking down the aisle first, yours will be a pale lilac; Mary Beth, yours will be a bit darker, like a regular lilac." The two women beamed, flicking their long nails as they imagined their manicures. "Janey...I know how much you love sparkles, so I thought you could go a shade darker than Mary Beth, a violet with a shimmer to it. Since you're the matron of honor, yours should be extra special!"

She tried to say all of this like it was a good thing. Like the idea of polish on her toenails and fingernails didn't make Jane want to puke up the danish she had just crammed into her mouth in order to stay silent.

Jane chewed slowly, swallowed, and took a huge gulp of her mimosa, disappointed to find she had already emptied the dainty flute. "Vivienne, you know I can't do that."

"Janey, please! I know you can handle this. It's just for a few hours! You can take it all off right after the pictures are taken!"

Jane slammed her fork down on the table, eliciting shocked gasps from Mary Beth and Sarah. "Damnit, Viv! How can you, you of all people, ask me to do this?! You know what I went through all those years ago! How hard it was and how much I struggled!"

"I know! I was there through it all. Who held your hands while you cried in the bathroom at school? Who stood by your side when you were being bullied by those hags every day? Your hearing? ME! I did that. I stopped wearing nail polish because you were so freaked out by it. I got rid of every bottle I had, and some of it was expensive brands. I was there when you finished therapy for fuck's sake." Vivienne's cheeks were flushed, and her chest was splotched an angry red.

"Wait, you're scared of...nail polish?" Sarah asked. "You had to go to therapy because of nail polish?!" Her mouth twitched, and Jane could see the beginning of a smirk on her lips. "Is that even a real thing? How can you be scared of something so ridiculous?" She started to laugh, Mary Beth joining in with her horse-like brays.

Jane's hands curled into fists, the women's guffaws taking her back to high school when she beat the girl who had smeared the nail polish on her. Before she could snap at these two bleached blonde pieces of shit, Vivienne's voice rang out sharply. "HEY! Stop that right now. First of all, it's a real thing. People have all kinds of phobias over stuff you wouldn't imagine. Some people are afraid of cheese, for Christ's sake. Seriously, I watched a documentary about it. This poor guy couldn't even be around pizza. Can you imagine? I would die! Second, don't make fun of Jane. That's beyond rude and hurtful. Third, you're all my friends. I wanted all of you here for Sam and I's special day. I don't give a fuck if you get along. Get over yourselves. If you care about me at all, you'll get your shit together."

All three women had the decency to look chagrined. Sarah even uttered a stiff "Sorry" in Jane's direction. Jane acknowledged her with a nod.

"I'm sorry, Viv. You're right, we need to focus on your day. You know I'll do anything for you."

"Even paint your nails and get a pedi?" Vivienne asked hopefully.

Jane signed. "No."

"But, Jane, just listen for a sec. Please?" Vivienne pleaded. Jane nodded her head, resigned to the fact her friend probably wasn't going to let this go. "You did so great in therapy all those years ago. Remember the first time we walked down the nail polish aisle after you started exposure therapy?" Jane reddened; the memory wasn't pleasant for her. "It was hard! Sure, you cried and had a bit of a panic attack. But you made it through. And the next time it was better. And it kept getting easier. You even got so much better that you could be around people wearing nail polish again. You never had a problem with *me* wearing it again! You faced down a monster and didn't even flinch. You saved my life. This is nothing compared to that."

"That's not the same thing as having it on me, though. You know that, Vivienne. You know what happened when I tried to wear it," Jane murmured softly, her resolve starting to weaken. "And I wouldn't have hesitated to pull that trigger." Sarah and Mary Beth gawked at her, clearly unaware of what the lifelong friends were talking about.

"You have all those tools at your disposal," Vivienne insisted. "Deep breathing, you can meditate while you get it done. Remember the song you used to sing to calm yourself down?" She began humming a few off-key bars of "Tuesday's Gone." She looked beseechingly at Jane. "And most important, you'll have me here to help you through all of it. Just like I always did."

Jane closed her eyes, gritting her teeth. Just the thought of polish touching her was enough to kick her heart rate up a notch. She inhaled slowly, counting to seven in her head, held her breath for five counts, and blew out through pursed lips. Once, twice, three times. She slowly opened her eyes to find herself being stared at by everyone at the table. "Okay," she muttered.

"Okay, you'll do it??" Vivienne asked. When Jane nodded, Viv leaped out of her seat and smothered her in a huge hug. "Thank you, thank you, thank you! Now everything really is perfect!" Sarah and Mary Beth applauded, causing Jane to roll her eyes, although she was still buried in her friend's embrace, so they were none the wiser.

🦷🦷🦷🦷🦷🦷

Jane sent Jake a quick text. *She talked me into it. Fuck.*

His reply was almost instantaneous. *Are you sure this is a good idea? Will you be okay?*

I'm going to have to be. I can make it. It's only a few hours. Luv u.

Luv u. I'm here if you need anything.

Wandering back toward the mini buffet table, Jane

made herself another mimosa. She poured strong again. She was going to need it to make it through this nightmare.

ᗺᗺᗺᗺᗺᗺ

"Okay, Jane, are you ready to try this?" Dr. Gardner looked at her with kind eyes, tucking her short blonde bob behind her ears.

Jane stared at the bottle of nail polish on the table. She glanced nervously at her psychologist, who gave her an encouraging nod.

"Remember everything we've talked about and all the hard work you've done. Deep breaths. Calm your mind. It can't hurt you. You have successfully managed to see it, be around it. You purchased this bottle." The chords of "Tuesday's Gone" were playing softly in the background.

Jane steeled herself. "I'm ready."

Grabbing the bottle from the table, she unscrewed the lid of the bright, glittery purple nail polish. Dr. Gardner had suggested she try it with her favorite color to make it a bit easier. Maybe something to look forward to, having it on her nails. She slowly brought the brush out, wiping the excess polish on the edge of the inner rim. Bringing it closer, she could smell the strong scent. Her breath hitched. Her palms began to sweat.

"Easy, Jane. You can do this. Just like you practiced with an imaginary brush. Then you tried a brush dipped in water and did great. This is simply the next step. Big, deep breaths, just like I taught you," Dr. Gardner encouraged.

Slowing her breathing, Jane carefully stroked the brush over the pinkie nail of her left hand. Staring at her finger, she suddenly felt nauseous. Acid bubbled in her gut, and her vision started to turn red. She could feel the liquid on her nail, suffocating it, causing it to itch like mad. Can a nail even be itchy? she wondered.

Suddenly, Jane shrieked like a banshee. "GET IT OFF!" She began crying hysterically, tears pouring from her eyes and snot dripping from her nose like a leaky faucet. She desperately began tugging on the nail, trying in vain to rip the whole thing off.

Startled, Dr. Gardner quickly grabbed the nail polish remover she had brought, just in case, soaking a cotton ball. "Jane!" she shouted, trying to get the sobbing girl's attention. As she reached toward her client, the girl hissed and took a wild swing at her arm. Her voice became firmer. "Jane, it's okay; we can take it off. See? I have the remover."

Jane looked at her and nodded. Dr. Gardner gently took her hand and wiped the polish off. She'd torn off a good chunk of the nail, and her finger was bleeding. But the second the color was completely off, Jane no longer felt the itching sensation. She could breathe again, her vision clearing.

It took Jane several weeks to bounce back from this episode. She never wore nail polish again.

♔♔♔♔♔♔

Jane meandered toward the bathroom, needing to pee after her third mimosa, sipped on while she got her hair done. Dee and Dum got their makeup done while Viv had her mani/pedi time. She had shown Jane when it was done, and she had done her matronly duty and told the bride how beautiful it looked. And she wasn't lying. The shade of purple Vivienne had chosen was perfect. Jane didn't have an issue with the polish on the others. But it would be her turn soon, and she was still trying to figure out how she'd let that happen.

As she approached the bathroom, she heard Mary Beth and Sarah around the corner, speaking in hushed tones.

"Afraid of nail polish? Whoever heard of such a thing?" Sarah sneered.

"I *know*. I Googled it, and it's not even a real thing. I could only find fear of fingernails, which is also totally messed up, but at least it's not a fake disorder. She's probably just making it all up for attention. I mean, look at her. With all those tattoos, you can tell she just wants people to look at her. What an attention whore."

Jane seethed. *Jesus Christ, it's high school all over again.* Attention whore? Fake disorders? Who did these axe wounds think they were?

Sarah chimed in. "Of course, she's also probably jealous of Vivi."

Vivi? Fucking vomit, Jane thought.

"I mean, look at her trashy husband. He doesn't even have a real job," Sarah sniffed. "What kind of person tattoos for a living? He probably learned how to do it in prison. You know Jane is jealous because Vivi's marrying a successful man with a real job and an actual education."

Jane almost came unglued. How dare they talk about her husband that way! Jake owned and operated the most successful tattoo shop in the city. He'd never been arrested, let alone incarcerated. Clients drove from hundreds of miles to be inked by him, and his books were packed solid with appointments for months out. Jane's beautiful tattoos were proof of her husband's talent. Sam was a teacher for fuck's sake, not the King of England. And Jane guaranteed Jake made more in a week than Sam did in a month. *Those ugly bitches! I'll fucking kill them!*

Strolling around the corner, Jane came face to face with the bridesmaids. "Oh, hello. Imagine seeing you both here. Interesting conversation?" Her tone was laced with sarcasm.

Their eyes widened. "Oh, Jane! You startled us. And doesn't your hair look so pretty?" Sarah gushed, clearly trying to cover up the fact they had been badmouthing her.

Jane glowered at them until they edged around her and fled back toward the bedroom. "Stupid cunts," she muttered, finally making it into the bathroom.

🦷🦷🦷🦷🦷🦷

Vivienne grinned at Jane. Her hair and makeup looked flawless; she barely even needed the blush she wore since she was already flushed with happiness. "Are you ready for your mani/pedi? I can't tell you how much this means to me."

Before her best friend could tear up and ruin her makeup, Jane gave her a fleeting smile. "As ready as I'll ever be." She looked at the technician, the nail trolley holding dozens of implements, and the bottle of shimmery, violet polish. "Okay, here we go," she muttered under her breath, taking a seat for her torture session. *Thinking about it like that definitely isn't helping.*

As the woman began to massage her feet, Jane had to admit it felt good. *Why haven't I done this before? This would be a godsend after a marathon.* She relaxed a bit in her chair, everything going much better than she had anticipated. Vivienne hovered around with a worried look, but when she saw her friend was doing so well, she left to get dressed. Jane basked in the hot towels around her calves and didn't even mind her feet being scrubbed with the pumice stone or foot file. *I can do this!*

When the nail tech grabbed the nail polish bottle, Jane felt her heart skip a beat. She immediately began her breathing, closing her eyes and trying to clear her mind. The woman gently touched her foot. Jane swore she felt the moment of impact between the purple liquid and her toenail. Her breath came faster, and she started to sweat. *I can't ruin my makeup! Get it together. I faced down an abusive asshole and threatened to kill him without batting an eye. For Viv, for Viv,* she repeated to herself. She fumbled for her phone and opened her playlist. The gentle rhythm and soothing lyrics of "Tuesday's Gone" began to play softly as she held the phone up to her ear.

Jane made it through the pedi. Her toenails felt itchy, but she was surviving so far. She pushed the memories of taunting laughter away. She kept reminding herself she could take it off in a few short hours. The manicure was similar to the pedi process. She liked the hand massage and other treatments, but the second the polish came out and onto her nails, she wanted to jerk her hand away and punch the smiling little woman in her stupid face. The music wasn't helping, she couldn't control her breathing. Jane closed her eyes, forcing her mind to go somewhere else.

"All done!" the tech said brightly. She placed everything back on the trolley, leaving bottles of nail polish and the tricks of her trade behind, in case any of the women needed a last-minute touch-up. Mary Beth, Sarah, and Vivienne were dressed and putting on their jewelry. Viv looked delighted with Jane's purple tips and toes.

"I knew you could do it!" she exclaimed. I'm so proud of you, Janey!" She went into the massive walk-in closet in search of her shoes.

Jane sat motionless in the chair. Her heart was beating so rapidly she thought she might pass out. She could feel the makeup begin to slide off her face, a casualty of her nervous sweating. Her breaths came in shallow pants. Lifting her shaking hands toward her face, Jane stared at the purple at the ends of her fingers. She felt hot all over. Her toenails were on fire. Her fingernails were burning, a raging inferno that she had to get off. Right now! She looked desperately around for a bottle of nail polish remover, but that seemed to be the one thing that didn't get left behind.

Sarah glared at Jane. "I knew you were faking it," she hissed. "Stop trying to steal Vivi's thunder. I can't believe she isn't making you cover your skanky tattoos."

Trying to pick off the fast-drying, chip-resistant polish, Jane froze. She slowly raised her head and stared at Sarah. The snarky woman looked into Jane's glassy, crazed eyes and slowly began backing away.

All Jane could see were her cruel classmates, taunting her and darting at her with bottles of polish. She screamed, a long, primal wail. "GET IT THE FUCK OFF ME!!!" Snatching a glass fingernail file from the table, she lunged at Sarah, grabbing her by her bottle blonde updo. Sarah shrieked as her head was wrenched back. "You think I'm faking, you bitch? I'll show you faking!" Jane stabbed the file into one of Sarah's flinty blue eyes, feeling it pop as she pushed it deeper into the orb. Sarah's shrieks turned into screams of anguish, blood and vitreous oozing from the wrecked eyeball. Jane laughed hysterically and yanked the file out, quickly stabbing it into her other eye. Sarah's cries reached an ear-splitting pitch but were silenced as Jane shoved the glass file into her brain.

"What the fuck are you doing??" Mary Beth shouted as Vivienne dashed out of the closet. Jane turned toward the bridesmaid with a snarl, her hands coated in fluids. She seized the woman and began punching her in the face, smashing her nose and nearly fracturing her orbital bones with the strength of her blows. Mary Beth gurgled on her own blood as it poured down her throat, crying and begging Jane to stop. Jane turned and grabbed the damned bottle of violet polish, twisting the lid violently off and pouring the liquid into Mary Beth's eyes, rubbing it in with her hands. Snatching the quick-drying spray, she shot the aerosol down her victim's throat, hoping it would kill her.

"Jane, stop! Oh, my god! What have you done??" Vivienne had tears streaming down her face. She was standing in the corner of the room by the king-sized bed, staring at her friend in horror.

"You!" Jane snarled, no longer in her right mind, the burning of her fingers and toes the only thing she could comprehend. "You did this to me! This is your fault!" Dashing across the room, she jerked one of the metal trays off the trolley and charged at her best friend.

"Janey, stop! Please!" Vivienne begged. "Why are you doing this? I'm sorry, I thought you'd be okay, I swear!" She screamed as the heavy tray swung down, connecting with her skull in a resounding crack. "Janey, please," she mumbled. "You saved my life once. You're my best friend...I love you..."

Jane brought the tray down again and again. Blood spattered the walls and ceilings, coated her face, and made it hard to hold on to the slippery metal. For a moment, recognition flashed in her eyes. But then the burning sensation quickly engulfed all reason.

Desperate for relief, Jane's eyes fell on the cuticle nippers and small scissors that lay scattered on the floor.

ᗯᗯᗯᗯᗯᗯ

Jake meandered down the hall toward the bedroom. It was his job to get the girls when it was time. He was feeling a bit tipsy from the sun and the booze. The groom, groomsmen, and several wedding guests had spent most of the day on the beach, far enough away that they couldn't easily see into the house with its many windows. Vivienne was adamant that Sam not see her until she walked down the sandy aisle.

With plenty of sun, drinks, and the music cranked, the pre-wedding festivities were in full swing most of the day.

The door to the bedroom was shut, and it was eerily quiet. The hair on the back of Jake's neck stood up, and he instantly felt more sober. *Shouldn't I be hearing laughter and shenanigans? I know Jane doesn't like the other two, but surely, she kept her cool and didn't tell them off. She knows how much today means to Viv.*

He knocked on the door and waited a few beats. Hearing nothing, he announced, "Jane? Vivienne? It's Jake. It's almost time for the ceremony to start. Jane? I'm coming in."

Turning the handle slowly, Jake eased the door open. He couldn't comprehend what he saw. The room looked like a scene from a slasher flick. Blood sprayed the walls, ceiling, curtains, the furniture.

Choking back the urge to throw up, he opened the door further, his eyes landing on the body of Sarah. Something was sticking out of her eye. Mary Beth lay not far away, her face a bloody mess splotched with purple. It didn't look like she was breathing.

In the corner, a body was propped near the curtains. The head was a pulpy mess (*oh God, is that brain on the wall?*), and she was unrecognizable. But Jake knew it had to be Vivienne. The gore-soaked wedding gown could only be hers.

"Oh, God. Oh my God! Jane? Honey? Please be okay!" Jake called into the room. He stilled when he heard something. What was that? Was that singing?

Walking around the bed, Jake found his wife.

She sat on the floor, spattered in crimson, a bloody pile of sparkly violet toenails lying at her side from where she ripped them off with the nippers. He stared in horror, watching as she tried to snip her fingertip off with a pair of small scissors. When he saw that most of her fingertips were bloody, with the nails only partially remaining, he couldn't hold it in any longer. He turned and threw up, hot bile sizzling his throat.

"Jane?" he whispered.

She didn't look up. Jake didn't even know if she knew he was there. He stared at her as she lined up the scissors with her thumb. He tentatively reached out a hand. She was smiling, rocking back and forth while she sang a soft tune, something about Tuesday and being gone with the wind.

14

ATHAZAGORAPHOBIA

BY SAVANNAH R. FISCHER

he door slams into the wall as my husband storms into the bedroom. *Ugh, what now?* I groan to myself. The interruption forces me to put down my tablet, closing the door on a spicy scene in the latest hockey romance.

"What do you want, Ty? Can't you tell I'm busy?"

"Busy?" He blusters, working himself up now.

"Yes, busy. It's been a hard day of momming, and now I just want to be here, in my safe place. Alone."

The last word hangs between us, shuddering on the precipice of a world-ending argument. But I can't take it back—I won't. After all, I've done nothing to deserve my husband's attitude. Nestled safely in my nest of blankets and pillows, surrounded by my books, I haven't even ventured out of the room today. So how is he *possibly* upset?

"A hard day," he scoffs, "You don't deserve to be called a mother, Lou! You just sit in bed all day, tapping away on your screens. When is the last time you cooked? Woke up before noon?"

"Come on, Ty. That's not fair! You know I'm depressed"

"Not fair?" The vein in his forehead bulges now, his eyes feral as he lashes me with more vile slander. "I'll tell you what's nor fair. You roll over in the morning, and the first thing you do is text *HIM*."

The accusation hits me square in the chest. *How does Ty know about Chad? I've been so careful.*

"You're so wrapped up in your own bubble, you don't even know if the kids make it to school. What was it you said—you *guess* they made it?"

"They're old enough to fend for themselves," I snap back, bristling under his verbal assault.

"They're seven and ten for Christ's sake! They shouldn't have to 'fend for themselves' when their mom stays at home!"

"I do a lot around here!" I shriek.

"If by a lot you mean lay in bed, spend money, and cheat—yeah, sure. You do *a lot.*"

"How dare you? All you do is work and play video games!"

"Are you serious right now, Lou? Like, do you hear yourself?"

"What do you want from me, Ty?" I can't keep the exasperation out of my voice. It's always *something*. Nothing I do is good enough. He knows I don't like to cook. He makes enough money; I don't have to work. And seriously, those kids *can* fend for themselves. They don't need me to cater to their every whim.

"I want a divorce, Lou. The kids and I deserve better."

He rambles on and on, but I tune the rest out. *A divorce???* But who will take care of me? My mind swirls around me. Maybe Chad?

"We're leaving, Lou."

I don't know how long I've been staring off into space, or even when I left the bedroom, but Ty has the girls and their bags by the front door.

"I want you out in two days. That's plenty of time to get your shit and get out. You'll be hearing from my lawyer."

The kids don't even look back as they follow Ty to the car. *Ungrateful brats!* The door slams behind them, leaving behind a blessed silence. Still, my blood boils. How dare he? After everything I've done for this family! I fetch my vibrator out from under the blankets and return to my hockey romance. Once I've orgasmed, *something Ty never did for me*, I check my phone. It's finally late enough for Chad to be off work. I fire off a demand for him to call me ASAP. It's a matter of seconds before my phone rings.

"Hey, baby girl," his deep voice rumbles in my ear.

"Omg, Chad. You're *NOT* going to believe what Ty did to me!"

Before he can respond, I'm unrolling my scroll of grievances, from his stupid late night video game raids to his demand that I leave *MY* house. I barely take a breath, but Chad just *gets* me. He's sympathetic and outraged.

"Ty is an idiot. How could anyone treat you that way?"

"I don't know. But it gets worse."

"Worse? Did he hit you?"

"No, but I was scared he would. He was feral." Tears fall so fast, I choke on their salt, "He knows about us."

"Oh shit—"

The line goes dead.

"Chad? Chad?"

I call back, but he doesn't answer. My barrage of texts remain unanswered. *What is going on?* Irritated, I throw my phone across the room, relishing the cracking of the glass.

Ty will have to buy me a new one. With nothing better to do, I grab my laptop and take to my online chat rooms.

"Ty just abducted the kids..." I type to my friends.

There's nothing like sympathy from the internet to soothe the soul.

♌♌♌♌♌♌

Alone, I'm all alone. The hallway is dark, with a glowing door illuminated at the end. I make a run for it, but invisible hands grasp at me. When their fingers fail to touch me, my assailants raise their spectral voices instead, lobbing lie after vile lie my way.

"Lazy! Unfit mother!"

"It's not my fault!" I scream back in defense, "I'm just so depressed."

"That doesn't give you the right to sleep with my husband!" My ex-best friend Josie screams.

"You're a whore. A cheat! And a god-awful mother," Ty shouts.

"I told you to straighten your hair or you'd look like a pube-head," chastises my mother.

"You're a narcissist," my ten-year-old accuses.

"You bunch of spoiled, ungrateful assholes!" I cry back at the voices, "I've given so much to all of you, and this is how you repay me?"

Somehow, I made it to the end of the hallway. I open the door, ready for escape—but instead, find myself on the edge of a cliff.

"Bye, bitch," Chad sneers before invisible hands push me down into the fiery depths of hell.

♌♌♌♌♌♌

I wake up drenched in sweat, but safe in my own bed. My fingers grasp around for my phone, but come up empty—that's right, I threw it. Terror stabs my heart like a knife. The edges of my vision darken as the walls close in, threatening to crush me. I'm alone and forgotten, just like in my dream. This can't be happening. I—

A notification dings on my tablet, cutting through my fear. A few taps bring my home screen to life. No missed messages—I'm hurt. It's like no one cares about my suffering. Hot tears stream down my face as my deepest fear threatens to bubble to the surface. Alone. Forgotten. Unimportant. Nothing. No, that can't happen. I won't let it!

I fire off a couple messages to Chad, then a Facebook post about emotionally unavailable husbands and ungrateful children that's sure to elicit sympathy from my followers.

ꢺꢺꢺꢺꢺꢺ

The next morning comes with a rush of serotonin. My post is filled with women lamenting their useless spouses and lazy brats. Comment after comment validates me. *See, the universe agrees—you're an asshole, Ty.* As if on cue, a fresh message dings on my tablet.

"I see you're not answering the phone. This is my final message to you, Lou. I will be at the house tomorrow with a sheriff if needed. The kids deserve to be in their home. All further communication will be through my lawyer."

He can't fucking be serious! This is *MY* home. Rage flares as I check the clock. It's already 2pm—at least I don't have to worry about the spawn crashing in through the front door and setting off another migraine. Yes, I could get used to this.

Another notification pops on my screen, freezing me in

my tracks. No—it can't be. Someone is disagreeing with me on my post!

"Maybe your husband would be more helpful if you stopped screwing other guys. XOXO- Lexie"

Who the fuck is Lexie?

Before I can reply to her blasphemy, another notification dings.

"Yeah, I heard she slept with her best friend's husband!"

"Yes, she caused Josie and Kevin's divorce!"

Before I can stop it, there's a flurry of activity on my post. As much as I hate what they're saying, at least they're noticing me.

I never slept with anyone who didn't want it, I sneer as I reply to the vicious attacks on my character. These nobodies just don't understand me. It's not *my* fault their husbands and boyfriends have wandering eyes. If they just kept him happy, he wouldn't have to look elsewhere. Ah, these internet arguments give me life. I just wish people would take some fucking accountability for their actions.

Around eight, I realize I haven't eaten anything. Dammit, Ty's not here to make me a sandwich. I roll out of bed begrudgingly, lamenting my ill fortune the whole time. My slippered feet slap the ground, letting my rage echo through the empty house. I hate being alone this long. How could Ty do this to me? He knows my secret, my deepest darkest fear— athazagoraphobia—an intense fear of being forgotten.

A peanut butter and jelly in one hand and an energy drink in the other, I shuffle back to my room. My chats are oddly quiet, and my post notifications have descended into a dogpile of verbal assaults. So-called keyboard warriors looking to take me down when I'm at my most vulnerable. I hate them all.

My focus slips, this book just isn't holding my interest

anymore. I mark it as read and move onto the next one. As the clock clicks closer to midnight, I realize I still haven't heard from Chad. Furious, I open my messages, only for my heart to drop. There's only one new message.

"Your asshole husband told MY wife. Thanks for ruining my life bitch," followed by the generic "you can no longer contact this user."

No, no, no, no, no. This can't be happening. This has to be a sick joke! Chad isn't married, he's a single dad, but he left his wife during COVID. We had so many conversations about their brutal divorce. *Was it all a lie?* Incensed, I turn to my chat rooms—only to find every single one empty.

Erika has left the chat. Daisy has left the chat. Veronica, Jessica, on and on it goes. *What is going on*??? A quick check of my socials reveals a similar phenomenon. My followers are down by several thousand, my friends count by hundreds. That's when I see it—a fucking post from Ty.

"I'm saddened but not surprised to wake up to such heinous words about myself from a woman I once loved. If she had simply attacked me, I never would have felt the need to make this post. But, by including our children in her tirade, I have no choice but to defend them against their mother. Ultimately, this will be decided by the courts. But, in short, Lou has neglected and abused both me and our children for years. I was blind, until my youngest asked me yesterday 'Daddy, why does Mommy hate me?' I made the decision to get my kids to a safe place while this plays out. Lou, if you're reading this, do yourself a favor and get help. Please."

His post has over 50k likes, with people calling me all sorts of names. *Oh, so this is how it's going to be!* The age-old fear niggles at the back of mind, threatening to pull me under. Alone. Forgotten. Useless. No! I settle in for a long night of posting and arguing in the comments. I will never let Ty have the last word. I will not be silenced, or worse, forgotten.

ᗰᗰᗰᗰᗰᗰ

A series of sharp knocks wakes me in the morning. My tablet reads 9am. *What the actual fuck?*

"Lou Denver, if you're in there, open up. This is the sheriff."

I snatch my robe and let my slippers smack their way to the source of the incessant banging. The world turns shades or red as I throw the door open to find Ty and two men I don't know on my doorstep.

"Ma'am, I'm Sheriff David, and this here is Deputy Thomas. We have here an emergency injunction for you to clear the premises."

"Excuse you?"

"Ma'am. A judge ruled it is in the best interest of your children for them to be in a safe, stable environment. With their father. In their home," Sheriff David's eyes bore into me, burning me with their hatred.

"I don't know what vile lies my husband has told you, but—"

"Ma'am, with all due respect, I don't write the orders, I just enforce them. Now, I am going to escort you inside to collect your things and make sure you do no damage to the property. Your husband has been generous enough to put you up in a hotel for a couple of days."

If looks could kill, all three of these men on my porch would be dead. Ty—generous? He's kicking me out of my home. Him and the kids can go elsewhere. I cross my arms and glare.

"I'm not leaving my home."

Ty shakes his head, raking his hand through his dark hair.

"Ma'am, you can either gather your things and leave voluntarily, or I can escort you to my car while my deputy packs you a bag. Make your choice."

I step forward, jabbing my nail into the sheriff's face.

"This. Is. My. Home."

"Ma'am," his voice drops dangerously low, "I am recording this entire interaction, and I can guarantee you, a judge will not look kindly on assaulting a police officer."

"I. Am. Not. Leaving."

I enunciate each word as its own sentence, sinking my nail into the sheriff's gut with each syllable.

"Have it your way," he growls, spinning me around and cuffing me on the front lawn, "You have the right to-"

He drones on and on, but all I can focus on is the deputy raiding my house, letting Ty inside. Cameras flash as the neighbors gawk. It's not every day your favorite neighbor gets arrested for doing nothing.

"I'll have your badge," I hiss as Sheriff David manhandles me into the backseat of his cruiser.

"I'd like to see you try, little missy," he retorts, slamming the door.

Alone Forgotten. Neglected. The panic attack drags me under, everything fading to black as I hyperventilate.

❧

"Doc, I haven't had a good night's sleep since Ty started this stupid divorce," I pout to the therapist.

"So, these nightmares started the night your husband left," Dr. Paige drones on, arching an eyebrow as she scribbles on her clipboard.

"Yes. When Ty abducted the kids and kicked me out of the house."

My therapist pinches the bridge of her nose and lets out

a deep sigh before returning her gaze to me. I don't think this self-righteous bitch likes me anymore than I like her.

"Remember, Lou. We have to be intentional with our words. Your husband did not abduct your children."

"How dare you?" I shriek, "you're supposed to be on my side!"

"No, Lou. Per the court, I'm to evaluate your competency to determine what, if any, custody should be recommended. Your husband leveled some pretty serious accusations and provided some compelling evidence. I—"

"He's a fucking liar!"

"Ok. Walk me through it. Let's go statement by statement, and I want you to reply simply with true or false. Can you do that?"

I huff, fixing a glare on this lady with the green hair. *Green hair!* On a court-ordered therapist! Who allowed this?

"You haven't held a job since you got married. True or false?"

"True—Ty told me I didn't have to work."

"Let's keep it to just true or false, please. I just want to establish your version of the truth."

"Over the course of your marriage, you've conducted multiple affairs. A physical one with your best friend's husband, and one on the internet with a married man named Chad Thumb, for starters."

"I'd hardly call them *affairs.* Ty just couldn't give me what I—"

"Next question," Paige cuts me off, "did you make your ten-year-old get both herself and her seven-year-old sister ready for school every day while you slept?"

"True—I mean the brats are old enough to—"

Paige glares at me with a barely concealed venom. I'd hardly call her a neutral party. She's jealous of me, just like all the other fuckers working for Ty. Without skipping a beat, she continues the barrage of questions.

"Did you assault a police officer and refuse to leave the premises in defiance of a direct order?"

"False. There was no assault."

"Lou, there's video evidence that we reviewed, proving otherwise."

"This is all a frame job by Ty and his new girlfriend! I can't believe Becky wants my sloppy leftovers. If she wants shrimp dick and my brats so much, she can have them. I-"

"Enough," Paige slams her pen down on the table between us, "This is our third and final court ordered appointment. I have never in my professional career met someone so narcissistic. I will be recommending your husband for full physical and legal custody. It is my professional recommendation that the only way your children can recover from the trauma you've caused them is by completely removing you from the picture."

"How dare you?" I screech, "I deserve my babies. I gave birth to them!"

"And you haven't done a lick for them since," Dr. Paige snaps back, "Get out of my office."

ꗞꗞꗞꗞꗞꗞ

I toss and turn on the lumpy mattress, squaring off against the creeping darkness. *Breathe in through the nose. Breathe out through the mouth.* The air shoots out in a ragged gasp. Fear's icy grasp grabs me by the throat, stealing the remaining air from my lungs. I'm choking on nothing. My eyes snap open, but the chorus of voices haunts me.

Alone. Forgotten. I haven't had human contact in weeks. I lost my husband, my lover, my friends, my kids. Tomorrow, I'll be homeless. Fear refuses to release its grip on me. I thrash, my flailing arms colliding with something cold and metallic. *Ah, sweet release.*

Mindlessly, I chug the energy drink, my fifth of the day. Instead of soothing my racing heart, it has the opposite effect. Nausea clenches my gut while my jaw locks painfully. My heart races faster, faster, faster. A cold sheen of sweat breaks out on my forehead. My breath comes in shuddering, hitching gasps. I don't understand. As darkness overwhelms me, I realize I'm going to die in a cheap hotel room, forgotten and alone. My worst fear, realized by death itself.

Fuck.

15

PITHECOPHOBIA

BY DYLAN WELLS

*B*esides a few lights on in the windows, Wild Oaks Apartments looked abandoned in the night. Weather-worn shutters drooped over unkempt hedges, and the fire escape had fallen unhelpfully to the overgrown lawn. The entry light had burned out so long ago, spider webs caked the fixture's remains. Thankfully, the summer moon's white light was enough for Chad to see around him, though there wasn't much of a view—a cornfield, a singular long-dead oak tree, and the distant lights of civilization. The silhouette of a child peered down at him. A second, larger figure entered the frame, and a muted argument began and ended with a darkened window. Huh, guess it was past someone's bedtime, but Chad welcomed evidence that people lived here, and he wasn't lured out to get murdered. He gripped a wax-paper bag in one hand and pressed the doorbell for 219.

A woman's voice, indecipherable over the static, came from the intercom.

"Food delivery." Chad grimaced, hoping his voice was clearer for her.

After the lock *clunked*, a low buzz sounded. Chad opened the door but hesitated at the threshold. A dim red glow from an exit sign at the end of the hall provided little illumination. Anything could be hiding in the darkness. The things he put himself through in hopes of a tip.

"Just a few more weeks of this," he promised himself.

He took a tentative step forward and a block of fluorescent lights turned on. One of the long tube lights was more purple than the others and flickered. He stepped farther in, and another section of lights clicked on. Motion sensors. Relieved, Chad strode confidently toward a staircase he could now make out.

Numbered doors lined the hallway, some with welcome matts and shoes, others with wreaths left from Christmas even though it was July. People's doors did little to block what blared from their televisions, and the lingering scents from dinners reminded Chad of high school. Just before he stepped onto the stairs, a dog barked right next to him.

"Oh, shit!"

He leapt away so his back pressed against the opposite wall. The apartment's battered door was slightly ajar, and a dog's nose poked at the opening, huffing Chad's scent. Or more likely the sub in the bag. After a few moments, it became clear the dog was more curious than aggressive, so Chad side-stepped out of its sight then headed up the stairs.

Startled like that by some old mutt? Chad shook his head. Ridiculous. His dog Zipper would be ashamed of him. Why was he so tense? On edge? He needed a break. No. He needed a whole new life. This was all too much. After surviving classes that broke his brain, a first job that numbed it, he had this. Door-Dashing. Sure, the pay wasn't great and sometimes people were mean, but driving around offered solace, decompression, processing. He could recite math formulas to himself, relive old arguments, or sing along without shame for his wavering voice or music choices. As a bonus, his dad was usually asleep in front of the television by the time Chad got home. In a few more months he'd transfer his credits to a state school, then the rest of his life, his *real* life, would begin. As long as he saved up enough money for a security deposit, he'd be free. First things first, though, he had to deliver a meatball sub. One day at a time. One step at a time. He'd get there.

Apartment 219 was right at the top of the stairs, thankfully. He set the bag down and flipped to the app to take a picture and be on his way. One bag of food and one drink. Shit. The drink. The one still sitting in his cup holder.

"Damnit," Chad said. The door whipped open to reveal a mousy-haired woman. She glanced at the food.

Chad gave her his best sad-puppy smile. "Sorry, I forg–"

"There's supposed to be a drink."

"Yeah, I just forgot it in my car. I'm gonna go get it."

"Better hurry. It's already affecting your tip." She tilted her head, ready for a fight. "In case you were just going to steal it."

"No, no." Chad showed her his palms as he backed away. "I'll be right back. Promise."

He jogged down the stairs and down the hall, fearlessly trusting the motion sensors to light his path. When he emerged from fluorescence into starlight and took a deep breath. It was one of those nights where the whole of the world felt at his fingertips and reminded him that none of this mattered. Not the forgotten drink. Not the wear and tear on his car. There was a whole universe out there! Maybe he'd treat himself and make this his last run of the night. He wouldn't go home, of course, but maybe he could just find a field, smoke some weed, and bask in the feeling of the infinite.

He snagged the Styrofoam cup from his center console

and twirled his keys on his finger. A small rustle from one of the overgrown hedges distracted him enough that the keys flew from his fingertip. They arced through the air as if in slow motion, glinting in the moonlight before falling into that same hedge.

"Ah, shit." He carefully tucked the drink in the entryway before going in after them. "Come on. Where are you, keys?"

In the darkest recesses, he pressed his face into the branches as he felt around. Nothing, just the rustle of his fingers and the sound of something dripping. He fumbled his phone out of his pocket and turned on the flashlight. Teeth. Glinting eyes. Chad threw himself back until a wall stopped him, mouth agape. A couple feet away, an opossum matched his expression. Chad, being of a little higher intelligence and much larger size, managed to collect himself first.

"Sorry, little buddy," he chuckled. "I didn't mean to scare you. I do need those keys, though."

Because, sure enough, his keys were caught in the tangle of branches right over the terrified opossum's head. After a brief negotiation, Chad gingerly plucked the keys free and extricated himself from the bushes only for his heart to plummet into his bowels.

"No," he whispered. Rivulets of soda ran like blood down the one step. He'd made sure it was safe. How had that happened? The cup wasn't just scuffed or even smashed; it was disfigured. Torn open and shredded. Goodbye, tip.

A low grunt snapped his attention back to the world around him. Even with adrenaline-dilated pupils, it seemed darker now. A low inhuman sound rose in pitch and volume, followed by a thump as a vaguely human figure emerged from the fallen oak tree. It definitely wasn't human, though. It was thicker, stouter, shaggier, with longer arms and much shorter legs. Adrenaline flooded Chad's body. He smashed all the door buzzers, hoping for someone to let him in. The figure edged closer. Chad couldn't wait. He needed to run. His car was close. Only a dozen or so yards from him. He could make it. He could—

Something slammed into his side, knocking him down. His breath exploded from his lungs making his scream little more than a wheeze as his blood spread over the pavement.

ᗯᗯᗯᗯᗯᗯ

Rose dragged herself to the edge of her bed and allowed her body to flow off the side to the carpeted floor with a muttered curse. Immediately, the downstairs neighbors responded by banging a broomstick on their ceiling. Did Rose complain when she had to stuff a pillow over her head to block out the screams from her neighbor's late night horror marathons? Or when her upstairs neighbor's kid played a rollicking game of dropping bowling balls? Well, yes, but she didn't pound on the wall like a child. She marched right up there and lightly tapped on their door in hopes they wouldn't actually answer then balked when a teenage boy did like a responsible adult! It was like they didn't even want her to exist. Not that she disagreed, but until she threw herself off the building or took a bunch of pills, neither of them would get that wish.

She gazed at the water stains and cobwebs on her ceiling, coming to terms with her predicament. She was, unfortunately, now fully on the floor. While the slide off the bed seemed like the most efficient way to get out of it, she now had that much further to get to her feet.

"Better hurry." Rose's closed door muffled Aubrey's voice. "It's already affecting your tip!"

For being a waitress who often ranted about being shorted on tips, Aubrey sure did like to nickel-and-dime when she was a customer. She said it was because, as a server, she knew good service. Really, it was because deep down (not even that deep) Aubrey was an awful person, one Rose dreamed of being free of. Moving in together was supposed to be a fun solution to a desperate problem (Aubrey's desperate problem) but the person Aubrey was in small doses and the person she was the rest of the time was vastly different.

With a herculean effort, Rose rolled to her feet. She left the sanctuary of her bedroom just as Aubrey pulled out a few crinkle-cut french fries—Rose's fries because Aubrey said she didn't want any—before handing the grease-spotted bag over. Judging by the amount remaining, it wasn't her first theft.

"Don't give me that look." Aubrey grinned as she crushed a fry between her teeth, coating her lips in grease. "I just took a couple and it's, like, three times the calories you need anyway. Really, you should be thanking me."

It wasn't worth the fight. Aubrey went straight for the jugular. Like hiding a pill from a dog, Rose tucked her annoyance in a handful of fries and swallowed it down. Rose put one of the few remaining fries in her mouth and went to the couch, leaving Aubrey alone by the door.

"Ugh, where is my drink?" Aubrey stalked past Rose to peer out the window. The parking lot and entry way was just out of sight with the angle, but that didn't deter her. She pressed her face into the screen, giving a wordless, aggravated whine. Then the door buzzer startled them both. "Finally!"

She went back to the intercom and pressed the button to allow entry. Judging by the set of her jaw, that poor delivery man was in for it.

"Did you hear they caught a tiger in Oconomowoc?" Rose offered as a distraction.

Aubrey loved high-drama stories. The more "what the fuck?" the better. It was laughable that a years' long endeavor to arrest an exotic animal trafficker was botched so badly some of the animals escaped. Rose pictured a cartoonish stampede of big cats, lemurs, and brightly colored birds bowling the federal agents over. She kept higher primates out of her mental movie to keep it from turning into a nightmare, though. It didn't make sense for a Midwestern girl to be wracked by pithecophobia, but the lack of monkeys and their stronger ape cousins as native fauna made it the best place for her. Those bastards were terrifying.

"Yeah, I'm the one who told you about it," Aubrey said, which was not true. "That's why I've stayed in rather than head downtown. I'm not going anywhere until they catch everything, or winter comes, and the freeze kills them."

"The guy lived in Green Bay. Miles from here. You're like when the Twin Towers got hit and everyone here thought this dinky corn town was the next target, blacking out windows like it was the Blitz."

"Listen," Aubrey's smile was small but playful. The hardness in her eyes shifted from steel to diamond. "The risk might be low..."

She didn't need to finish the phrase. Rose laughed and, for one warm moment, Aubrey was who Rose remembered as a friend.

A scream came through the wall, anguished and violent. Rose jumped and a meatball threw itself out of her sub, splattering her legs and floor with a violent slash of marinara.

"Fucking scream queens." Aubrey glared at the shared wall. The music in whatever movie the neighbors were watching swelled, and an explosion rattled their pictures in the hall. "It's almost fucking midnight. And why is it always horror? Why not a rom-com every once in a while?"

"We probably don't hear it when they watch rom-coms." Rose fetched the roll of paper towels to clean up the meatball's suicide.

"Then they're not watching the right kind of rom-coms." Aubrey grinned suggestively before allowing herself to collapse against the door with a whine. "Where is my drink? What is happening in the world, and why is it conspiring against me?"

"Maybe he just left in the entryway."

"If he did, he didn't message about it." She punched at her phone. "There. Done. No tip at all."

"Aubrey, he drove like twenty minutes to get here," Rose said. "We have sodas."

"But not fountain Diet Coke. And that's what really matters. I hope he learns his lesson."

Something lightly thumped against the door, followed by a gentle scratching.

"See? What if that's your drink now and you just shorted him for nothing?" Rose said.

"It's too late, buddy! You should have ru—" Aubrey turned and ripped the door open then jumped back with a strangled scream.

It wasn't the delivery guy with a drink, but a creature in the shadows. Dark, wiry hair. Large, emotive brown eyes staring back at her. A monster. No. Aubrey's words flew through her mind. It was one of the escaped animals, something she'd never heard of, one that had huge teeth and a lust for blood. It took a step forward and Rose blinked, cursing herself for an idiot.

"Oh, it's just Mr. Buttons." Rose couldn't keep the baby-talk from her voice. The large elderly black terrier wagged its whole body and pressed itself into Rose's legs. "Did you get out? Did you? Did Walter not shut his door all the way again?"

"Ugh, get him out of here. He stinks and I'm allergic," Aubrey said.

"Are you a stinky old dog?" Rose asked the dog. He did, but she wanted to see if he thought so.

"Rose," Aubrey admonished.

"Come on, Mr. Buttons," Rose affected an English accent as she guided the dog out the door. "We mustn't bother Cruella any longer."

"Not funny. And look for my drink!"

Rose hoped to spot the drink just to kick it. She looped her finger through the ring on Mr. Buttons' collar and led the old boy down the stairs. Of course, the supposedly eco-friendly lights didn't register her. They never did. Though one flickered dark purple at the far side of the hall by the exit, giving the hallway an ominous ambiance.

Thankfully, Walter lived in the first apartment off the stairs, so she didn't have to venture into the darkness. As expected, his door was slightly ajar, and the TV blared local news.

"...there's no telling how many animals escaped," an anchorwoman said. "But experts suggest at least two dozen and only five have been recovered so far in the weeks since the investigation. Authorities say most of the animals are harmless, but to not approach any animal that is not native to this area and to reach out to the police for support."

"Walter?" she called. "I have Mr. Buttons."

She gently pushed on the door, and it swung open. Mr. Buttons whined but padded in.

"Walter?" she called a final time. The old man was close to blind and hard of hearing, so she could be there all night, and he'd have no idea. With Mr. Buttons safely inside, she reached around his door to the inside doorknob and twisted the lock before pulling it shut, wincing as she touched something sticky. She looked at a dark red smear on her palm in horror. There was nothing grosser than mystery sticky.

A low sound interrupted her, somewhere between a grunt and hoot. Could Mr. Buttons have slipped past her as easily as he did Walter? And now she'd locked the door and couldn't get him back in. Oh well, he'd just have to spend the night, and Aubrey could go fuck herself. And look for her drink? Rose peered down the hallway. Nope, not there. Except, she did see something in the flickering dim purple light. She squinted her eyes, willing it to come into better focus and just be a garbage bag someone was too lazy to take to the dumpster.

"Mr. Buttons?"

The light at the end of the hall turned on with a click, illuminating the shape. The information her eyes presented her with was so incongruent with her daily life her mind reeled like a slot machine, morphing and twisting it from Mr. Buttons to a crouched rotting corpse to a pile of black laundry an instant.

The light went out.

Her nervous system overran with competing instructions. A closer section of light clicked on. It stood motionless. Blood splattered its face and fur. It was impossible. *Impossible.* They were in the middle of nowhere, rural northern Illinois, a daytrip from where the animal trafficker lived.

The lights flickered off.

The stairs were behind her, only three or so long steps away from where she stood. All she had to do was turn around then go up the stairs two—no, three—at a time. She'd left the door unlocked. She'd burst through the door and slam it behind her. Safe. She watched herself do it over and over. A section of light only a dozen or so yards away clicked on. Its fur glistened in the cold white light.

Rose tensed as the animal shifted its weight. Then Rose fucked up. Even though she lived in rural Illinois, even though there were only twenty people in her graduating class, even though she'd barely left the state, she knew it was a threat. A challenge. But she'd done it anyway.

She met its eye and didn't look away.

She leaped back as it sprung forward, screeching, the sound drowning out the click of each section of lights turning on as it grew closer. Rose gripped the banister to slingshot herself up the stairs. She made it four steps in her first leap, and she fell forward, catching herself before scrambling up the remaining stairs. Her door was right there. Right there!

She threw herself into it. For a panicked second, she knew Aubrey had locked it. Aubrey was paranoid and vindictive. She'd think it was funny to make Rose beg, but the joke would leave Rose dead. But after the slightest catch, the knob turned and she toppled in, kicking the door closed behind her. The monster screamed as it slammed into it. Rose locked every lock just as the doorknob turned and the whole of the door rattled.

"What the fuck?" Aubrey demanded. "What is that? What did you do?"

"Just help me!" Rose screamed; her full bodyweight leaned against the door. Miraculously, Aubrey did.

"You better fucking stop!" Aubrey roared through the door. The next impact jarred Rose to her bones. Its scream pierced her skull like a pick.

Rose shushed her. Maybe without further provocation, it would lose interest. Go away. Know it had won.

"What is happening?" Aubrey said, full volume.

Another violent impact and a splintering sound. Rose told her to shut up with only her eyes.

"Rose! Tell me what is going on!" Aubrey yelled. Another impact caused a dark line to appear in the door jamb by the deadbolt. "Is that a fucking monkey?"

No. Rose's *Animal Planet* knowledge told her as much. Monkeys had tails. This was an ape. The most violent and unpredictable one. It was a fucking chimpanzee.

"Just shut the fuck up for a second," Rose hissed. "Wait 'til it leaves."

Aubrey opened her mouth to speak again, but for once, whatever she saw in Rose's glare finally stopped her. After a few more desperate tugs and pounds at the door, the chimpanzee grunted, then only the distant screams of the neighbor's scary movie could be heard.

Rose waited a couple breaths then carefully stood, pausing to see what effect each movement, each creak of the floor, each shuffle of clothing had on the chimp outside. Buoyed by every lack of response, she ushered Aubrey down the hall and into her bedroom before explaining what she encountered. Aubrey looked at her without blinking for a long time before speaking.

"You can't be serious." Glee at how stupid she found Rose brightened the fear from her face.

Rose ignored her and called the police. The dispatcher scolded her for wasting community resources and hung up on her.

"Fuck." Rose dropped her arms to her side. So much for calling the authorities. A burst of screams from the neighbors punctuated her desperation. "It's just Mr. Buttons again." Aubrey's volume raised as the neighbor's movie must be at its climax, the final fight with the boss for the crescendo of screams and crashes. "Or something else. I was joking when I said we needed to be careful. I know you can't take a joke, but this is ridiculous. You're delusional! There are no chimpanzees in Marengo!"

A thick, all-too-human hand coated in dark, coarse fur burst through the thin drywall and grabbed Aubrey's hair. She screamed, hands flying to the chimp's fist. Rose leapt forward, but the animal pulled Aubrey off balance. The top of her head and hands disappeared into the wall. Rose grabbed a pair of scissors just as Aubrey's scream turned from terror to pain and what remained of her hands slipped into view. The chimp's other hand grabbed another handful of Aubrey's blood-soaked hair, but Rose sliced the strands close to Aubrey's scalp.

Hysterical but free, Aubrey propelled herself from the bedroom, slamming the door in Rose's face. That *bitch*. Rose risked a glance behind her as her adrenaline-clumsy hands fumbled with the doorknob. The hole to the next apartment was now about a foot around and the chimp's bloody grin turned its screeches into laughter. A lump in a pool of blood on the ground came into view as the chimp double-fist-punched another chunk of drywall away. It wasn't until Rose ripped open her bedroom door and followed Aubrey's trail of blood down the hallway that her brain put the pieces together. That skinless lump was once her neighbor, arms blunted to stubs.

It didn't take long to catch up to Aubrey. She pawed at the front doorknob with what remained of her hands, coating it in blood. Most of her right hand's fingers were gone, the left was missing parts of her pointer and most of her index.

"Help me! Get me out of here!" She looked back at Rose.

Rose's hand slipped on the blood, so she used the hem of her shirt to grip the knob. Finally, it turned.

"Go, go, go!" Rose pushed Aubrey to go down the

stairs. Only idiots ran upstairs where there was no escape. Down was outside. Down was Rose's car. Down was how they'd get away.

The chimp leaped over the railing and landed in front of them, blocking the way down. Idiocy it was. Rose pulled Aubrey around the stairwell to get to the ascending side.

Shrieks and hoots serenaded their stampede up. By the time they made it to the third floor, the chimp was upon them. Time slowed as Rose looked behind her with no breath to spare for a scream. This is what she wanted, right? To die? Then why did she just want one more day? One more time to feel the wind on her skin and a chance to finally write that book always relegated to someday? In this frozen moment, strands of Aubrey's bloody hair floated around them both, her eyes wide and terrified. Behind her the chimp was mid-leap, arm outstretched, teeth bared. What remained of Aubrey's hand found hers.

Flashes of memory flickered like an old movie through Rose's mind. Laughing in Chemistry class. Aubrey splitting her sandwich in half when Rose didn't have one after track practice, singing along to a banger in a club, getting all the words wrong, and not caring at all. All of Rose's annoyance at Aubrey vanished. All the slights, the demands, the complete lack of accountability. It didn't matter anymore. This was it. Rose squeezed Aubrey's hand, forgetting her missing fingers. At least they'd die together.

Aubrey wrenched her arm down, pulling Rose forward. Instead of a steadying hand on Rose's back, she pushed. Rose tripped on the top step and sprawled onto the third floor. Time lurched back into rhythm and Aubrey leaped over her, footsteps fading as she ran down to the fire escape door at the end of the hall.

That *fucking bitch*.

"Aubrey!" Rose screamed from the depths, full of

betrayal and fury. The chimp landed on her, scratching at her face. When she brought her hands up protectively, the chimp pulled one into its mouth, chomping through the meat of her hand beneath her little and index finger. As easy as that, the digits were gone almost to her wrist. Blood sprayed them both and then all Rose saw was teeth, yellowed with plasma and dripping her blood. It was coming for her eyes, her face. It took everything Rose had left to turn her head. It tore through her cheek and its teeth clacked on hers.

As the chimp pulled back, a flap of Rose's skin smacked back into place. Then the maw blocked out her vision. The last thing her eyes would see would be their own destruction.

Something collided with the chimp's head with a ringing *thwung*. Its body twisted off of her with the force of the blow and she scrambled back.

"Come on!" A young male voice shook with adrenaline. She scooted herself toward it without taking her eyes off the dazed chimp.

"Come on, come on," the voice hissed. She crab-walked across the threshold into his apartment, only regaining herself when the door slammed. In an instant, Rose was on her feet, peering out the peephole. For the first time, the blood running down the chimp's fur was its own. It was still wobbly, but looked up at the peephole like it knew Rose was just on the other side. Then, thankfully, something made the chimps' head swivel, and it lumbered off. Numb, Rose turned around to her rescuer.

Gone were the sullen, downcast eyes, and mumbled responses. A baseball bat splattered in blood took their place.

"What the fuck was that?"

"A goddamn chimpanzee!" Rose said. Or rather, tried

to say. The gash through her cheek made speaking painful and difficult. She went to press her hand against it, but horror stopped her. Her hand was barely anything. Her voice broke. "Oh god."

"Here." The young man lunged to grab a kitchen towel, which he thrust at her. She held it dumbly, so he took it back and wrapped it around her hand, staunching the flow of blood. He told her to hold on and disappeared down his hall before returning with a roll of paper tape. While she stood in shock, he bound her injuries, comically inexperienced but gentle.

"The police didn't believe me," she said. "They're not coming. No one is coming."

He looked at her for a moment, then dropped his gaze. The endorphins that thrust him into heroism faded. He was just an awkward teenager again.

"Lucas?" a child's voice called. The young man, Lucas, turned. A little girl in a pink princess nightgown and mussed hair came into view. "I had a nightmare."

She froze when she saw Rose, eyes widening.

"She's fine. Go back to bed." Lucas donned the annoyed-older-brother mantle.

"Is she okay?" She was sweet for someone who likely jumped everywhere she went when Rose was trying to sleep. Rose attempted a smile before realizing it probably made her look even more horrifying.

"Ava!"

Ava *hmphed* and stomped back down the hall.

"Mom's on nights," Lucas mumbled to the floor.

Rose nodded, but the domestic scene forced her out of her shock and back into terror. Their door stood no better chance against the chimp than hers did. All Rose wanted was to hide, to curl herself into a ball and wait for rescue.

But rescue wasn't coming and somehow, she was the adult in this insanity. Goddamnit, they were doomed.

Seven minutes later, Rose and Lucas were in position. It would have been five, but Lucas had the gall to remind her she was now missing the fingers needed to hold on to the rope of clothing tied together. Rose, in turn, reminded him he wasn't even old enough to drive so there was no way she was putting him in harm's way. At least not directly.

Careful of her torn cheek, she checked the peephole. The lights timed out so she couldn't make out much besides her blood splatter by the stairs. If the chimpanzee was right there, there wouldn't be time for her to get in position. She shifted to adjust her view through the peephole, straining to make out the chimp's shape in the darkness. Nothing. Good. She slowly released a breath. This was going to work. It was going to be okay.

The lights clicked on and eyes in a gory stew slammed into view. Rose recoiled.

"Oh god," she whispered, then she flew back to the peephole.

It was Aubrey, trying to speak, but without her bottom jaw her tongue flopped uselessly. Her face was ripped off into her hairline, showing muscle and bone. She raised her arms up to hit the door. Only the palm remained on one and the other ended at the wrist.

She hadn't escaped. She needed Rose to save her. Rose always did. Signing onto an apartment she couldn't afford so Aubrey didn't get evicted, swallowing every put down when Aubrey had a bad day, giving her endless rides when she got a DUI. The pull to rip open the door and drag her into the apartment grew so strong it hurt. But Aubrey needed her.

"What is it?" Lucas shoved her out of the way. He jerked back with a string of words Rose would inform his mother of in any other circumstance. He reached for the doorknob. She stopped him. If she kept saving Aubrey, they'd all die.

Lucas met her eyes and nodded once. She tugged at the harness they'd fashioned out of sweatpants and held fast on the rope of bedsheets knotted as tight as they could pull them. A distant shriek came through the door. It was time.

Lucas opened the door fully and hid behind it. Aubrey lay at the threshold, dead eyes staring into the fluorescent light. A gurgled breath bubbled out of the gore. She wasn't dead. She just didn't have eyelids. She couldn't shut her eyes.

Rose drew a few quavering breaths that did nothing to bring oxygen to her lungs. Her whole body shook, and she gripped the sheets with her still-good hand. She carefully leaned over Aubrey to peer down the hall. Only one section of lights was on a dozen or so yards down. Centered, as if under a spotlight, the chimp played with a flap of skin. Not just flesh. There were eyebrows. It was playing with Aubrey's face.

"Hey." Rose's voice betrayed her and didn't make a sound. She cleared her throat, which caught the chimp's attention then tried again. "Hey!"

It still wasn't quite the battle cry she'd intended, but it was enough for it to look at her fully. Rose met its gaze and held it, bared her teeth and gave a strangled scream. She thumped her injured hand against her chest. It was a painful mistake but did the trick. The chimp stamped and shrieked in response then charged, triggering blocks of lights as it came closer.

Its speed was surprising, and she barely had time to get deeper into the apartment before it was only a couple yards away. She ran through Lucas's living room, stepped onto the coffee table, and leapt. Time slowed again as she twisted her body so her back shattered the glass. She fell, momentarily weightless. The chimp, enraged, followed.

Their trajectories threw them away from the building, but the bed sheets cut Rose's journey short. She grunted at the sudden stop. In a twinkling shower of glass, the chimp reached for her. The rage left its eyes, and Rose knew it didn't want to be this way, stolen from its mother's arms. Kept for novelty instead of love, forced away from and punished for its nature. It had just wanted to be free, to look at the stars in the sky and relearn its mother tongue. It never wanted to be here, to become this. Rose saw herself reflected in its eyes and, for a moment, reached back. But it was too late. Rose would never get the sound of its compact body hitting the ground out of her mind.

By the time flashing red and blue lights filled the parking lot, the chimp disappeared. It'd taken its broken body and soul and vanished into the corn. Months passed. Then a year. Beyond a few tracks early on, no sign of the chimp or the chimp's body was ever found. When Aubrey finally got out of the hospital, face forevermore hidden behind a veil, she messaged Rose about rooming together again. Rose left her on read.

16

SCIOPHOBIA

BY AJ HUMPHREYS

*I*t was the correct call—letting me write this down. Especially in the safety of the shadows under my bunk. Thank you. I'll take your advice and ease into it.

So, the 90s. What an odd time to grow up. As a planet, we were just beginning to connect as individuals. Like we now possessed the power to communicate near instantaneously without the aid of anything but a computer. "Globalization" wasn't even a term in most kids' lexicon yet, and still we were the generation exploring this phenomenon through the birth of the World Wide Web. I think it was that level of free access to information across the globe that led my sister and her friends to the legend of Shady Sheila.

I certainly did everything in my power to search after the incident. For over a decade, I let the fervency of an addict battling withdrawal possess me. And yet, I never found even the slightest hint of a clue to a puzzle that MIGHT unearth the truth behind what had stolen my sister from me. Well, not what. I'm pretty sure I know WHAT.

I just didn't know *where* it had taken her. But I have a rather good idea these days. Hence, why we're here; why I'm writing this.

The shadows. MY shadow. That's where she went. I know you won't believe me. No one ever believes me. I'm simply the *crazy* little brother. But this is the exact same thing I told my parents and the police officers that fateful October evening in 1994.

It's been thirty years, and I still can't escape the shakes and tears born of that night.

I digress.

Sciophobia, you want to call it. I think AUTO-scio-phobia would be more apt. See, I love the shadows. The shadows keep me safe from my own shadow. But I defer to you. After all, you're the expert, Doc.

Don't worry, I'm still going to say my piece.

I don't fear other people's shadows. Only my own. I've tried explaining this, but I'm still not sure if you are like all the others yet, Dr. Zintavan. The jury's still out, as they say. But I want you to believe me, and while hearing it from the horse's mouth is one thing, I appreciate you allowing me to jot this letter down because it's revealed to me how impossible it is for me to tell this story in its entirety without succumbing to tears. And likely another emotional *breakdown*, no, episode.

I'd like to get out of this place and go back to my house and my dog, Bert. He's all I have in this world. And you're the decider. I'm well aware you won't make that decision until I've given you what you want to hear. Which is the truth. I know.

And this is one-gazillion percent the truth.

I promise. On Bert's life, I promise.

ᙁᙁᙁᙁᙁᙁ

October 30th, 1994. The night before Halloween, my folks were leaving me home alone with my older sister Daphne for the first time. And only time.

It was a Saturday. Mom and Dad were going to some masquerade party. I remember because Dad had this beaked half mask that I now can't help but associate with the image of a medieval plague doctor. I think Mom's had feathers, colorful ones, but it didn't have the remarkable beak that my father's did.

Daph was fourteen, and though she always got up to mischief, my parents were hardly aware. They trusted her. But maybe they shouldn't have. Maybe if they hadn't trusted her and instead asked old Mrs. Hopper next door to watch us, then maybe no one would have died. And maybe, I wouldn't be afraid of whatever had taken her returning from my shadow once more.

Sorry. I know. Maybes, what-ifs, and a five-dollar bill will get me about as much as a draft domestic.

But... *Never mind*. I know.

So, my folks leave Daphne in charge, and the first thing she does afterward is grab the kitchen phone and call her friends, Karen and Rachel. Within the hour, both girls were at our house, contributing to a fledgling argument about which movie they were going to watch. Daph and Rachel wanted Halloween. But Karen was squeamish. Not to mention obsessed with a certain young actor named Tim Roth. So, she had brought along her older brother's bootleg copy of Reservoir Dogs.

At fourteen, I'm not sure either movie was appropriate for my sister and her friends, but certainly neither was suitable to my ten-year-old mind.

Thankfully, I was happier with a book in my hands, anyway.

With it being the night before the former movie's namesake, Karen was outvoted. I caught bits and pieces of John Carpenter's iconic score flittering up from the basement, while taking advantage of my free rein over the rest of the house.

I remember the girls making a ton of noise. Their shrill shouts echoed up the basement stairwell as they tried to scare one another in the shadowed darkness of our parent's "home theater."

Since that day, I have seen the film. Not exactly scary. But the bias of living through the explosive age of computer-generated imagery may have something to say about that. I like the newer films a bit more.

Despite the noise, I mostly read. I liked reading and Rachel had just brought me a copy of "Watchers" by Dean Koontz. Another bit of media I'm not sure my parents would have approved, but Rachel loved to read and regularly lent me books she thought I'd enjoy. So, I always trusted her with recommendations. None of them ever traumatized me. Not that I believed the written word could scar me back then. But after what happened later that night, the thought of something as trivial as printed text racking me with anxiety or a panic attack is hilariously laughable.

Which I should get to. I feel like I've set the scene thoroughly enough for you. I know you'll have questions regardless. Maybe I'll even address some as you continue reading.

෴෴෴෴෴෴

Movie time ended and once the girls settled down, I moved from whichever room I'd been reading in, itching for some company, hoping Daph wouldn't shoo me off like a buzzing gnat. It was always a fifty-fifty chance whether she'd consider me family or a foul, toxic waste polluting her precious air.

This time, I was family.

Daphne was happy to see me. She looked up from the family computer. I hold on to that image. A pure smile that bled into those bright eyes framed beneath her iconic 90s bangs. To me, that's the definition of genuine joy. And it was at seeing me. But I'd give that sight up in a heartbeat to have my sister back. Even all these years later.

Why couldn't she have just been annoyed, like a normal teenage girl? Why couldn't she simply have wanted nothing to do with me?

Sorry.

You said to just keep writing. So that's what I'm doing.

I have no clue what website they were on. Probably one of those early sketchy forums or chat sites from the dawn of mass internet access. Irregardless, rather regardless, (you taught me that) this was the moment they beckoned me over to join them.

That's when they asked if I would help them play "Shady Sheila." Like it was a game. It wasn't. On the surface, it was a far more involved version of "Bloody Mary." But rather than a mirror, this summoning relied on shadows. In this case, MY shadow.

Nowadays, as you've observed, the comfort of darkness offers me a reprieve from these fears. After all, it's the brightest lights that cast the darkest shadows.

♕♕♕♕♕♕

We made our way down to the basement, where the girls carried out a meticulous set of instructions they'd uncovered. I should mention, I have never found these rules anywhere online. The only copy I believe existed were those handwritten notes that my sister copied into her X-Files notebook.

I still have it. The notebook, that is. Or I should. Depending on what's been done to my house since my confinement here. But the rules are long gone. I burned those motherfuckers YEARS ago. Sorry for the language. It's just... I can't be any more clear about this.

PLEASE don't go looking for them.

I don't even like vaguely outlining them like this for you. However, I know all too well that the Devil is in the details, and these details are as clear as ever in my mind, which is where they will stay. It's in everyone's best interest.

ᗺᗺᗺᗺᗺᗺ

Here is what I am comfortable sharing.

The first rule required the gathering of four participants. Specifically, a trinity of maidens, forming an unbroken loop around the fourth individual and their shadow. Daph and Rachel had mocked Karen to some effect because of a recent rumor floating around the school.

"Guess we can't do it if Karen's with us." They'd teased her.

"Shut up, you guys!" Karen was nearly crying, visibly approaching her wit's end with the provocative lies.

She was, in fact, still a "maiden" (I think), but high school rumor mills have always been detrimental to the mental health of their students. And this rumor had been circulating ever since Karen broke up with her boyfriend. I can picture his smug face, but not his name, for the life of me.

The girls and I gathered a seance-like collection of candles, before arranging them all around where I would stand, as well as on the periphery of the triad. Satisfied, Daph went around lighting each one with a box of matches. That sulfur stench accompanying the ignition of each match has stuck with me all these years later.

It would return later.

However, there is something about that setup, which to this day I can't reconcile with what I know to be true. The way we'd positioned all those candles could not have possibly created a singular shadow.

But it did.

And I'm getting ahead of myself again.

The next rule was even more particular than the last. Within the circle-to-be-formed, the shadow couldn't be any longer than a number that I do not wish to divulge. But because of the girls' heights, only I was going to fit the bill. So, Daph grabbed our dad's bright yellow tape measure and Rachel quickly worked out the math to make sure we carried everything out correctly.

I'll add, this process really took some time. God, they were meticulous. Because the next thing I knew, we were spending what had to be at least thirty minutes looking for lanterns and flashlights, messing with the lighting, and yeah, it was way more effort than I'd expected when they called me over. But they were adamant about needing to get my shadow just right.

It had to be dark. As dark as possible. Like pitch black. There shouldn't be anything visible within the bounds of the shadow. Which was a lot harder to do than any of us expected.

Maybe we would have given up if Karen hadn't gone

and been creative, gathering several black jackets from the hall closet. We continued to make do with what we had, meeting each precondition. The final step was successfully measuring the dark after image with the yellow serpent's tongue of the tape measure.

Then came time for me to perform the ritual.

Again, I plan to be vague here. You do not need the specifics. I PROMISE.

So, it starts with me repeating the name, "Shady Sheila," a specific number of times in a chant-like rhythm. Know that this is not something as simple as saying, "Bloody Mary" into a mirror three times. Each utterance seemed to distill the meaning of the words until they were hardly more than a rhythmic blend of sound.

The next part is where things get incredibly, I don't know a better word than WEIRD. Supernatural, maybe? Because no one told me to say what I said next. But the words came from *my* throat, in *my* voice, and in rhythm to *my* monotonous chanting of that name, "Shady Sheila."

"Shady Sheila, Shady Sheila, Shady Sheila, Shay-dee She-La, let the darkness lady see ya, this is what you asked for, the lady born of ichor. Shady Sheila."

I didn't even know what the word ichor meant at that point in time. Yet, I know I said it. I remember the word leaving my mouth. But it's like I was a puppet and something else had reached into my innards, cavorting around the nooks and crannies, until it slipped its dark grasp into my jaw and spoke through me.

Before my very own eyes, my shadow grew deeper. Darker. A level of black so unfathomable it creeps under your skin, gnawing at primal instincts buried deep by evolution.

Then the candles went out. But they didn't just flicker out of existence like some cheesy horror film. My shadow consumed them. It swelled like a bulbous balloon—inflating until it devoured all the light in the basement, leaving behind an eternal emptiness.

A scream echoed out from the darkness. I'm pretty sure I was already scared, but the sound of one of the girls' painful cries petrified me. The weight of that wicked gloom forced me to my knees before toppling me down to the fetal position. I distinctly remember trying to shove my kneecaps into my eyes and finding more light behind my eyelids than I did beyond them.

Until this moment, I'd been distracted. Lulled into the prestige that came with the territory of the cool kids. Just the thought of how awesome it was that my older sister, who was in HIGH SCHOOL, was willing to include me, still gives me jitters. Well, not just Daph, but her friends, too. Neither girl dissuaded her from including me in these pre-Halloween festivities. They needed me, and that felt good.

ᗰᗰᗰᗰᗰᗰ

I had to take a quick break. This is just a lot.

Again, I didn't really scare easily. Nothing in the real world seems as scary as the images some stories had let creep into my thoughts and dreams. And I'd gotten over all those with ease. Even the dancing clown only troubled me for a weekend earlier that month.

But as I laid there, trying to form a smaller and tighter ball of security like the pill bugs that enraptured me as a child, I struggled to tell myself this was all an elaborate prank.

That's why they wanted to include me. Surely, they meant to scare me. That would explain the jovial sister I'd seen. It was the glee of a schemer.

Unfortunately for all involved, they had genuinely wanted me to be a part of their spur-of-the-moment spooky season shenanigan.

I peeked over my knees, hoping to see light return to the world. Instead, a hellish darkness swept across my vision. It swatted away any lingering thoughts I'd held regarding the lights going out as part of the girl's scheme to scare me.

A sulfuric stench greeted my nostrils as if seeing the darkness triggered its release. Not dissimilar to the feeling of being puppeted, the stench dug into me, burrowing down my sinuses with the heft and agility of a subterranean arthropod.

But that's nonsense. Right???

I thought so many things that you would call rationalizing. My ten-year-old brain had already cemented certain facts I'd learned from my sister and the world. The supernatural wasn't real, being chief among them. That was saved for books, TV, and movies. Those types of things didn't happen in your childhood basement. The most fun, safe, and reliable place a kid could ask for. At least, that's what I thought before the entity scuttled its way through me with that stench that appeared to signal Sheila's dissatisfaction with my existence.

It hated me. There's no explaining how I knew that. I'd never felt such a visceral wave of unrestrained malice in my young life. And I haven't since. So, I retreated to the safety of the fetal position once more. This was the most rational action at that moment.

Maybe you share the sentiment of most. That this is all a fantasy of my mind. Repressed trauma or something nonsensical like that. A blackout, so I wouldn't remember what Daphne did. That's how every other psychiatrist, therapist, social worker, and whoever else I've spoken with seems to think.

Why would you be any different?

That's *my* question to you, Doc. Why should I trust *you* with this?

Not that it matters. I've already scribbled down this much. I mean, I could shred it. *Or burn it.* Okay, I couldn't do that. Burn it, that is. Not in this place. Maybe in the 90s when cigarettes were rampant indoors. But not now. And I won't shred it. This is my story. I've stuck to it this long. Why change that now?

🦷🦷🦷🦷🦷🦷

I know, I know, I left you hanging. I just—God, I needed a break. The idea of a cigarette sounded too nice, and I was getting that fidgety itch that required the use of my fingers. But... I can't go breaking the streak. It'll be a year without, next month on the thirteenth.

I'm stalling.

Here it goes...

When I composed myself enough to brave another glance over my knees, the screams and cries in the distance had all but faded into the mild whimpers of broken creatures resigning themselves to their helpless demise.

The room was dark. But it was normal-dark. It wasn't the endless trench of blackness that had gluttonously devoured us moments before.

Except the source of that abyss still stood there. Lingering. Waiting.

Shady Sheila.

I don't know that I could describe her fully, even if I wanted to. But I know I can do her—IT—better justice by writing it down. At least, I hope so.

She was a small silhouette against the night that infected

our basement. I don't know how I can better say that. That she, it... IT was an *IT*.

Okay.

It had the frame of a woman no bigger than ten-year-old me. So maybe five-foot, at most. But the edges were, without a doubt, feminine. When it had been alive. If it ever had, I think it was a girl. I don't know what she did to end up in that bottomless exile of shadow, but I knew in my bones that it was elated to have escaped that domain.

An abrasive, peppermint-like wave exuded from Sheila. Not the scent exactly, but the experience. The way a potent dose can slap sobriety through each of the bodily senses. That sickening sulfuric stench lay beneath it, curdling the air in what was beginning to feel like an abandoned mausoleum.

Yet, there were still more repercussions for summoning Sheila from that foreign realm. It expected something in return. Whatever the girls thought would happen, they should have at the very least expected the most quintessential horror cliche. That this was a transaction. Like all the fucking books and movies depicted. Maybe that's hindsight talking. We were just kids, after all.

To this day, I'm not one-hundred percent certain what this thing wanted, but I wish I had been the one that found out. Because then Daphne wouldn't have.

Now, I know you've garnered "all" the information ahead of time. The OFFICIAL information, I should say. Daphne killed the girls and ran away. Something about mental instability based on what they found in her diary. Which is *bullshit*. The line that I'm sure you've seen by now was, "there are days where I feel like I'm two people." That, amongst other things, allowed those useless pigs to pin it all on Daph.

Even though the case isn't technically closed, the cops

aren't doing shit. Not this long after. Maybe a cold case sort of detective. But I doubt it.

Sorry. That's very pessimistic and crass. But what four-teen-year-old girl, or guy, didn't feel that sort of way? Did you, Doc? Did you sometimes feel that you were living two lives as a teenager? Cuz, I get that. I get it even more now.

To me, that's the self-awareness of a woman in this world. Women are thrust into the horrors of this life long before us boys. Men. Whatever.

Point is Doc, the next line in her entry that day was, "I have to be the older sister, the responsible and structured one. But with my friends, I can be loose and wild and free, and I just love it." She went on writing about how she simply wished Mom and Dad understood she wanted a little more freedom and for them to not be so strict with her all—

Again, I digress.

So, regardless of how you've heard it, there is the official story, which makes now as good a time as any to tell you the UNOFFICIAL truth, as Fox Mulder might have said.

ଘଘଘଘଘଘ

I can picture it to this day. Its shadowy hands tore through the air as if the entity were trying to swim down toward me. Despite the depths of its darkness, the shadow-thing had formed. Its twiglike fingers capped in scale-like series of sharp spines that pulsed as if in time with the tenebrous veins of a heart concealed in shadow.

But Daph was strong and fast. She ran the...crap. What was it??? The full lap. And she was a cheerleader. That's how all three of them became friends. Daph brought in her fellow cheerleader Karen and then bonded with the straight-A shot-put thrower, Rachel. That's just the way it'd been since they were in fifth or sixth grade.

Yeah, I know. That doesn't matter to the story. I started so strong too.

It's those fucking fingers. The way they waded through space, spreading Sheila's stink, desperate to impale me with those pulsating barbs adorning each digit. But Daph, like I said, was quick and strong. Remember, that's why they thought she could have overpowered the other two girls. But that isn't what happened.

Daph was impaled on the thing's fingers. In my mind, I have this memory of her skintight shirt wriggling with the pulse of something invading her body. Something tuberous and littered in spindly appendages that skittered beneath the fibers of muscle and sinew until a faint sound welled out of my sister's horrified silence. Something akin to a small dog clacking its nails across hardwood.

A gleeful cackle erupted from where Sheila's mouth should have been. Terrifying joy filled the room with a burgeoning gravity that threatened to squash me beneath the boot of a demented cosmic force.

I think IT had gotten exactly what IT wanted. Which wasn't me. I simply made the perfect sized tunnel for IT to crawl through, escaping whatever abyss could possibly have imprisoned such an entity. And in return, I don't believe it expected a quid pro quo.

No. There was never any intention to bestow compensation for our deeds that night. No magic wishes or a pot of gold.

It was committing a crime. It needed a scapegoat. No, a placeholder. A *thing*. That could take its place. Like the old switcheroo. You know that Indiana Jones trick with the bag of dirt and the weighted pedestal?

But the entity's seething fury at the form of a boy in

place of a proper offering had doomed us. Because, in all that noxious air that my lungs continued to heave through, I felt a panic far more alien than my own.

Wherever this being had escaped from, I don't think it was at the top of the food chain. See, it only wanted my sister. It didn't try taking the other two.

But when both girls bravely clung to Daph, it attacked. The pair began wailing as if the mere aura of the shadow slithering up my sister's insides, consuming her figure, sliced into their hands with rusty, jagged hooks. Despite the gory assault on their palms, and the agony slitting their vocal cords, they clung to their friend, desperate to pull her back.

That may be what hurts most. The world thinks my sister killed those two girls. When, with unwavering conviction, only I know they were heroes. Tragic heroes incapable of cleaving themselves free of Sheila's hooks. The idea of fish dangling in the air has always clung to this moment. And just like the transients of the sea, Rachel and Karen floundered and flopped until it was too late.

That's when the thing tore into them. Literal shreds of skin, muscle, and clothing rained down on us. Yet, each shadowy finger worked with the speed and precision of a surgeon wielding white-hot scalpels to slice through butter.

I watched with helpless terror as my sister sank into the infinite emptiness of my shadow, which hadn't so much as wavered from my standing silhouette. It was like one of those radioactive afterimages from Chernobyl.

Whether it was Sheila or my shadow, I can't be certain, but it spread along Daph like creeping fungi. Draping over her, submerging her head, and consuming her until what little of her outline remained dwindled into the depths of that bottomless cosmic gelatin. My final sight of my sister isn't even my sister. The blackness had already engulfed her, draining her of color like a cartoon and leaving behind a horrid, featureless face and an inexhaustible scream.

I don't know.

If I could explain it with perfect science, wouldn't that make it more likely it was a lie? The fact that I stand by what I saw, despite knowing the holes in my story, should mean something. But you're the doc, Doc.

🦷🦷🦷🦷🦷🦷

The next thing I remember was my mom holding me as paramedics stomped with their heavy black boots across the linoleum floor. I wasn't in the basement anymore. I was on the couch swathed in a towel. One of the fancy ones reserved for house guests. I remember thinking I was going to get in trouble for dirtying the soft, white fabric with the blood and slick carnage coating my clothes. Thankfully, I think my mom saw that on my face. Her lips tickled my ear as she hummed our favorite B-52s song. Simultaneously offering the reassurance of stroking my hair with her soothing touch.

It's funny. Amid all the nightmares, the bloodshed, the therapy sessions, you name it, I still remember that moment of comfort and reassurance from my mother. What does that say? I don't know.

But I do know one thing for certain.

My sister hadn't trailed those bare, bloody footprints through the house and out the door.

🦷🦷🦷🦷🦷🦷

That sucked. I hate that you made me relive that. But I understand why.

Everything after is mostly moot.

I was briefly questioned at home. Then in a weirdly sterile room the next day at the police station, and then by the local news twice. I didn't get to say much to the reporters either time. Dad couldn't have his son spouting ridiculous heathen nonsense for the entire town to watch during dinner.

So outside of him, Mom, a handful of police officers, and an overcurious nurse, you're the only one to get the entire story. Something tells me you won't be the first to believe it, though. But that's the truth.

That's why I can't stand the sight of my own shadow, and how I knew this day was coming.

I could feel that same oppressive gravity weeks before the event at the library. Imagine that. Being on edge for weeks, not knowing where the threat would come from, but that it was coming.

And this is why I—*rightfully so*—FREAKED THE FUCK OUT when I heard those kids in the library talking about playing a game called "Daphne Darkness."

I thought all sorts of crazy things the moment those words crept down my ear canals. But I knew only a single truth with any certainty. It HAD indeed been a switcheroo, and now, somehow, Daphne was trying to get out. But I don't think it was Daphne. I think Daph died the moment that THING dug its fingers into her sides.

The shadows have her now. My shadow.

I believe each of us offers the opportunity to be a key. Well, anyone who can block just the right amount of light can be the key. Keys to open doors to dark and dangerous places. And that night, we opened a cell that was sealed for good reason.

Somehow, someway, we let what was once a girl named Sheila back into this world, and in return, my sister took the escaped entity's place. Now she wants out. Or, no, something else wants to return to this world. Whatever has possessed my sister's body and soul these last thirty years is now ready to be let loose. And I couldn't allow that to happen.

This is a conviction I've held for decades.

If she gets out, someone else must go in. That SHOULD be the way the rules work. I know you don't think that justifies my actions, but I swear they do. The information couldn't leave that building. That's why I locked the doors. That's why I poured the gasoline. And that's why I made sure it was dark when I lit the match.

There are no coincidences in this world. Of all the places, these children attempt this game in MY library. No. Something cosmic and ancient was pulling at strings. But I denied it that night, sealing the victory for all humanity.

You should have seen the way those shadows ran as the fire grew. Cowards. Pathetic bastards hid in corners and tucked in fetal positions, unable to flee or stand and accept death proudly. Mine, most of all, shivered in a weak grey mass, flickering indiscriminately atop the pavement. Daphne would not be returning through my shadow. No, sir-ee-bob.

Then I heard the screams, and just like before, they erupted from the depths of darkness. Only this time, it was my turn to surprise the enemy. To catch them off guard and watch as they were devoured in the searing maw of flame.

In those screams, the wave that left the burning mass of shadows and architecture exuded a sweet musk of fear. But I'm not sure that will be enough to dissuade future attempts to set foot in our world or take another life.

Many will not see the heroism in my actions. I don't expect this to change people's opinions about what I did. If it was wrong or not. But one life stolen thirty years ago was already one too many. This way, no one was lost to the shadows that night.

Those grieving families and loved ones can live out their days knowing exactly where the souls of their loved ones rest. Something I'll never have.

So, if I'm being honest, Doc, which is what I have been throughout this ordeal, I don't care what your final decision is. I don't. Not anymore. Writing this out has made everything abundantly clear.

Thank you for that, at least.

There's only one sure-fire way to prevent my shadow from opening again. And seeing how this facility of yours specializes in preventing such an action; for the time being, I can only hope that it ends with Daphne.

17

TRYPOPHOBIA

BY ANDREW ADAMS

"*T*o what do I owe the pleasure today, Ray? I haven't heard from you in a few weeks." Dr. Olivia offers a warm smile and beckons for him to have a seat. Her walnut desk is cluttered with reminders of upcoming meetings and sticky notes stuck to her calendar since her life is generally chaotic and she never had the chance to write them down. An amber pill bottle sits beside her computer mouse, and she quickly brushes it into the top drawer. She was already long overdue for a dose but got interrupted when Ray walked in and didn't want to be seen taking anything in front of the on-and-off addict.

He sighs and shuts the door awkwardly behind him with his left hand. The right is tucked into his jacket pocket. "I've been struggling, Doc."

"My clients typically reach out *because* they're struggling, not disappear." She chuckles and discretely attempts to straighten a stack of papers as Ray sits, accidentally uncovering a pack of cigarettes and her nearly full ashtray. "Nevertheless, I'm happy you're here. What's been on your mind?"

Ray's face is gaunt and pale compared to his usual appearance, a typical looking man of about thirty and average weight. He's thinned considerably in the recent weeks, and he's fidgety, unable to focus his attention on any one thing in the office. "I wish I could show you, but I ... I just can't. I can't look at it or something bad might happen. I might die."

"Interesting. So, you're saying you've seen this ... ailment before?"

He begins to shake and clatter like a bag of bones, not unlike a previous visit when heroin withdrawals had forced him into convulsions that resulted in an ambulance escort. "Yes ... I've seen it. I can't look again. I just can't."

"Understood, Ray. But did you die then?"

"What?"

"You said you might die if you look at this mysterious curse of yours. Did you?" She leans forward with her hands clasped and a cluster of wild hair dangling in front of her face.

"Well, no, but—"

"No, you didn't die. That's the thing about fear, Ray. It makes us think and behave strangely as if some alien entity took control of our bodies. Fear is the death of joy—it will fester within us in a frenzy if we allow it to, like a parasite that feeds on happiness alone. You want to be happy ... don't you, Ray?"

"Yes," he says as he quivers with the most violent shaking coming from within his jacket pocket.

"So, let me help you. Tell me what's wrong. I won't be much use until I know what we're up against. Are you using again?"

"No, not today." Ray slams his eyes shut and takes shallow breaths through his nose for several seconds without saying anything else. His elbow shakes vigorously as he begins to remove the hand from its pocket, and he holds a tight fist with white knuckles before him for her to see.

"Your fist?" Olivia asks. "Looks normal to me. What's wrong with it?"

"It ain't my fist—it's what's inside."

"Can you show me, Ray? Let me see so I can help you. Remember, fear makes us behave strangely."

He nods with his eyes still pressed shut tightly enough to seem like the lids have sealed together and disappeared entirely. His arm and fist tremble even more heavily as he covers his nose and mouth with the left hand. "Here it is."

"Please, Ray. Show me."

He opens his fist and points the palm toward Olivia with his fingers extended straight upward. A perfectly healthy palm, though the sweats glistens beneath the office lights.

"I don't see anything," she continues.

"You don't?! Where'd they go?! Oh God!"

"Easy, Ray. Take a deep breath with me ... In ... Hold ... and out. I'm only saying that your hand appears to be completely fine like it should. Have a look for yourself."

"I can't. Not after what I saw already." He bites his shirt collar and appears to be on the verge of tears. "It's ... the worst thing I've ever seen, and I saw a man's skull blown out by a bullet before when he used up all the dope he was supposed to sell."

"Well, I don't see anything there. You trust me, don't you? Have I ever led you astray?"

"No."

"No, I haven't. Let me give you something to help you relax so we can continue talking." She opens the top drawer to remove the same translucent amber bottle and reads the side label before giving it a shake. *Alprazolam. Take by mouth twice daily.* "This one here." She swallows hard, fiending for one herself.

"Fine."

Olivia stands from her ergonomic office chair, though even her heels don't provide much extra height to her slight frame from the seated position. She approaches the water jug and pulls a flimsy paper cup from the side dispenser then lifts the blue tap to fill it. "Here you go, Ray."

He flips his left hand upward to accept the small white pill and pops it in his mouth then takes the water cup from her. "Can I smoke in here? Smells like cigarettes already."

Olivia's face flushes in embarrassment, wanting to make a thousand different excuses, but she instead returns to her desk. "Sure. Do you need one?"

"No. Got my own." Ray downs the rest of the water and pulls a pack of red Marlboros from his chest pocket. He flips the lid and fishes one out with his tongue and lips then lights it with his right hand still outstretched. "That's better."

"I'm glad. Can you at least tell me what was wrong with your hand? What did you see? How did it feel?"

He takes another deep breath and sighs accompanied by a cloud of smoke. "A cluster of holes across my palm. I saw seeds within some of them like the parasites you mentioned before. Then those seeds turned into tiny groups of insect-type eyes with their own sets of clusters each, all staring at me like some sort of ancient creatures. Something infectious. I tried scraping at my hand to remove them, but the holes only grew bigger and deeper. Darker. Seemed like my flesh had begun to decay and the rot would set in soon enough. Maybe something would hatch inside those cells and pour from my hand. Baby spiders maybe. But the itch was too much to bear, and I washed my hands a thousand times for nothing. I can feel them crawling around in there." He takes a deep draw from the cigarette as his eyes and expression soften. The medicine must've begun to kick in.

"Trypophobia. You've developed a fear of clusters of holes."

"Whatever you wanna call it, I need it gone. Now. I might do something drastic if the holes don't disappear soon."

Olivia's eyes widen. "Drastic? Like what?"

"Can't say because I don't know. I can't take much more."

"Very well," she scoffs. "How about this—let me shake your hand to prove that it's fine."

"No! You can't touch it!"

"Ray, let me show you that everything is safe. That's why you're here. If you're right then I would be infected too, yes? But I suspect my hand will be perfectly fine just as it is now."

"I can't!" He recoils the hand while keeping his elbow tucked into his stomach to maintain distance.

"Ray, I'm sorry to pull rank like this, but ... Doctor's orders." She winks and approaches him, her high heels clip clopping as they leave a trail of circular indentations in the carpet. He turns his head and tucks his chin into the left shoulder. Olivia grabs his clammy hand and rubs her palm deeply into his. He squirms and she smirks. "See? No parasitic gangrenous rotting flesh! I'm fine, Ray, and so are you."

"Ain't you listening to me? I *feel* them burrowing into my skin! Tiny tapeworms gnawing into the meat and bones and tendons. Do you hear me? I *feel* them!"

She stares into his desperate eyes as they cry for help alongside his vocal laments, and she wipes his sweat on her skirt before returning to the desk. "Ah."

"What? Ah what?"

"This is much more complicated than simple trypopho-bia. Of course. You're suffering from post-traumatic stress disorder, which likely triggered your current aversion."

"PTSD? How?" He inhales the cigarette deeply and allows the affected hand to dangle over the edge of the chair.

"Your addiction. I believe these holes of which you speak stem from the trauma you suffered from using. The burrowing represents the needles you injected into your skin; the creatures represent the poison in your system, and the anxiety you're suffering now stems from the sickness you experienced during withdrawals. Go on. Look at your arm and see."

Ray tucks the cigarette into the corner of his mouth and carefully pulls his right sleeve up to the bicep. He stares at his heavily scarred forearm filled with track marks in silence for several seconds when his face morphs into some-thing from a lucid nightmare. "Take it off! Get my fucking arm off of me right now!" He smashes it on the edge of the chair multiple times, and Olivia hears either a bone or board break as he attempts to mutilate himself. "Cut my fucking arm off! Cut it off! CUT IT OFF!"

"Calm down, Ray! It isn't real!" Olivia hastily retrieves the amber bottle from her desk drawer again and rushes to him. She dumps two more pills into his open mouth and forces his lips shut and rubs his throat until she feels the Adam's apple rise and fall. Then she pulls his jacket sleeve down again with her palm rubbing against the pock-marked skin all the way down, and she covers his eyes for as long as it takes him to relax.

"I'm okay now. I feel better."

"I think we should break for the day. No use continuing if it's going to cause you harm." She opens a separate desk drawer and grabs a white pad of paper. "I'm going to write you a prescription for now, but we need to meet again ASAP. I'm available at the same time tomorrow. These are only meant to stop you from going over the edge, not for recreational use." She gulps, knowing she couldn't even follow her own advice.

He nods glassy eyed and dull in the face then rises to take the paper and leaves the office grim and silent like a corpse. Olivia exhales sharply, having not dealt with such an unhinged patient since her early days as a prison shrink. She opens another drawer and pulls out a fresh gold package of cigarettes, Benson & Hedges, and unwraps the cellophane then flips the lid in exasperation. Twenty tightly-packed circular holes stare back at her with ground tobacco leaves inside each of them, the shadows and crevices seeming to magnify as if something dead or decaying might be hiding inside like tiny parasites. Or perhaps a hundred spider eyes could be leering, having laid even more clusters of eggs in the cigarettes to be discovered in horror later. Olivia groans at the thought and lights one up anyway.

♔♔♔♔♔♔

It wasn't until the drive home from the office that a tingling sensation began to tickle Olivia's right palm pressed against the steering wheel. The feeling was subtle at first, like the lingering impression after scratching an itch, only it didn't go away. Her hand felt like something was embedded in the skin as if she had touched some old fiberglass, or maybe there was a small wood splinter stuck in there. She hadn't handled either material—and she knew it.

The itch began to burn like irritated skin that had been rubbed raw. Olvia tried to ignore the sweat which made the steering wheel slick and nauseating to hold onto as her hand slid across it. She swallowed the discomfort as little more than symptoms of intrusive thoughts propagated from Ray's affliction. It's happened before, when patients with such vivid imaginations and descriptions of those phobias burrowed into her head. The power of suggestion.

There was Phoebe the claustrophobic, who detailed being trapped in a totaled car for several hours after rolling it on a seldom-travelled road one night. Olivia felt her own throat tighten at the thought of laying conscious in a metal death trap, only hoping that help might come eventually. And then it passed just as quickly. But nothing had ever left a lasting impact like Ray's story and the burning in her palm, which caused her to nearly hit three other cars on the way home when the pain crescendoed. It felt like she would die if her hand didn't get washed immediately.

She made it home and now sits in her front yard panting, having driven diagonally through the grass and stopping just before crashing through the wooden fence. Her hand still grips the steering wheel tightly, not yet indulging those errant thoughts physically. "I'm fine. You're fine, Olivia," she whispers into the rearview mirror. "We're perfectly fine. Everything is just fine."

She tucks her right hand into her jacket pocket like Ray and dashes into the house and throws her belongings across the foyer. She's begun to sweat bullets from her head that run through her foundation and drip on the tile in powdered globules. "Your hand is fine, Olivia. Look at it."

Her elbow quivers and aches as she raises her fist and takes a final deep breath before opening it ... Nothing. But the burning remains.

Olivia sighs and beelines for her cigarettes on the dining room table and lights up right there in the house. The open pack stands upright, roughly half-empty with staggered empty spaces between the remaining smokes. She inhales deeply and chokes when she looks at the pattern, then flicks the lit cigarette into the kitchen in a panic.

A new wave of pain in her palm forces her to flip it over once more, this time with the same cluster of holes embedded in the skin as were packed into the container of cigarettes. Olivia dashes for the sink and runs the hottest water over her hand that she can stand. Then she turns the water just a bit hotter and fills her cupped palm with blue dish soap to scrub ... and scrub ... and *scrub*.

She grabs the sponge and scours and buffs the skin raw, yet still the burning remains. "There's nothing wrong with your hand, Olivia. Deep breaths." Her voice is unsure as it warbles, sounding quite unlike the professional woman who spoke to Ray with such confidence about his affliction earlier. She cycles through box and pursed-mouth breathing, then five-five-five and four-seven-eight breathing to no avail. The efforts immediately shatter once she looks at her hand again and sees the pattern of tobacco leaves skittering as if some dirty little insect crawls its filthy body through the cover of darkness—the darkness inside her rotting skin.

Back to the sponge it is, scrubbing so hard her knuckles grow tired and begin to fail. She flips it over to use the rough side for further persuasion when the yellow labyrinthine holes of the soft half cause her to dry heave and stuff the sponge into the garbage disposal and turn it on. Small bits regurgitate into the sink and land among the soap bubble remnants that still lie grouped together in bunches of spheres. One of the largest bubbles pops and causes her to fall flat on the kitchen floor, the back of her head taking the brunt of the impact.

Olivia stares blankly upward as an aura of phosphenes and spinning circles overtake the white ceiling. "No ... No! Leave me alone!"

She scrambles to rise woozily and dashes for her purse

in the foyer, digging through it like a rabid animal to find the pills. The precious amber bottle that reads *alprazolam* on the side will surely fix all that ails her, just as it has every other time she's needed it. Empty. She accidentally gave Ray the last of her desperately-needed stash, which was meant to last until tomorrow when the refill would be ready.

"No, goddamnit! NO!" Falling against the wall and crumpling to the floor, she resorts to tears with her right hand outstretched to avoid touching anything, knowing she won't be getting pharmaceutical relief anytime soon. Ray is the only person who might have any sort of answer.

The phone rings through the earpiece several times in her left hand, and she grows more agitated with each one as if the continued sounds solidify her doom. No answer. Voicemail.

"Hey, Ray! It's Dr. Olivia, and I... erm—wanted to pick your brain a bit more about your condition. Maybe you could call me back, hopefully right away, and tell me a bit more about it? Like what am I—I mean you—going to do to resolve it? Please call soon, like really, really soon. Thank you!"

She ends the call, and the screen reverts to a digital keypad of twelve patterned circles. "Fuck!" she screams as she tosses the phone and inadvertently slams her head backward into the wall. The second time doesn't feel any better.

"Doc? Are you alright?" Ray reaches out with his right hand to stand her upright. "Don't worry. I've got you."

Olivia rubs her forehead and inhales deeply through her nose to steady herself. "Ray? What the hell are you doing here?!"

"You called me ... remember? I came to help you."

"Thank God you came, Ray. What am I supposed to do with this? What's happening to me?!"

"Shh ... Quiet now, everything's going to be alright."

He brushes her hair behind her ear and rubs the afflicted palm on her cheek, its skin clammy and calloused, leaving behind a smear of discharge. "I have all the answers. No need to worry."

"Please tell me! I need to know right now because I *feel* them! The eggs are going to hatch inside my skin!"

"Easy now, easy. There's one simple solution to make it all stop." Ray leans in slowly and kisses her sludgy cheek with the hand still pressed on her cheek, then he whispers soothingly into the uncovered ear, "All you have to do is kill yourself." He pulls back and presses his face into hers, his eyes now resembling the close-packed hexagonal cells of a fly's eyes like honeycomb, and something seems to stir and crawl beneath.

"No! Get away from me, fucking get *away* from me!" she screams and kicks and claws, but his grip only tightens. Olivia begins to drown in the dense array of repetitious cavities, each cell beckoning with microscopic parasitic appendages that cause her to feel as if she's coated in scurrying spider legs.

"No! NO!" She bellows and opens her eyes. She's flat on her back and realizes she's been smacking herself in the face. The sting of the infected hand burns from the temple to the jaw and everywhere else she touches, too. She looks at the palm again and sees irritated holes with red rims and pus running from them. They've grown to encompass most of the skin from fingers to wrist. The disease must be stopped before it spreads further.

Olivia stands and staggers. A decision must be made quickly. She runs haphazardly back into the kitchen which is littered with visible patterns and holes. Porous wine corks sitting on the counter. The six pack of beer she and a friend shared the night before, all of the bottles sitting in two rows in the cardboard container with the caps off. The grout spacing around the floor tiles. Even ordinary solid objects like the refrigerator and pantry appear now to be developing sickly holes. Mocking her. Calling.

"I'm *fine*. I'M FINE!" Olivia closes her eyes and breathes deeply several times once more. "I'm fine ... I'm okay ... Everything is okay." The darkness fills with oozing track marks, empty pill bottles, and dozens of unreachable alprazolam tablets patterned into hexagons. She sees insect eggs and corroded flesh and cigarette butts and scores of blinking eyes. Her naked body coated in circular arrangements of embedded black seeds and scaly lesions.

Her eyes jolt open, and she yanks the silverware drawer from the cabinet, pulling the slides out with it. Metal utensils cling across the floor with a sharp reverberation as they scatter across the tiles. She grabs a spoon first and slams her forearm on the counter just barely able to hold it still enough for inspection. The holes in her palm now appear to be bottomless with bold red rims and infection stirring from the skin. Green and purple bruises and rot make up the rest of the flesh surrounding the cluster.

"Get it out of me! GET IT THE FUCK OUT OF ME!" she bellows desperately, knowing nobody else will come to perform the operation. She digs the spoon into one of the holes and tries to scoop out its infected contents as if it were half a grapefruit. Blinding white-hot pain sears her vision, but she cannot stop. She scoops at the skin and pokes it sharply with the spoon like jabbing at a frozen drink. The flesh begins to break free in small bloody chunks that she drops into the garbage disposal for proper cleansing of the disease.

Blood bubbles and pops in the pitted mess of her palm, and she takes to stabbing it with a fork to kill the creatures that still scurry beneath her skin. The first stab results in unbearable pain as a metal prong strikes a nerve, but a bit of the itching subsides. Some of the parasites must've been killed. Another stab yields the same result, and her eyes begin to flutter and cross from the agony. She stabs both mindlessly and ferally again and again.

More holes. Bleeding, seeping holes in patterns of fours, yet still they shriek back at Olivia. The itching and burning persist, as does the tickling of tiny legs beneath the skin. This will not end with half-measures, nor can it continue any longer without permanent harm coming to her. The bread knife it is.

She fishes the wooden handle from the pile of silverware, a premium blade that she bought on a whim but never used. No more half-measures. Time to white knuckle her way to recovery. She saws through the first layer of skin slowly to establish a path in which to cut, her screams so loud they nearly drown out the pain. Blood reaches the outer dermal layer and seeps from the wound thick as syrup tapped from a maple tree and spreads across the counter beneath her arm. She drives the serrated blade back through her flesh, cutting muscles and tendons and ligaments as if they were little more than bits of a pork roast prepared for dinner.

Everything will feel better once the hand is severed, she reminds herself again and again. Everything will return to normal. The pain will linger for a time, but the inner peace will be worth the suffering and loss of appendage. She cuts through a large nerve and nearly vomits but grits her teeth and continues on. The creatures and parasites will die soon enough, she tells herself, quarantined in the dead flesh. That's worth losing the hand alone, if only they won't live for long.

The bread knife strikes bone and refuses to cut further. The blade makes a sound and vibration that resembles rusted steel grinding against another scrap of metal, with the creaks and screeches causing the same discomfort as nails on a chalkboard or aluminum foil grinding into her teeth fillings, like every ounce of pain she's ever experienced concentrated into one moment. It's unfathomable.

She cackles not out of humor but madness overtaking her. She imagines her teeth, jagged and pitted, exposed during her laughter and perfectly aligned in reciprocating horseshoe shapes. Her right hand instinctively shoots up to cover her mouth after a lifetime of using it for nearly every task, and it coats her teeth and lips in blood and infection and the *stink of death*. Suddenly all she wants to do, the only thing she can focus on, even above breathing, is dying by any means necessary.

Olivia shakes and gags then spits out her own blood that just may be rife with microscopic worms. She drops to her knees and screams and howls like a dismembered animal seconds before death, and she fishes through the pile of utensils for the heavy-duty cleaver knife and slams it through the notch in her wrist, driving between the carti-lage and joints with a chunky squelch.

"I'm free! I'M FREE! HAHA!" Olivia falls on her back with the world spinning from blood loss and pain and concussion, but there's an immediate sense of relief. The poison is gone. She allows her head to fall loosely to the side where the cleaver rests bloody beside the tile that broke under impact. A crimson puddle pools beside it where her right hand lies severed, resembling the pepperoni twist appetizers at her favorite pizza place. The hand—bone frag-ments jet beyond the skin with veins and vessels spurting like severed hoses, and ligaments wrap around them to create a cornucopia of circular chaos.

She leaps to her feet and stuffs the hand into the garbage disposal with the handle of the spoon, then pours in dish soap and bleach and every other kind of disinfecting chemical she can find behind it. She flips the switch. Bones crunch and ricochet about the disposal like grenade shrapnel. Red bubbles rise from the drain and fill her with a new type of dread that dwarfs anything she's felt before.

Olivia reaches for her phone and woozily types a text message that she only hopes is legible beyond her tunnel vision: *Help me, Ray ...*

There's a notification of a new voicemail at the top of the screen, received sixteen minutes ago. Her phone is still on silent mode from work. She plays it with the last of her strength.

"Hey, Doc, I have something to confess ... I slipped up in my sobriety as soon as I left your office. I couldn't handle the holes anymore, the fuckin trypophobia *or whatever you called it. But I have good news—the pain in my hand went away as soon as I did. Maybe I was just going through withdrawals, or fiending for a fix. You were right ... it was all in my head. Talk to you tomorrow."*

"Withdrawals." Olivia chuckles weakly and spots the empty amber bottle on the foyer table by the door. The phone drops to the floor on one of its corners and bounces away. She slumps to her side as the wrist stump continues to gush blood along the grout and line the kitchen tiles in a red-outlined checker pattern.

GLOSSARY

1. Eisoptrophobia: Fear of mirrors
2. Globophobia: Fear of balloons
3. Veloxrotaphobia: Fear of rollercoasters
4. Cacophobia: Fear of being ugly
5. Ornithophobia: Fear of birds
6. Urophobia: Fear of urinating (in public)
7. Apotemnophobia: Fear of amputation
8. Mysophobia: Fear of parasites/germs
9. Mottephobia: Fear of moths
10. Omphalophobia: Fear of belly buttons
11. Ablutophobia: Fear of bathing
12. Onuxophobia: Fear of nail polish
14. Athazagoraphobia: Fear of being forgotten
15. Pithecophobia: Fear of apes/chimpanzees
16. Sciophobia: Fear of shadows
17. Trypophobia: Fear of clusters of holes

MARI PITTELMAN

Mari Pittelman is a horror fan and writer who prefers rainy days to sunny ones and secretly hopes the monster under her bed wants to be friends. She is on track to realize both of her life long dreams: to write and publish as much as possible. And to be the neighborhood witch that children tell scary stories about, because she believes that every child deserves a local urban legend. Mari lives in Milwaukee, Wisconsin with her familiar; a cat named Lilith. They can usually be found lurking around their apartment ignoring as many responsibilities as possible.

MEL KITCHING

Mel Kitching (she/her) is a new horror author residing on the NY/PA border with her family. Mel has been a lover of all things spooky and macabre since she was young. When she isn't writing, you can find her on the couch with a book or behind the chair at the hair salon.

JOSEPH MURNANE

Joseph Murnane lurks at the mouth of a cave off the banks of the Eno River in Durham, North Carolina, with four hellish animal companions and an eldritch queen of terrifying beauty. They say you can see him there just before dawn, but only out of the corner of your eye, and only if he wants to be seen. He can be reached via blood dance, or if the trials prove too difficult, email works too. jmurnanehorror@gmail.com

MATTHEW LUTTON

Matthew Lutton is an up-and-coming author who currently haunts Marysville, Washington. Originally growing up in a sunny beach town in California, Matthew's imagination was sparked by the eerie and unexplainable happenings that would occur in the quiet corners of the city. He has always been fascinated with the horror genre, and began writing his own stories as a way to explore his dark and twisted thoughts.

Matthew's debut book, *10 Drink Minimum*, delved deep into the darkness of the human soul, exploring themes like fear, desperation, and madness. His second book, *Candy Dish*, gives the reader sinfully delicious tales reminiscent of Tales from the Crypt, the Twilight Zone and Black Mirror. His third book, and first novel, *The Morningstar Confession*, has garnered rave reviews, sparked intense debates among readers, and has earned a spot on many authors' and readers' book of the year lists.

JULES TERRY

Jules Terry is an Arizona cryptid and crazy cat lady. The mother of four lovely, little gremlins and menagerie keeper of pets ranging from cats, dogs, and chickens (with her husband, of course), she spends as much of her free time with her nose in a book, writing, or making art. Her love of horror started young and kept her parents thoroughly concerned. Jules enjoyed renting creature horror movies from Blockbuster, in addition to the bloodiest anime she could find. When not living out her bog witch dreams, she would curl up with books by Stephen King, Dean Koontz, or Dostoyevsky. Playing video games, namely Diablo or World of Warcraft, is another fond passion. Not much has changed, except a growing TBR and beloved weekly blog posts.

JAY BOWER

Jay Bower is a horror author living outside St. Louis, MO in the forest of Southern Illinois. He spends his time reading, writing, and convincing his wife the dark stories he writes do not involve her.

One time punk-rock skateboarder and heavy metal kid of the 80s, Jay approaches his work with the same indie attitude as those early punk bands.

He's the author of several dark novels and short stories. You can find him at jay-bower.com.

LISA BREANNE

Growing up in the PNW, there was no shortage of inspiration to fuel Lisa's love of the strange, dark, and unusual. During her childhood, she often spent weekends exploring abandoned places and ghost hunting with her mother. Her grandfather solidified her love of reading from a very young age. His words took her from the sands of Egypt to deep space or down in the depths of the Mariana Trench but in his lap, listening to him tell stories was her favorite place to be. When she's not exploring the world through the pages of a book, you can usually find her in the kitchen creating new and fun recipes from scratch, hiking one of the many incredible trails Washington has to offer or playing with her three amazing kids.

JYL GLENN

Jyl Glenn is a writer, editor, formatter, anthologist, poet, and a medical-legal writer and consultant. Her lifelong love affair with horror began at a very early age when she was left unattended on the weekend Poltergeist debuted on HBO. And then she figured out she could read any horror book she liked as long as she hung out at the public library, even if the librarian deemed it not to be age appropriate. Jyl was born and raised in New York and now lives in Tulsa with her dog. She loves creepy art, dark poetry, and pink dinosaurs. When she isn't dabbling in the macabre—she's most likely asleep. You can keep up with her chaos on her website at https://www.jylglennwrites.com, Facebook, or Instagram.

ANGEL RAMON

Angel Ramon is a weird author from the island of Puerto Rico. When he's not writing he enjoys trips to the beach and reptile watching. Angel is a reptile freak despite his mother's disdain for them. He has a few series out including Pina Coladas and Rats, Frogs and Margaritas, and his zombie series, The Fifth Survivor.

Despite his titles containing delicious alcoholic drinks, Angel is not a big drinker. The titles were just his clever way of making his books sound fun, hehe. He's a full-time author who takes care of his elderly parents and ensures they enjoy their golden years. When he's not writing or heading out to enjoy nature, he's out posting frog memes for the public to enjoy.

Many people have come forward admitting their Facebook feeds have been dominated by frog memes. Angel considers that a win. Go check out his books on Amazon today. Also, check him out on Facebook if books and memes are your thing.

DEREK THOMAS

After 55 years of living in the urban jungles of Dallas/Ft. Worth and Houston, Derek Thomas now dwells in a small central Texas town with his wife of 18 years and two precocious French Bulldogs; where he survives on tacos, whisky and Coke Zero. When not writing he loves to cook, garden and, of course, read and watch horror. He is particularly fond of Asian horror and Scanda Noir films and shows.

His first novella, Blood Brawl, was released in July of '24 by No Pants Publishing to excellent reviews, with a sequel planned along with two more releases in 2025, and a story in another anthology soon.

Derek is a proud liberal and continues to fight the good fight for any and all marginalized citizens, with a focus on supporting the LGBTQ+ community.

ZAQ CASS

Zaq Cass is a rabid consumer of all things genre fiction, especially horror, science fiction, and fantasy. He spends his nights haunting an old factory for pay and his days under the watchful eyes of several chickens. Alongside his wife (who puts up with his rants about subgenres with a grace and dignity that is unmatched), he lives in Indiana, keeping four children mostly content in the chaos that they reap upon the house. His first published short, *Character Creation*, was released in Judith Sonnet's SCREAMS anthology and he compiled *Error Code*, a horror anthology revolving around tech-based nightmares. In honor of the story he wrote for this, here's a picture of him from when he was actually a teenager.

DAVID K. SLATER

David K. Slater goes by many names, he likes it when you call him SlaterTheWriter or Mr. Night-Terrors. He writes, wait, why am I talking in third person? I'm not The Rock. I write what I like, I write what scares me, what makes me laugh, and what makes me cry. I've been told that if I write for myself I'll find my audience. So what about you? Are you my audience? My debut novel Air Conditioned Nightmare, is coming in 2025. Gage Greenwood said "It does for customer service calls what *The Shining* did for hotels." Get ready. You are not ready.

STEPHANIE HUDDLE

Stephanie Huddle is a heavily tattooed college professor and part-time editor who teaches her students about real-life human horrors in the criminal justice field. She has been a voracious reader since childhood, and while her go-to genre is horror, she also likes fantasy, psychological thrillers, and sci-fi. She's an avid runner, with several half and full marathons under her belt, and enjoys lifting weights. When not reading for work or leisure, Stephanie relaxes by watching true crime documentaries, horror movies, and any TV show about the strange and unusual. She's a fan of nachos, cats, the color purple, and talking llamas. She also has an extensive collection of nail polish strips, and the only time she has naked nails and toes is when she's between polishes.

SAVANNAH R. FISCHER

Savannah R. Fischer is the permanently exhausted pigeon in charge of two well-loved chaos gremlins. When not with her family, she can usually be found in her cave, wrapped in an oversized blanket and dreaming of spinach puffs. She wants to show her gremlins that they can do hard things, even when it's scary, like pulling the wrong lever and ending up in a pit of alligators. No llamas were harmed in the making of her works of horror. Savannah R. Fischer is the permanently exhausted pigeon in charge of two well-loved chaos gremlins. You can follow her on Facebook as Savannah R. Fischer and Instagram as s.r.fischerauthor. Signed copies of her books are available at https://srfischer-author.bigcartel.com

DYLAN WELLS

Dylan Wells is a full, 100% human being (promise!) who spends her days witnessing the real-life horrors of late-stage capitalism and nights dallying in fictional worlds. She now lives in Wisconsin with her cat and a constant sense of dread. More of her work can be found in Wicked Ouija Press' *Crumpled*, From the Ashes *Hootenanny Horrorshow, and* Crystal Lake's *Hotel Macabre, Vol.1*. You can follow her on Instagram @DylanDisappeared and friend her on Facebook at facebook.com/DylanDisappeared

AJ HUMPHREYS

AJ Humphreys is an emerging author of spooky thrillers, mysteries, and dreadful tales. The small-town serialized four-volume supernatural mystery saga, *Season of The Monster*, served as his debut within the publishing world.

A member of the Horror Writers' Association, AJ is also the founder, owner, and chief operating officer of Dark Journeys Press.

When AJ isn't writing, he can often be found outdoors, possibly walking eighteen holes with his parents, brother, or cousin. Otherwise, it's almost a sure bet he will have his best buddy, Kobe The Husky, at his side. Together, they both enjoy hiking and swimming. AJ operates as an amateur landscape and wildlife photographer, which fits in well with the pair's thirst for outdoor adventuring. AJ currently lives in Urbana, IL, working part-time to support his dream of writing full-time.

ANDREW ADAMS

Andrew Adams is the author of Son of a Serial Killer, Black Widow Blues, and several other titles of horror, thriller, and transgressive fiction. He is an ex-filmmaker, unabashed metalhead, and baseball fanatic in his spare time.

ACKNOWLEDGMENTS

Jylannah would like to thank their families, the Penguin Club, the Chaos Cartel, Bones Coffee, our haters, and the power of the full moon.

A very special (and probably annoying) thank you to Tommy Clark, our beloved Bearded Beacon of Bullshit, and our MMI family.

We also want to thank our wonderful authors for their amazing stories. And a big thank you to our readers—your support gives purpose to every word we write.

Much love to you all,

Jyl & Savannah

—May 16, 2025